THIEF OF LOVE

"It's not that the Major's a bad dancer. He didn't step on my feet. But I didn't feel . . . comfortable with him."

"And you do with me?"

She remained silent, but he noticed she made no effort to pull from their relatively close embrace.

"I'm sorry," he added with the proper note of contrition. "That was rude of me. Allow me to say that I hope you feel more comfortable with me."

"I do."

Her quiet words caught him off guard. "Pardon?"

"I do feel comfortable with you. Safe."

They were innocuous words, delivered in total innocence with no double entendre, not even a knowing twinkle in her eye. Yet they shook him to his core.

Safe? With him? He was a crook. Nothing was safe with him. Not women's jewels. Not women's hearts. Then why did he want to stop in the middle of their dance and kiss her? To assure himself this was nothing more than a simple, sexual attraction? That is what he ought to do. Stop dancing, kiss her and then walk away and get back to work.

They stopped in the middle of the floor.

But theirs was no simple kiss. As their lips met, they became the center of the universe, the other dancers revolving around them in a blur of color. The music faded, drummed out of Delgatto's ears by the rush of blood from a rapidly beating heart.

Her heart . . . or his?

Dear Romance Reader,

In July last year, we launched the Ballad line with four new series, and each month we'll present both new and continuing stories set everywhere from medieval England to the American West—the kind of passionate, romantic stories you love best, written by the most gifted authors. At the back of each book, we'll tell you when you can find subsequent books in the series that have captured your heart.

Debuting this month with a fabulous new series called *The Rock Creek Six,* Lori Handeland offers **Reese.** The first hero in a series of six written alternatively by Lori and Linda Devlin, Reese is haunted by the war—and more than a bit skeptical that a spirited schoolteacher can heal his wounded heart. If you liked the movie *The Magnificent Seven,* this is the series for you! Next, critical favorite Corinne Everett continues the *Daughters of Liberty* series with **Fair Rose,** as a British beauty bent on independence in America discovers that partnership is tempting—especially with the right man.

Alice Duncan whisks us back to turn-of-the-century California, and the early days of silent films, with the next *Dream Maker* title, **The Miner's Daughter.** A stubborn young woman hanging onto her father's copper mine by the skin of her teeth has no place in a movie—or so she believes, until one of the film's investor's decides she's the right woman for the role, and for him. Finally, the fourth book in the *Hope Chest* series, Laura Hayden's **Stolen Hearts,** joins a modern-day cat burglar with an innocent nineteenth-century beauty who holds the key to his family's lost legacy—and to his heart.

Kate Duffy
Editorial Director

Hope Chest

STOLEN HEARTS

Laura Hayden

ZEBRA BOOKS
Kensington Publishing Corp.
http://www.zebrabooks.com

ZEBRA BOOKS are published by

Kensington Publishing Corp.
850 Third Avenue
New York, NY 10022

First Printing: September 2001
10 9 8 7 6 5 4 3 2 1

Printed in the United States of America

One

Infrared beams.

Pressure-sensitive plates in the floor.

Triple redundancy alarms.

Few museums, much less private collectors, had protective systems quite this sophisticated. But this particular Georgetown collector liked to accumulate things that belonged to other people.

Funny, but it seemed crooks always had the best security systems. Of course, such precautions might stop most burglars, but they couldn't—wouldn't—deter the man known only as "Delgatto." After all, Delgatto wasn't exactly a criminal. He considered himself a redistribution specialist—rearranging the inequality of wealth between the greedy rich and the deserving poor.

It was harder than it sounded. Not all rich people were greedy and not all poor people were deserving. The expertise came in distinguishing the right candidates in both groups.

And at the moment, Delgatto had a live wire—a baby broker who cheated his clients, knowing they couldn't turn him in for fear of exposing their own less than legal behavior. If any man deserved to suffer a bit of forced divestiture, it was this guy.

A live wire, indeed . . .

Delgatto stared at the tangle of colored wires spilling out of the exposed panel like an unraveling rainbow. This type of caper was all in a day's work for an artist such as he. At least, that's what he told himself as he struggled to place the last jumper that would disable the alarm system.

He bit his lip.

All in a very *challenging* day's work . . .

He swiped his gloved hand across his brow, drew a deep breath, and made a fifth attempt to deactivate the system. This time, the alligator clip bit firmly into the wire and made contact. The control panel readout changed from *Armed* to *Disarmed.*

He almost laughed out loud.

The King of Thieves does it again.

The title would remain his yet another fine day. The pretenders to the throne could slink back to their urban jungles and return to boosting cars or snatching luggage at the airport. They had no class. No real talent. Most of them were merely one step above common street thugs.

Their motto: "Take from the rich and give to yourself."

How gauche, Delgatto thought. At the same moment, an image swam in his memory—the smug face of the young man who had taunted him only the night before. The young man was yet another challenger to the throne, a two-bit, wet-behind-the-ears hustler from the Jersey shore who thought he could pose a serious challenge as competition in the arena of property redistribution. Like most of his peers, the young man didn't grasp the concept of sharing the wealth.

Delgatto sighed. All philosophies aside, no matter how good The Kid thought he was—even if he did happen to be some sort of combination computer geek/master locksmith/trapeze artist/pickpocket extraordinaire—no one was better at breaking and entering and, more importantly, escaping undetected than Delgatto.

Nobody.

He checked the alarm panel again, admiring his handiwork. He'd instinctively sidestepped two in-line booby traps, not because he could see them, but strictly because he sensed they were there. It took more than raw talent, dumb luck, a steady hand and a sharp eye to do what he did. It took years of experience.

It took seasoning.

Delgatto sighed again. Who was he kidding? *Seasoning?* That was nothing more than the politically correct term for getting older in a young man's game. That's what The Kid had said—that at thirty-eight, Delgatto was losing his touch and should move over and allow the younger generation to take over. In some ways, Delgatto agreed. He was tired of being a cat burglar, tired of researching his marks, planning his strike, and executing the theft.

He was ready for the final caper.

The big heist.

The last hurrah.

But his criminal tenure wouldn't—couldn't—end until the moment he found his quest, the object for which he'd spent a lifetime searching. Until then, he had to keep up appearances and let the world believe he was nothing more than a common master criminal. Luckily, keeping up appearances meant letting one big-mouth punk learn his lesson.

The hard way.

The Kid had made sure everyone at the bar heard his wager that the "title" of King of Thieves would go to the man who stole the St. Saen's jewelry collection. How could Delgatto let such a challenge go unacknowledged, especially when the jewelry belonged to such an unscrupulous man as the baby broker? What a lovely way to kill two birds with one proverbial stone: rob from the evil while reminding The Kid that small children should be seen and not heard.

Delgatto moved cautiously down the hallway.

And good cat burglars are never heard—and never seen.

Best of all, once he fenced the St. Saen's jewelry, he could use the proceeds to provide a new roof and some sports equipment for a nice little orphanage in Philly. He smiled in appreciation of the symmetry of things—the crooked baby broker's wealth being used to fund an orphanage.

How appropriate.

Delgatto now stood only a few yards from sweet and, most likely, sparkling success. Turning back to the disarming job at hand, his highly experienced thirty-eight-year-old eyes spotted an almost invisible wire that snaked down the side of the door frame.

There was no time for celebration. Only part of the alarm system had been deactivated. The second half was so complicated that it'd be morning before he worked his way through the schematic, killed the right sequence of relays, and disabled the rest.

But where there's a will . . .

He shifted his specially altered goggles into place

and moved carefully across the carpet, avoiding all the pressure sensors that now, thanks to the enhanced lens, glowed a spectral green.

What you can't fix, you learn to avoid.

He sidestepped the splotches of color and bent his body into impossible angles. There'd be hell to pay if he broke one of the bars of light guarding the safe.

Once he reached the safe, he placed sensor pads on the door near the lock, then plugged them into the palm computer strapped to his forearm. All he had to do now was sit back and allow the sophisticated machinery to divine the combination.

Ah, technology. Ain't it grand?

One number, two, three . . . finally all eight digits glowed on the L.E.D. readout. He disconnected the wires, punched the numbers in sequence, and heard a decisive click. Success!

The safe door swung open to reveal several shelves filled with over a dozen black velvet cases—the celebrated St. Saen's collection. He opened one case, expecting to see a generous handful of loose diamonds sparkling in the meager light.

Nothing. It was empty.

He grabbed another case and opened it. Empty. His heart wedged itself tighter into his throat as, one after another, every case proved to be empty.

The owner couldn't have sold his collection without Delgatto knowing about it. Nothing moved in the northern hemisphere without Delgatto's knowledge. There was only one answer.

He did it. Delgatto's stomach soured. *The Kid beat me to it.* He stared at the stack of empty boxes, then leaned his head against the cool metal of the safe door.

Stymied.

Skunked.

Another flare of pain sliced through him. Here he was, worrying about his reputation when he should be worrying about failing the orphanage.

He sat down with a thud on the floor, narrowly missing one of the floor sensors. At the moment, he didn't care. He drew a deep breath, trying to push back the pain of his humiliation and allow logic to fill that void. Logically speaking, there was no way The Kid could have beat him to the collection. There simply hadn't been time for The Kid to research, plan, and then execute such a complicated caper.

Unless . . . Delgatto slapped his forehead with his gloved hand, his imagination providing the missing sound effect.

Unless it had been a sucker's bet and The Kid had already stolen the St. Saen's collection before they'd ever made the bet. As Delgatto thought back over the genesis of the idea, he realized The Kid had led him by the nose, vetoing certain targets and leading him to one inevitable and seemingly perfect conclusion—a collection of jewels The Kid had already stolen.

Brilliant.

He shook his head and pushed back the revulsion gnawing at his gut. Glancing into the yawning blackness of the safe, all he could hear were the words, *Pride goeth before the fall.*

And he was headed for a very large fall from criminal grace.

Suddenly, he noticed something lurking in the

bottom of the safe. It sat on the lowest shelf in the back, almost hidden in the darkness. Overlooked by The Kid? Not likely. Knowing The Kid's perverted sense of humor, Delgatto half expected a mousetrap or some other sort of device to ensnare his fingers. He pulled out his penlight and shone it into the safe.

A split second after the light hit on the object, he knew exactly what it was. His already rapid heartbeat suddenly tripled, his vision blurred, and his hands shook, making the beam of light jitterbug across the object.

It was a simple wooden box, adorned with a golden crest consisting of a royal lion standing on his hind legs with one front leg raised in salute, as if saying, "Hiya, pal. Remember me?"

Delgatto's breath caught in his throat.

How could he forget?

With trembling fingers, he felt around the box for tripwires or signs of a pressure trap inside the safe.

No wires. Nothing. No internal security.

Could it be this simple, after so many years of searching? After years of training? A lifetime dedicated to the recovery of this box and its contents? It was the very reason why he'd become a thief. As a schoolboy, his lessons had been diverse—everything from proper etiquette for royalty to the principles of pocket picking. He'd been brought up to believe he had one mission and one mission only: find and steal back an heirloom that had been taken from their royal family over a hundred years ago.

The Heart of Saharanpur.

Two-hundred-sixty-seven carats of green perfection and that many or more years of royal history behind it. This legendary, historic emerald was the sole reason why he'd been trained in electronics, security, gemology, and any and every subject that could make him a better, smarter, more successful thief.

He knew by heart every bit of information countless generations before him had gleaned about their missing royal jewel. He knew it all—every rumor about the stone, from its reported loss in the 1824 flood of St. Petersburg, its presumed fiery end in the horrific Hamburg fires of 1842, its supposed theft from the *Marie Celeste,* which was later sunk to disguise the crime, its brief appearance at a Virginia resort hotel, and its rumored destruction a few years later in 1894 in the fire that destroyed much of the Columbian Exhibition in Chicago.

The result of such intensive study and training had been a twenty-year career as a burglar—like his father and grandfather before him—breaking into and entering a variety of homes, museums, and stores for one purpose only: to recover the missing Heart of Saharanpur, the most important symbol of his family's royalty, lost to them for almost two hundred years.

He forced himself to breathe, having stopped at least a minute earlier. He even allowed himself a grin. The Heart of Saharanpur. Here. Now. His search was over. Triumph at last.

"Come to Papa . . ." he whispered, using two hands to pick up the case.

His senses buzzed. *Something's wrong.* He mentally calculated the probable weight of the stone and its ornate gold rope chain. The case was . . . too light. His throat began to close as he pried open the box's metal clasp. The hinges protested with a squeak as he opened the lid.

The Heart of Saharanpur was gone.

He groped in the dark recesses of the safe, hoping against reason that he'd overlooked it. His fingers grazed something, and he fished out a folded piece of paper.

His heart skipped a beat as he opened and read the scrawled words:

Time to retire, old man, and let the next generation take over. The King of Thieves is dead. Long live the new King of Thieves.

And it was signed *The Kid.*

Anger clouded his vision, changing everything from spectral green to blood red. This was impossible! No god could be this cruel, to let him come this close to his life's goal only to have it snatched away by a snot-nosed novice.

Fooled.

Bamboozled.

Turned from the King of Thieves to the Court Jester in one masterful stroke.

His career, his livelihood, his pride, his family's honor—all gone.

Blind anger filled him as he rose, pivoted, and took a step. He realized a moment before his foot touched the carpet that his rage had betrayed him. Great klaxons screamed, gongs thundered, shrill alarms pierced the air.

He'd stepped on a floor sensor.

Just my luck, he thought as he sprinted for the only exit amid ear-shattering sirens. *I can't even be a failure in peace.* Loud voices filled the hallway outside. Shouts. Dogs barking.

Humiliation and anger gave way to a stronger emotion—the need to survive at all costs. There was no time for one of his grander exits. All he had time to do was protect his face with his forearms as he dived through the window. As he fell with the shards of glass, bullets whizzing by his head, one thought captured his sole attention: *I'll get even somehow, Kid. You can bet your life on it.*

Three hours later, a bruised and slightly battered Delgatto had eluded three different sets of security guards, a pack of vicious guard dogs, four patrol cars, one helicopter complete with a halogen searchlight the size of the moon, and two hookers intent on showing him a real good time.

That's what you get for hiding in a bad neighborhood, he told himself. But wanted men couldn't be choosy. A check of the local news showed that a hidden camera he'd sworn he'd deactivated had caught at least one good shot of him, full face, and the picture had been broadcast to every federal, state, county, and city cop in a five-state area. Reagan, Dulles, BWI—every airport from the largest to the smallest private landing strip would be under close watch.

Luckily, the commuter traffic started impossibly early. He'd managed to blend in with the morning crowds that filled the Metro and get to Union Station, where he hoped to continue hiding in plain sight by mingling with the business commuters headed to New York for the day. But the placement of three District Police officers at the entrance to the tracks changed those plans.

He ended up heading south and managed to put a hundred miles between him and the scene of the crime before he had to abandon the train . . . the hard way. Thanks to an observant commuter with a cell phone, he'd been fingered, and he knew the cops would board at the next station.

He managed to leap from the train, clear the tracks, and hit a bog that absorbed the worst of the impact, allowing him to escape injury of everything but his dignity. His dignity as well as his body was covered in something he tried to tell himself was just mud.

Really smelly mud.

Although he was more comfortable in the jungles of Manhattan than the backwoods of Virginia, Delgatto took to the wilds in hopes of shaking the cops he instinctively knew were on his heels. It wasn't until he literally stumbled over an old advertising sign on the edge of the road that he realized where he was.

"Hope Springs," he read aloud. "It certainly does. . . ."

Day passed and faded into night, forcing Delgatto to take shelter. Now he sat in the dark, shivering, half out of fear and the other half because of the bone-chilling temperature.

Hiding in the ruins of an old hotel in the snow wasn't his idea of deluxe accommodations, but it was all he had at the moment. Lucky for him, someone had rousted the bums out a couple of nights ago, leaving their empty cardboard shacks behind. He chose the sturdiest one, hoping it would give him some small amount of protection from the elements.

A series of trip wires connected to cans loaded with rocks became his second level of protection. He'd be alerted if anyone entered the ruins.

For the first time that night, Delgatto tugged off one leather glove and bared his hand to the freezing cold. It was small comfort to know he'd left no fingerprints behind at the scene. He pulled the wooden box out of the front of his shirt. After a lifetime of searching for the family treasure, he couldn't leave the empty box behind, and had instinctively stuffed it his shirt as he ran for his life. Through some miracle, he'd managed to protect it when he jumped from the train.

He gingerly opened the box and touched the soft lining of the case. Age and wear had browned much of the black velvet, especially in places where the nap had been rubbed away. An indentation indicated where the Heart usually rested; a smaller serpentine slot showed where the chain would have fit. He stroked the empty spot absentmindedly, circling it with the tip of his forefinger.

A noise echoed outside, drawing his nerves into a sharp knot. His first and most demanding instinct was to rid himself of the evidence of the aborted theft. Looking around, he spotted a large hole in the wall. Jamming his hand back into its glove, he leaned into the hole, hoping to discover it was a suitable hiding place for himself, but it was already filled with an old scarred wooden chest. Maybe not a hiding place for him, but one for the jewel box. Prying open the lid, Delgatto dumped in the empty box, then blew the dust back over the fresh glove marks.

He scurried away, melting into the shadows, ready to bolt if the noise proved to be the sounds of police searching the ruins for the late great King of Thieves, reduced to common criminal status. A few minutes later, he realized the sounds originated from two homeless women in a cat fight, either battling over a man or a can of beer—he couldn't tell which, judging from their drunken expletives. Evidently, not all the squatters had been evicted. Luckily, the two women wandered away, evidently finding a second man or a second beer. Everything grew quiet once more and he had the unerring feeling he was alone, again.

He returned to his fortress of squalor and fished the wooden chest from its hiding place. To his surprise, he realized the box held more than the purloined jewelry box. Inside was an old dueling pistol, a shiny sheriff's badge, some sort of brass nameplate, and a pair of busted handcuffs that looked like they'd barely survived the Inquisition.

He eyed the oddball collection. Some of it might be useful. Maybe he could use the badge to fool the local yokels into thinking he was a county cop—but not if he brandished those broken cuffs.

But the pistol was the real find. He knew good workmanship when he saw it. He lifted it from the chest and examined it more closely, admiring its expert craftsmanship. He gripped the hilt, testing the gun's balance and weight. Not bad. He aimed it across the ruins, sitting on an old stone wall, then slowly lowered the gun.

Was he insane? He'd spent his entire criminal career without a gun. It'd meant the difference between the gentlemanly art of burglary and the hostility of armed robbery. There was only one way he'd use a gun now.

Hock it, his conscience ordered. *Hock it and get yourself out of this Motel Rack and Ruin and into something more your style.*

He replaced the gun into the chest, but in doing so, something jabbed through his glove and stung him on the finger. He recoiled, stripped off the glove, and looked down to see a drop of blood welling up on his fingertip. Pushing aside the items in the chest with more care, he spotted a broken gold neck chain hiding beneath the sheriff's badge. The chain's last link jutted up at an angle, its dangerous point ready to spear yet another unsuspecting forefinger.

Gingerly picking up the chain, he held it up in the moonlight for a better view. *If I didn't know better, I'd swear this was the chain from the Heart of Saharanpur.* He'd read everything available about the jewel, found every drawing of the set, memorized every description. Was he so tired that he was starting to see things?

Letting his imagination get the best of him?

But Hope Springs . . . The name sounded familiar.

The chain glistened despite the stingy light. Delgatto's eyes blurred for a moment, and he rubbed them with his other hand. Then, to his surprise, he yawned.

Jeez, I didn't realize I was so tired.

Usually he stayed awake for twenty-four hours or more after a caper, successful or not. Adrenaline had a way of sticking with a guy.

His arms grew heavy, as if the chain itself was gaining weight. He dropped it back into the wooden chest with less care than he wanted.

What's wrong with me? His brain fought for control,

but his body grew more sluggish. He slumped against the wall, trying to support himself, but found it increasingly harder to stay upright.His mind raced ahead, despite his body's unwillingness to function.

The chain.

There had to be something on the chain. A drug? A wave of nausea poured over him.

A poison?

He slumped over sideways, unable to hold himself upright. The chest tipped over, but the only thing to spill out was the jewelry case, which landed inches from his face. The impact caused the case to spring open and some of the inside lining to come loose. Struggling to focus, he spotted the corner of a small microchip hiding behind the lining, and a telltale chemical odor permeating the old fabric.

The Kid set me up. Drugged me.

The area began to glow with a golden-green glare that hurt his eyes. He tried to turn away, but his muscles were paralyzed.

Above the sound of blood roaring in his ears, he could hear someone approaching, setting off one of his can and rock alarms. The Kid must have booby-trapped the velvet lining with a drug absorbed through the skin and maybe had even added a tracking device.

Delgatto knew when he awoke, he'd be tucked away in a nice jail cell, his whereabouts having been leaked to the police by an unknown informant on the phone who would know the exact GPS coordinates of a sleeping thief.

Damn.

* * *

Delgatto knew he wasn't responsible for his drug-induced dreams. Everything was cut loose—his libido, his id, his ego, and, for certain, his imagination.

His very wild imagination conjured up a companion, a woman, but not the sort of woman he usually dreamed about. He usually dreamed about exotic redheads in black garters or blond beach bunny bimbos. The woman in this particular dream bore no resemblance to either archetype. This one was prim and proper, reminding him of his fourth-grade schoolteacher.

"Miss Brewer?" he said in a slurred voice.

"Please, Mr. Delgatto, we haven't much time." She glanced anxiously at a watch pinned to her starchy white shirt. "This is the third time I've told you. It's Sparrow. Esmerelda Sparrow. Listen to me, please. Do you remember the Heart of Saharanpur?"

He nodded. "Gone. Poof. Vanished." He seemed able to say single words. What about a whole sentence? He squinted in concentration. "I didn't steal it. The new king stole it. Stole my crown, too." He sniffed. "And my family honor."

She nodded as if he was indeed a good fourth-grade student who had given the right answer. He felt all warm and cozy inside.

She knelt down beside him. "Do you remember the last time anyone ever saw the Heart of Saharanpur?"

Dim-witted or not, he still remembered the yellowed newspaper article his father had made him memorize at the tender age of eight. "At a masque—masqwue—" His mouth wasn't working well, but his memory was improving by leaps and bounds. He fought to say the word. "At a mas-que-rade ball in

1890. Christmas. Chesterfield Resort." He tried to stave off a sudden wave of sleepiness. "Wait! Chesterfield . . . Hope Springs. It was here. Right here in this ve-e-e-e-e-ry spot."

"How would you like to go back to The Chesterfield during her glory days, Mr. Delgatto? How would you like to go back in time to the last place where anyone ever actually saw the Heart of Saharanpur?"

In his haze, her words sounded logical. Reasonable, even. What a delightful solution! Go back in time. Find the Heart of Saharanpur. Steal it long before The Kid was ever even born. Steal back his family's honor. What a plan.

He tried to compliment her on her scheme and to volunteer for the trip, but he was too busy floating to talk. Instead, he smiled his agreement.

"I thought you'd like that." Her thin eyebrows arched in thought. "But you need another identity. Listen to me. Your name will be Robert Galludat, and you're a French count. You do speak French, don't you?"

He tried to answer with a rather boisterous, *"Mais oui!"* but his lips refused to cooperate.

Miss Sparrow clucked and sighed. "Well, we'll work around that somehow. Now remember, Robert Georges Galludat . . ." She said it the French way, "ro-bare," which was close enough to "robber" to make Delgatto start laughing.

The echoes of the laughter filled his ears as he fell into a deep sleep and dreamed impossible dreams with sparrows flying around backward, carrying clocks in their beaks. And Freudian dreams of entering long tunnels that glowed and spun around like a tornado on its side.

Better to laugh now, he told himself.

He'd wake up soon enough and find himself in jail.

"Monsieur?"

Delgatto tried to push away the voice and the hands that accompanied it.

"Compte Galludat?"

He tried to pull away from the inky darkness that claimed him, but it seemed so comforting. "Whah?"

"Excusez-moi, mais votre nom est-il le Compte Galludat du Paris?"

He was in jail? In France? OK, maybe in Montreal? But the woman in his dreams—she'd mentioned something about speaking French. He struggled to remember faded memories and fuzzed facts. He was supposed to be French, wasn't he? But why? Extradition to France? They didn't still use the guillotine on their criminals, did they?

He opened his eyes and stared into a woman's face. Although concern flooded her features, there was something captivating in her eyes, a look that held his attention and kept him from slipping back into the warm, lush darkness where he'd been hiding. But Master Thieves—especially royal ones—didn't believe in love at first sight, right? Especially not with female Canadian Mounted Police. Talk about oil and water . . .

Her voice was soft and musical. "*Je m'appelle Emily Drewett. Vous êtes le compte, n'est-ce pas?*"

He knew enough French to get by. Evidently, by her accent, that's about all she knew, as well. She wanted to know if he was some count. He looked up into her green eyes and found the only answer that seemed appropriate at the moment, an answer he hoped would make her smile. Right now, that seemed the most important thing for him to do—please her.

He cleared his throat. "Yes . . . er . . . *oui,* I am ze count."

Her smile broadened and the angels sang.

The pretty young woman clapped her hands together in obvious relief. "Oh, good. You speak English. I didn't want to torture you any more than I had to with my French."

"T-torture?" he repeated.

"Oh . . . to torture—to bring deliberate pain. But we don't torture people here at The Chesterfield." She took a quick, almost surreptitious glance at his lap, then looked up again. A fine pink tinge washed over her features. "I'm sure your time here will be quite restorative."

"R-restorative . . ." He glanced down at his blanketed lap. Did she know something he didn't? He fought against the cobwebs that covered his brain, strained to see around the spots that swam in his vision.

She continued. "Let me call an attendant." She turned away and signaled to someone behind her.

Delgatto managed to come to his senses long enough to take stock of where he was. A train car, done up in red and gold and . . . *Are those gas lights on the wall, or those bulbs that flicker to simulate flames?* He squinted. Real gas jets. He splayed his hand across the seat beside him. Red velvet. Everything so real . . . so new!

His vision sharpened as the aisle was suddenly filled by a huge, unsmiling man in white.

Delgatto's angel peered from around one of the man's massive arms. "This is Franz, our finest attendant. He'll carry you off the train. We have a chair waiting for you."

Before he could get the words "A chair?" out of his mouth, the behemoth reached down and plucked him from the seat with the ease of a father carrying a small child. Delgatto began to protest, but the young woman cut him off with a gentle but efficient smile.

"Sir, I understand your reluctance to be tended to in such a manner, but it's been a long trip. Certainly you don't want to risk reinjuring yourself after so much inactivity. I'm sure after only a few sessions in our hot springs and mud baths, you'll be on your way to full recovery and will walk once more."

"Er . . . recovery . . ."

Delgatto closed his eyes, unwilling to see the world whirl by from his lofty perch. *OK, let's recap. One, she thinks I'm a French count; two, that I can't walk. Hmmm . . . this might work . . . at least until the real count comes.* He heaved a mental shrug. *In for a penny . . .*

"I'm sure I'll recover . . . eventually," he offered weakly in his best "suave but vulnerable" continental accent.

A moment later, Franz carried him down the steps and placed him with surprising gentleness into something which bore more resemblance to a chair with wheels rather than a wheelchair.

"I'll see that a porter delivers your luggage to the hotel, and the bell staff will make sure it reaches your room with due haste." She dipped her head and offered him a small curtsey. "It's been a pleasure, *monsieur.*"

He reached out and snared her hand. "You're coming with me, aren't you?"

This time it wasn't a mild pink tinge that filled her face, but a total, unmistakable apple-red blush.

"Oh no, sir. I'm not . . . I mean, I'm not allowed . . ." She came to a verbal standstill, turned even deeper red, then stammered, "I must go," and dashed up the steps back onto the train.

Franz began to push the chair across the train platform and Delgatto fought the urge to spring from the chair and follow her. It wouldn't do to blow the scheme right here and now over a woman whose name he didn't even know. He had a mission, and that didn't include chasing after women who weren't much more than blushing schoolgirls, butchering the king's French.

"Women," he muttered to himself with a sigh.

Franz, his heretofore silent attendant, released a similar sigh. "Vomen . . ."

Two

Emily waited until Franz and his charge were on their way in the guest wagon before she stepped from the shadows of her hiding place. Although confused at first, the count had seemed a pleasant man. He was certainly a handsome one. Then she thought about the blanket covering his legs. How it must frustrate him to be relegated to such a reduced physical state—such an otherwise strapping, virile-looking . . .

Emily felt her cheeks flush with heat.

Such unseemly thoughts.

And about a hotel guest, too.

The Major would have her head if he could read her thoughts. He had many attributes, but luckily mind reading wasn't one of them.

She released her errant thoughts in a breath that hung as a frosty cloud in the cool, crisp air. Cold weather had been late coming this year, and they'd reached the winter solstice without even as much as a flake of snow. She glanced up at the clouds gathering at the mountain tops. Perhaps snow would come at last.

Then Emily made the mistake of letting her glance drop from the cloud-shrouded mountains to the road leading to The Chesterfield. As the guest wagon turned onto the private drive, she could just make out the outline of the count in his wheeled chair.

Poor man. . . .

Despite two years in service at the resort, she still endured overwhelming pangs of sympathy and regret whenever she saw an otherwise healthy individual suffering an unfair affliction or injury. Sick people came to The Chesterfield Resort with a variety of attitudes: Some placed all their faith in the restorative powers of the hot springs, some were highly doubtful of the potential benefits.

However, those who possessed hope tempered with a healthy dose of wariness for miracle cures most often seemed to prosper from the treatment—either through physical improvement or their acceptance of physical limitations. They were the ones Emily enjoyed dealing with the most—the pleasant guests who didn't yell or throw things or create unnecessary messes.

As a hotel maid, Emily held tidy, undemanding people in high esteem. But invariably, the section of rooms that fell within her responsibility attracted some of the messiest, nastiest-tempered guests in the entire resort. Hypochondriacs, Miss Sparrow called them. Emily suspected the Major situated them in her area on purpose, if for no other reason than to bedevil her.

However, Miss Sparrow had explained that the Major placed great faith in Emily's quiet talents and pleasant demeanor. In fact, he'd deliberately assigned his more difficult guests to stay within her area of responsibility, knowing that the hot-tempered or ill-mannered would gather no additional fuel for their fiery tirades from Emily's actions and reactions—or lack thereof.

But Emily believed Miss Sparrow gave the Major far too much credit. The man had never liked her, pure and simple, and it all stemmed from her very first day on duty. He'd been mangling a quote from Socrates and, since she knew no better, she'd offered the proper wording. It was then she learned two important rules: one, no one was allowed to speak during morning muster unless directly asked a question; two, no one corrected the Major.

Ever.

Especially when he was obviously wrong.

He also appeared to hold some secret resentment against educated women, having himself, as he frequently stated, ". . . matriculated on the field of battle."

Duly armed with knowledge of his bugaboos, rules, likes, and dislikes, she'd managed to evade his wrath for the two years since, but had never quite escaped his watchful eye. And now that she had reached the end of her contract, he still appeared as if he fully expected her to violate a staff rule, perhaps as a deliberate gesture of farewell. In any case, he seemed content, even anxious to see her leave.

Emily didn't look forward to informing him of her radical change in plans. She reached into her apron pocket and pulled out the telegram she'd picked up at the train station only moments before meeting the count's train.

She stared in quiet dread at the words:

TOWN QUARANTINED STOP FAMILY ALL FINE STOP DON'T COME HOME STOP WILL WRITE LATER

Don't come home . . . Emily's stomach soured. If she couldn't go home, then where *could* she go? The Major would never agree to an extension of her contract. He'd already hired her replacement and arranged for the young woman to arrive on the next train. She knew for a fact that the girl was scheduled to take over Emily's duties as well as her living quarters.

No job, no home, no money . . .

Emily pulled her cloak around her tightly and began the long trek back to the resort, where her two rather plain carpetbags sat beside far finer luggage at the bell stand. Rupert, the porter, had been so sweet, insisting on carrying her bags as if she were a highfalutin' guest rather than a maid. She corrected herself—a former maid.

She sometimes suspected Rupert had a crush on her, but luckily the industrious young man had no spare time to devote to an enamored heart. He was little more than a sweet boy with a head full of grand ideas and a vest pocket filled with paper containing elaborately scrawled diagrams and schematics. The Major was forever scolding Rupert about the scraps of papers that peeked out of every pocket and ruined the lines of his otherwise impeccable uniform. The Major also disliked the ever-present pencil tucked behind Rupert's ear at a rather jaunty angle.

Emily sighed.

There was only one Rupert, a resort favorite, definitely unique and often quite handy to have around. Everyone knew he had an unquenchable thirst for information and was forever taking notes about the smidgens of conversations he overheard in the elevator, especially information about the stock market.

A shrewd but affable young man, everyone knew, from staff to guests, that if you needed something special or out of the ordinary, or the latest gossip, you went to Rupert. Even the Major reluctantly acknowledged that and, on rare occasions, utilized the young man's distinctive talents.

Rupert was lucky. He had a secure, even unique, berth at The Chesterfield. Then, there was Emily, who could be replaced at a whim, and by an untrained girl at that.

She sighed and continued to trudge up the shortcut path. Perhaps Miss Sparrow could give her some advice. The woman was quite different from anyone Emily had ever met, but she was definitely kindhearted. If anyone could talk the Major into hiring an extra maid, it was Miss Sparrow.

Emily drew in a sharp breath of crisp, cold air.

I hope. . . .

"I'm so sorry, Miss Drewett." Miss Sparrow offered a sympathetic sigh. "There's nothing I can do. The Major has made up his mind."

A tear slid down Emily's cheek despite her best efforts to steel herself against crying. She didn't appreciate people who used emotions, false or otherwise, to sway others. The difficulty lay in determining when an emotion was honest or when it was made up.

"I appreciate everything you've done for me, Miss Sparrow. I'll go back to town and see if there are any positions available as a maid or a shop girl or . . ." Her lip trembled uncontrollably and she tightened it in hopes of conquering her obvious weakness.

"But you'll still need a place to live." Miss Sparrow tapped her finger against her cheek. "And if I'm not mistaken, you've already wired that last paycheck home, haven't you?" She thought for a moment, then brightened. "Why, I believe I know the perfect place for you to stay. Follow me."

Miss Sparrow didn't look back as she marched out of the room in her usual no-nonsense manner. Emily scrambled to keep up with the woman as they climbed the back staircase, reserved for staff only and leading to the top floor of the Tower.

Emily's thoughts raced ahead.

Sometimes they had special guests in the top floor suite who required extra servants to press ball gowns or watch children. Once they'd even had an Eastern potentate who had required six round-the-clock staff members to fulfill his rather eccentric food requests, bedding restrictions, and unusual requirements for comfort.

Maybe the rajah was returning.

Emily shivered. *I hope not. He has beady eyes . . . and a harem.*

"So." Miss Sparrow pulled out her special master key from her apron pocket, unlocked the door, and flung it open. "Will this do for accommodations?"

Emily had never actually been inside the suite. Rajah notwithstanding, only the most high-ranking, most experienced staff members were ever assigned to work here. She stepped in tentatively at first, but then curiosity gave her enough strength to take a second bold step into the room.

The sight took her breath away.

It was the single most magnificent room she'd ever seen in her life. It was filled with magnificent furniture that gleamed with a perfect polish, wall tapestries that must have cost a fortune, a Persian carpet that looked as if it'd never experienced a single footprint. A grand piano sat in one corner, covered by a decorative floral shawl and sporting a silver candelabra polished to a high gleam.

Miss Sparrow evidently noticed what had captured Emily's attention. "Do you know the story about the piano?"

Emily shook her head. "No, ma'am."

"Years ago, we had a concert pianist staying here to recover after a horrible riding accident. Sometimes in the middle of the night, we'd all hear the most marvelous music coming from the suite. We learned later that the man was playing in his sleep. When awake, he couldn't play a note, believing his injury had ended his concert career. When told of the nightly concert, he scoffed, calling everyone liars and worse for making up such stories.

"Then one day, he stumbled upon a small boy trying to pick out a tune on one of the pianos downstairs. The tune in question was one of the pianist's own compositions, one he'd never performed in public. It was only then that he realized the child must have indeed overheard the tune in the middle of the night. The man sat down and began to play for the child. Soon, everyone within earshot, guests and staff alike, gathered for one of the most beautiful and most poignant concerts we'd ever heard. When he departed, the musician left his magnificent piano to the resort in gratitude."

Emily sighed. "That's such a sweet story." She ran her fingers lightly over the piano keys. "I will never be able to look at a piano like this again without remembering that tale."

Glancing at the thin layer of dust on her finger, she reached into her apron pocket and pulled out a small dust cloth, intent on cleaning the keys.

Miss Sparrow reached out and grasped Emily's wrist. "You shouldn't do that."

Emily withdrew obediently. "Yes, ma'am." She paused, daring herself to ask the obvious. "But why?"

It took only a small twinkling smile to make Miss Sparrow appear years younger. "Because you're not here to clean. You're here to live."

Emily's dust cloth fluttered to the floor like a thistle in the wind. She waited until she was able to catch her fleeting breath before she allowed herself to even think, much less speak. "Live?" She gulped. "Here?"

Miss Sparrow's smile broadened. "Yes, Emily. Here."

The piano bench remained steadily in place as Emily dropped to it in a rather unladylike manner. Her elbow hit the keyboard, resulting in a dissonant chord. She jumped up, almost knocking over the bench. "I'm sorry, I'm sorry," she repeated, almost breaking out in tears.

"That's all right. No harm done. And I'm being serious. You can live here."

"I can't possibly . . . Here? It's too . . . too . . ."

"Too small?" Miss Sparrow suggested, a twinkle in her eyes.

Emily glanced at the cavernous room, knowing it was only one of several *other* cavernous rooms that formed the penthouse suite. "Merciful heavens, no. Too large. Too grand." Her voice faded to a hoarse whisper. "Too good for the likes of me."

Miss Sparrow rolled her eyes. "Stuff and nonsense. You're a well-bred young lady with proper manners."

"But I'm a maid . . ."

The woman shook her head. "Not any longer. Your contract has run out. Now you'll become a guest of The Chesterfield, courtesy of the owner, Mr. C. William VanderMeer—"

Emily managed a strangled gasp. "Mr. VanderMeer?"

Miss Sparrow ignored the interruption. "—whose plans to visit his property have been delayed due to his wife's ill health. Apparently, Mrs. VanderMeer is sick and tired of traveling during the holidays and is refusing to leave their home in Philadelphia until at least late January, so the suite will be held for their delayed arrival. It was actually Mrs. VanderMeer who suggested that a deserving employee be allowed to stay in the suite at their absence as a sort of Christmas present. So . . ." Miss Sparrow made a grand sweeping gesture of the room. "Happy Christmas, my dear. You are the deserving recipient of their largess."

This time, Emily missed the bench entirely and sat heavily on the plush Persian carpet.

"H-h-happy Christmas. . . ."

Delgatto stared at the slightly balding man who stood before him, clicking his heels in attention. The man did everything but salute.

"Ah, Monsieur Galludat, welcome to The Chesterfield. I understand you do speak English. Excellent." He continued without waiting for confirmation. "I am Major Payne, and I'm the manager. I've seen to it personally that your rooms meet your specifications. I believe you'll be quite pleased with the accommodations. You'll have an attendant available on call around the clock. Your physician's instructions have been hand delivered to Dr. Ziegler, who has outlined a course of therapy for you, including sessions in our hot springs and mud baths. I believe you will find The Chesterfield to be a highly restful yet restorative place to spend the holidays."

"Holidays?"

"Christmas, sir. How do your people say it? Jwah-you Noel?"

"Joyeux Noël," Delgatto corrected, after cutting through the man's terrible accent. "Yes, Christmas." So it was still December. Maybe still the twenty-first—the same day he'd left his own time. Something turned in his stomach. *The day I left my own time . . .* A bolt of electricity shot through his body.

My God, I've traveled through time!

He drew in a shaky breath and looked around the lobby at the gleaming brass, the polished wood, the old-fashioned clothing. This wasn't some carefully maintained or newly restored hotel. These people weren't actors in costumes.

It was all real.

It was both real and *old.* Real old. He corrected himself. *Not old. New.* His brain began to hurt as he sorted through the terminology that should accompany such a conundrum.

"Monsieur Galludat?" Major Payne squatted beside the wheelchair. "Are you all right, sir?"

No, I'm not all right, you idiot. I've traveled back in time.

The man turned to a staff member behind the desk. "Ring for the doctor."

"No." Delgatto almost didn't recognize his own voice. "No, I don't need a doctor." A sense of self-preservation helped him reclaim his composure and fall back into his more familiar mode of maintaining the ruse with fast thinking. *Damn straight I don't need a doctor. If he examines me, he'll realize there's nothing wrong with my legs and the scam will be up before it ever gets started.* "I'm just tired . . . tired from the trip. If I could . . . rest . . ."

"But of course, sir." The Major raised an eyebrow, flicked one hand, and two people snapped into place behind him, the behemoth who'd carried Delgatto out of the train and escorted him to the hotel, and a younger man dressed in a bellhop's outfit. They both stood at military attention. Payne didn't even turn around to address them. "You've met Franz. He'll be your personal attendant. If you need any aid in dressing or your toilette, Franz will be at your disposal twenty-four hours a day. There are bellpulls located in several places in your room. Any of them will summon him." Payne paused to glance behind his shoulder. He seemed perturbed by what or who he saw. "Where's O'Riley?" he demanded.

The younger man standing behind Payne flushed. "Taking his break, I believe, sir."

Payne stiffened in response, but recovered quickly. "Rupert, see that Monsieur Galludat's bags are delivered to his room and unpacked. Immediately."

"Yes sir, Major." The young man scrambled away, heading toward an impressive pile of luggage and trunks that he began to load on a shiny brass cart.

Payne glanced at the young man with mild disapproval, then turned his attention back to Delgatto. "If you need anything, Monsieur Galludat, don't hesitate to inquire at the front desk, and please, sir, ask for me personally. We at The Chesterfield are quite proud of our quality and speed of service." He performed a precise bow at the waist—"At your service, sir"—and backed away. Although short in stature, the man marched back to the lobby counter with a swagger and bravado that would have done General MacArthur proud.

Or maybe a peacock.

Suddenly, they were on the move again, with Franz providing the strength to muscle the wheelchair toward a first floor hallway. Luckily, the big man was one of few words, so Delgatto didn't have to listen to idle chatter or, even worse, come up with appropriate responses that wouldn't violate whatever rules of nature governed time travel.

Time travel.

He swallowed hard. It was almost too much to comprehend. One moment, he'd been on the run from a botched burglary. The next, he was hurtling a hundred years back through time. And now here he was, being treated like a royal invalid in a resort hotel that was nothing but shambles in his own day. He closed his eyes and the image of the Heart of Saharanpur swam in his mind.

The Heart was here. Somewhere. Just waiting for him. He could feel it.

For a fleeting moment, the image of a pretty young woman replaced that of the Heart. It was the woman from the train, the one with the riveting eyes. He shook his head, as if he could shake away the image and return his attention to his primary responsibility: finding and stealing the Heart of Saharanpur.

He opened his eyes and glanced down at his blanketed legs. So just how was a partially paralyzed French count supposed to case the entire joint, find, and then steal the Heart? He liked *Rear Window,* but he didn't intend to use it as the basis of his own crime.

They came to a jarring halt in front of a door marked "Room 19." Franz bent over, folding his considerable bulk into an awkward angle as he attempted to twist the key in the door lock. Although Delgatto didn't recognize the man's words, he fully understood the sentiment of a curse born out of frustration and delivered in some Slavic language.

After a moment, the door swung open.

Somehow, the young bellhop had managed to beat them to the room and was busy lining up an impressive assortment of trunks and carpetbags against the wall. Glancing around the room, Delgatto had to admit he'd stayed in more palatial places before, but for a hundred-year-old hotel room, this one wasn't bad at all. It was spacious and featured an assortment of furniture which in a century or so would be highly valued antiques. Of course, none of them were particularly accessible to a man in a wheelchair, but that sort of sensitivity was years away.

"Nice room, eh, Mr. Galludat?" The young man smiled as he bullied the last trunk into position. He walked over and briskly opened the brocade draperies to let sunshine flood the room. "Great view, real quiet, and since it's on the first floor, you don't have to worry about the stairs or waiting for the elevator."

The young man pointed out other features in the room, the various bellpulls that would summon Franz the Silent, and the door that connected to the servants' hallway and the one that led to the next room. "You can lock it on your side and no one can get in from the room next door. But you don't have to worry about the servants' door. It's always locked and only the staff on duty assigned to you will have a key." He thumbed over his shoulder at the behemoth filling the doorway. "That'll be Franz and whoever is assigned to spell him, and the maid assigned on this floor."

The young man paused artfully, making it plain he expected a tip but not holding out his hand in a crass gesture. Delgatto patted himself down, wondering if his costume came complete with change. He discovered a coin in his vest pocket and held it out for the young man.

The man's eyes grew wide when he glanced at the coin. For a moment, Delgatto wondered if he'd tipped a twenty-first century amount to a nineteenth-century man—perhaps a virtual fortune—but his fears were quickly put to rest. An entranced grin filled the young man's features.

"Is this a French coin?" He held it up for inspection. "A *real* French coin?"

"A franc," Delgatto offered, hoping he was right. It could be anything, a yen, lira, a ruble . . . who knew?

"Magnificent!" The young man polished it on his sleeve. "One of these days I'm going to Europe, you know. To make my fortune. Now I already have some of their money." He offered Delgatto a brilliant smile. "If you need anything special, sir, you just let me know. My name's Rupert. Just ask for me. I'm the only Rupert around here."

"*Merci,* Rupert." Delgatto belatedly remembered

to use his patented unidentified Continental accent. "I'll make sure to remember that." He nodded toward Franz. "Why don't you two go on so I can familiarize myself with my new"—he almost said "digs," but stopped himself in time—"accommodations."

Rupert crooked his forefinger at the behemoth and the young man practically genuflected as he inched out of the room. It was almost as if he'd been taught never to turn his back on either a cripple or a Frenchman or perhaps both.

Delgatto couldn't help but breathe a sigh of relief when the door clicked shut. He reached over and flipped the lock.

So far, so good.

He started to rise from the wheelchair, but damned near fell to the floor. His heart thundered and fear squeezed his throat. What if there really was something wrong with his legs? He pulled himself back into the chair and ripped off the blanket.

At least he still had legs.

He poked his thigh with his forefinger.

Do I feel that?

He poked it again. Something. He felt something. He slapped his leg, this time distinctly feeling a faint sensation. He did it again, the feeling growing somewhat from near nothing to one his grandmother used to call "pins and needles."

He was so intent on proving that his legs had merely been asleep and were slowly coming to life that he jumped at the sudden sound of someone rapping on the door.

"Mr. Delgatto? It's Miss Sparrow."

He stretched out his right leg, grimaced, and flipped the inner lock of the door. "Come in."

When she entered, he ruefully tapped his knees. "Forgive me for not getting up, but my legs fell asleep. For a moment there . . ." He felt a flush creep up his face.

"You feared you suffered from the real Monsieur Galludat's unfortunate malady?"

He nodded. "You had me going there for a moment." He scanned the mountain of luggage. "Whose stuff is this? His?"

She smiled. "For all intents and purposes, yours. I assure you the clothes will all fit."

He tested his left leg, finding it responsive, albeit prickling in pain. "As much as most people believe clothes make the man, I've found that a fat wallet goes a lot further. How can I afford this place? I think I gave my only coin to the bellboy as a tip."

"You have plenty of coins, Mr. Delgatto."

"It's Delgatto," he corrected.

"Beg pardon?"

"Not Mr. Delgatto. Just Delgatto."

"Your Royal Highness the—"

He cut her off with a curt wave of the hand. "No. Never say that name. It's not mine. It can never be mine until I find the Heart of Saharanpur."

"You want it very badly, don't you?" She tilted her head. "For your family's honor."

Delgatto shrugged. "It's rightfully ours." He narrowed his gaze. "Are you suggesting you might know where it is?"

A sad look settled over her face. "That would be terribly convenient, wouldn't it? For me to know its exact location so you can steal it back and return to your rightful time." She glanced at the watch pinned to her apron. "The portal is still open for another hour, at least."

He started to rise, but she waved him back down to his seat.

"I'm afraid it will not be quite that simple a task."

He noticed she didn't exactly answer his question, but something she said posed an even bigger question in his mind. "I *can* go back, right?" *Oh, man . . . talk about a question I should have asked before I agreed to come here.*

She nodded. "Of course." She hesitated for a moment, then added, "but not until the summer solstice."

"June?" he sputtered. A movie image flashed in his mind of a calendar with its pages being flipped by a stiff breeze. "You mean to tell me that once I get the Heart, I still have to wait around here until June to get back to my own time?"

She allowed herself a small smile. "You're very sure of your abilities as a thief, aren't you?"

He didn't answer. Gentlemen thieves didn't brag about their abilities. Real success in his business meant no one ever really knowing what he did or how he did it.

And especially why.

"June . . ." he mused aloud. "I'll need funds to support me until then." He stood up, testing his legs, which now prickled in welcome pain. Lurching toward the nearest steamer trunk, he opened it to reveal a row of drawers on one side and hanging clothes on the other. At least he'd have the right clothes. He pulled out a jacket and held it up in admiration.

"Snappy dresser, this Monsieur Galludat." He pulled out the matching trousers. "Hmm . . . with the proper props, I suppose I can work a 'play now, pay later' dodge. But how do I explain"—he waved at his legs—"this?"

Miss Sparrow adopted a suitably sympathetic expression. "An unfortunate riding accident on your English country estate."

"Which, of course, explains my excellent command of the English language," he supplied. "Good thing, too. My French is somewhere between rusty and nonexistent."

The sound of raucous laughter in the hallway commanded their attention for a moment. As the noisemakers faded away, Miss Sparrow grew somewhat agitated. She reached into her apron pocket, pulled out an envelope, and pressed it into his hand.

"I can't stay. It's really not appropriate for me to be here."

"Why?"

She shrugged and stepped toward the servant's door. "This is a different time and place than you're used to. Different rules of etiquette and propriety. I must go."

She opened the door, checked the hallway, then slipped out of the room.

"A different time and place," he repeated to himself. *You'd think she dealt with time travelers on a regular basis.*

He turned the envelope over in his hand and examined the inked calligraphy letters on the outside: *To Monsieur Robert Georges Galludat.*

He opened the envelope and an elegant cream-colored, deckle-edged card slid out.

The Chesterfield respectfully requests the honour of your presence at its Tenth Annual Christmas Masquerade Ball on December twenty-fourth at eight P.M. in the Grand Ballroom.

The Christmas ball. The last time anyone had ever seen the Heart. He glanced at the wheeled chair he'd abandoned in the middle of the room.

Great. An invitation to regain the Heart of Saharanpur had literally fallen into his lap and here he was, saddled with a persona of limited ability.

What was he supposed to do?

Roll around in his wheelchair on the dance floor, trying to get a sneak peek at the décolletage of every woman at the ball? His seated vantage point alone would make it highly difficult.

Maybe the count could have a miraculous recovery just in time for the ball. A Christmas miracle.

He shook his head.

Talk about suspicious behavior.

He read the invitation again, his attention suddenly riveted to the words, *Masquerade Ball.*

The whole scheme unfolded in his head as if it had been stored up there in reserve for just such a situation. It was a sweet deal. By day, he could be an affable crippled French count, harmless because of his unfortunate affliction. He might even make a brief appearance at the ball, wheel around and meet and greet, then retire early because of the strain of the excitement on his delicate constitution.

But another masked man, one with the full use of his legs, could appear, sweep the ladies off their feet, admire their cleavages with undisguised lust, and charm them out of their priceless heirloom necklaces.

Have mask, will travel.

Once he stole back the Heart, he'd get the hell out of Dodge or Hope Springs or whatever this place was called, lay low until spring, maybe do some traveling as Galludat, then show up here in time to take the Summer Solstice Express Train back to the future.

He flopped onto the four-poster bed, stretched out, and laced his fingers behind his head.

Oh, man, is this going to be sweet.

Three

Emily dabbed at the juice that trickled down her chin. "These strawberries are so sweet. I don't think I've ever eaten any that tasted this good. Where do you suppose Chef Sasha finds them?"

Cornelia Furman flopped into the chair by the foot of the huge bed. "No one knows. For all his bluster and noise, he's quite a secretive man, you know. All I've heard is that the food comes on the train every day and that he tends to hurl a piece or two at his assistants when he's angered by its poor quality." Cornelia gave the bed a critical once-over, her gaze lingering on the coverlet. "You didn't sleep in the bed. Why?"

Emily grinned. "Perhaps I'm one of your neater guests—one who makes up a bed after herself."

Cornelia made a rude noise. "None of my guests make up their own beds. I wouldn't be that lucky. They're the sort of people who do nothing for themselves." She made a comical face. "The nouveaux riches." She uttered a sharp bark of laughter. "Believe me, they're definitely not old money. Sometimes I wonder if they actually expect me to hold the handkerchief to their noses when they sneeze."

She eyed the bed again. "No, you didn't sleep in

this very grand but very lonely bed." She scanned the room, her attention settling on a settee that fit within the curves of the grand piano. "You slept there, curled up like a child, clutching your pillow for company."

Emily stared at her friend. "You never cease to amaze me, Cornelia. As usual, you are right. I couldn't bear sleeping in such a large bed by myself."

A sly smile spread across Cornelia's face. "Perhaps you will have better luck . . . be less lonely at the Christmas Ball."

"Cornelia Persephone Furman!" A sudden heat flashed up Emily's neck and across her face.

Her friend rolled her eyes. "Don't look so shocked. The ball will be the perfect opportunity to find a rich and powerful man to sweep you off your feet." Cornelia looked down at her uniform and gave her apron a derisive tug. "And you'd never have to wear such hideous apparel as this again."

Emily pushed her breakfast tray aside. "What wealthy man in his right mind would mistake a maid like me for a lady of means and breeding?"

"It could happen." Cornelia pursed her lips in a secret smile. "I have a new guest on my floor," she said, like an older sibling dangling a sweet out of the reach of a younger one. "An invalid, but a very handsome man despite his infirmities."

For a moment, a face flashed in Emily's mind—the French count she'd met at the train. Although she'd seen him probably at his worst, he still had a charm about him, and certainly he was rather handsome. What would she do if someone like him began courting her? How would she act? What would she say? What would she—

"I can tell by the look on your face." Cornelia laughed. "You've seen him already. Very dashing, don't you think?" She leaned forward, joining Emily and creating an air of near conspiracy. "Wouldn't you suppose a man like him would cherish a beautiful woman who found him almost as attractive as his ample fortune?"

Emily stiffened. "You make me sound like a gold digger."

"Gold?" Cornelia scratched her head in puzzlement. "I'm not so sure if he has gold. But judging by the quality of his clothes, he certainly has access to some sort of substantial fortune. Now whether it's a gold mine—"

"No, that's not what I mean. A gold digger. You know, a woman who uses her charms to entice a rich man."

Cornelia wore a confused look. "There's nothing wrong with that. If you're not born into money, then how else are you supposed to get it? As my mother always said, it's just as easy to fall in love with a rich man as a poor one. My grandmother did. And my mother did. And I plan to, also, someday."

"No, I'm talking about women who use fake charm and offer false interest in a man. Your mother truly loves your father. If she didn't, she would have left him when he lost his fortune. But she didn't. With a gold digger, love doesn't come into the relationship . . . except, perhaps, the love of money."

The light began to dawn in Cornelia's eyes. "Ah, I understand now! It's like the fisherman who dangles bait in the water, waiting for the fish to strike.

When the hook is set"—she jerked an imaginary fishing rod—"he pulls in his catch. And then he cooks and eats it."

It was as good an analogy as any. "Something like that."

Her friend's devious smile deepened. "But your charms aren't false. You are an attractive young woman of obvious manners and education, staying in The Chesterfield's finest suite, who—"

"—who dresses like an off-duty maid because that's what she really is." *And no prosperous and handsome French count would be interested in the likes of me.*

"You mean that is what you *were,*" Cornelia corrected. "But perhaps there's something we can do to change that." She gestured for Emily to stand and twirled her finger, indicating that Emily should turn around in a circle. "Definitely something we can do."

An hour later, Emily stood beside a worktable at Maria's Dress Emporium, Hope Springs' finest dressmaker. Not only had Cornelia coerced Rupert to unearth a large chest from the hotel's storage area, but she'd enticed him to bring it down by wagon to the small alley behind Maria's shop and lug it inside. He blushed mightily when both Maria and Cornelia gave him simultaneous chaste kisses on his cheeks.

Emily eyed the chest, a stone of doubt planted firmly in her stomach. "Are you sure this is . . . right?"

Rupert dismissed their crimes with a careless wave of his hand. "We've been holding this trunk for six months in lieu of payment from Lady Arkling. She ducked out of a three-month stay without paying. It's about time it did us some good. And even better, it'll clear up a corner of the storage area for other things." He rubbed one cheek absentmindedly.

Cornelia used a small tool to pry open the lock, and it took all four of them to open the heavy chest and reveal a rack of clothes in one side of the trunk and a set of drawers in the other.

Maria reached in and plucked out the first gown. "The hotel bill is not the only thing that woman did not pay." The dressmaker ran a loving hand down the fabric of the gown. "I made this for Lady Arkling"—she turned and ran her other hand across the other dresses—"and this one, and this . . . and didn't receive a single penny in payment. So legally, these are my property."

Emily stared at the beautiful green velveteen dress Maria had liberated from the trunk. "As much as I might like wearing such a lovely gown, the Major might disagree with you about the ownership."

The dressmaker muttered something in Spanish which Emily suspected wasn't too terribly complimentary of the Major. Then Maria turned around and held the dress against Emily. "Green is not his color. But I think this one, as well as the others, would look lovely on you."

Rupert's blush deepened again. "Yes, ma'am. I concur wholeheartedly. Especially the bit about the Major. Green is definitely not his color." Before they could chide him for his unexpected interest in fashion, he tipped an imaginary hat. "And with that, I believe I must go." Rupert scooted out the door with a carefree whistle.

Left to their own, Maria and Cornelia insisted Emily try on each dress, clucked over each one, and declared each one prettier than its predecessor. But they weren't content with that. The two women poked, prodded, conferred, and pinned each outfit, adding bits of lace, taking some away, and making small changes to update the styles to current fashions.

As they toiled on the third dress, Emily finally spoke, letting her conscience free. "I do appreciate what you're doing, and these are certainly grand dresses, but isn't this a case of putting the cart before the horse? If the Major sees me walking around in such finery, he's sure to notice it, if not me, and realize that I'm still here. He might even discover Miss Sparrow has put me up in the top floor suite and then *her* job might be in jeopardy."

Cornelia, who had been kneeling to work on a hem, leaned back on her heels and tapped her forefinger against her lips. "You have a good point. . . ." After a moment's reflection, she stood. "Then what we need for Emily, first, is a fabulous Christmas ball costume. Something to attract the attentions of a rich man looking for a wife. Or perhaps a rich man who doesn't know he needs a wife—yet. Then"—she indicated the pinned dresses with a sweeping gesture—"you'll need all these other dresses as he courts you. Once the hook has been set in your prospective husband's mouth, the Major won't dare try to dislodge it by telling the man that you are no more than a lowly maid. How could Major Payne explain why you were living in the suite? And even if he could, your rich man will be so enamored of you that he will not listen to naysayers."

Emily tried to push the image of the French count's face out of her mind as she crossed her arms. "You have this all figured out, don't you?"

Cornelia smiled. "I always do."

* * *

The next morning, Franz-the-behemoth parked Delgatto at an empty table on the edge of the crowded dining room. A moment later, a waitress in a starched outfit scurried over to offer him a menu and a wide smile.

"Good morning, sir. Would you like to start with coffee or tea this morning?"

"Coffee," he croaked. Morning was not his strong suit, and he refused to gain strength until he downed a pot or two of black coffee. The maid reappeared with a silver coffeepot and poured him a brimming cup. The first sip was an eye-opener—not only was it steaming hot, it was some of the strongest coffee he'd ever had.

"It's our special house blend, sir. Would you prefer something different?"

Translation: *If you're not man enough to drink the hard stuff, we have some milder coffee in back for wussies.*

He coughed, trying to regain his breath. "Oh, no, this is fine." He took a second sip, hoping he could build some resistance to the inky brew. At least he didn't cough the second time. "Delicious," he managed between gasps.

A voice boomed behind him. "You may be in Virginia, boy, but this here is what we call Texas coffee."

Judging blindly by the accent, Delgatto expected a John-Wayne type to step into view. Instead, a small man slipped around to the front of the table. He wore a buckskin outfit that smacked of Davy Crockett in miniature, carried a large black cowboy hat in his hand, and wore a Texas-size smile.

"The name's Horace McKinney, from San Antone.

You new here, ain't you?" Then without pausing, he added, "Mind if I sit he-yah?"

Although Delgatto meant his nod to be in response to being new, McKinney made it appear an invitation to sit. Somehow Delgatto knew the man had pulled a similar trick on unsuspecting guests a dozen times before.

The little man straddled his chair with a bowlegged gait, plopped his hat on the table, then signaled to the waitress. "Bring me coffee and the usual, little darlin'."

To the woman's credit, she didn't wince openly, but she did betray her distaste by stiffening slightly. "Yes, sir, Mr. McKinney." She turned to Delgatto, her strained smile softening. "And you, sir? Have you made your selection, or would you like more time to consult the menu?"

"Just toast, please."

"Yes, sir."

"Nonsense," McKinney roared. "That's no breakfast for a real man. Bring him a couple of fried eggs, a rasher of bacon, and some of those grits I taught Chef Sashy how to make."

The woman showed only the slightest bit of hesitation.

"Now, don't you mind ol' Sashy, little lady. He may roar like a wounded bull when he's riled, but he's nothing more than a pussycat. Now run along and put in that order. And tell him to get the lead out."

As the waitress hurried away, McKinney leaned back in his chair, smacking his lips. "I wish I could convince Sashy to come back home with me to San Antone. We could sure use a new cook at the ranch house. I'd even put up with the man's hollering if it meant eatin' his grub. You in for a real treat, son." He continued without taking a breath. "Like I said, I'm Horace McKinney from San Antone. And you are?"

Delgatto offered the short man a deliberately limp handshake. "My name is Robert Galludat."

"Ro-bear? Is that your name or your profession? Ro-bear . . . rob-ber?" He shook with laughter.

Delgatto maintained his usual poker face despite the extra heartbeat. *A robber? Not exactly. I'm a burglar.*

The man continued. "Can't say I've ever met a man name of Ro-bear. They call you Bear for short?"

"In your country, it's usually pronounced Rob-bert."

McKinney's laughter evaporated and he caught Delgatto in a look that revealed something deeper than a simple Texas cowhand. "All right, Robbie. Now what's all this I hear about you being from France? I've been to Paris a couple of times and you don't sound like no *parley-voo* Frenchy to me."

And so the dance began.

Any story Delgatto made up now he'd have to remember and be able to repeat. "I matriculated in England."

McKinney's eyes narrowed. "An educated man, eh? Y'all don't sound like no Oxford grad, neither."

Delgatto met the man's skepticism with a careless smile, but meanwhile, he wondered just how many simple nineteenth-century cowhands from Texas would understand the meaning of the word *matriculate.*

Not many.

He offered an equally careless shrug. "My tutor was American. I picked up my accent from him."

The excuse seemed to assuage McKinney's doubts. He leaned back and released a loud guffaw. "Well good for you, Rob. I can't abide them snooty-sounding Brits, either."

Delgatto watched as the occupants of three different tables, obviously British citizens, stiffened in reaction to McKinney's loud exclamation. One gentleman directed a sympathetic look at Delgatto, which made him wonder if being accosted by McKinney was a ritual most new guests had to endure. And why did the man hide behind such a crass façade?

Perhaps the best defense in this case would be a strong offense.

"So you're from Texas." Delgatto gave the man a slow once-over. "I thought things . . ." He paused artfully to gauge the man's height or lack thereof. ". . . were supposed to be *big* in Texas."

McKinney seemed nonplussed by the implication. "Abso-durn-lutely. My ranch is so big it takes a week to ride from one end to the other. Mah house is durn near the size of this hotel and a might more comfortable. And mah"—he looked over Delgatto's shoulder at someone or something and paled slightly—"appetite ain't quite what it used to be. Tell you what, Bobby-Boy, I'll catch up with y'all later, you hear?" He pushed his chair back and moved with unusual speed and agility toward the nearest exit.

Delgatto turned around and saw the source of his distress. A handsome older woman was making a beeline toward the table, maintaining her ramrod posture as she wove between the other seated diners.

"Mr. McKinney, I need to speak with you posthaste!" Her ironclad voice suggested few people had the audacity to ignore her commands. Her steel-gray bun suggested those who did ignore her commands would suffer a schoolmarm tongue-lashing that would cow even the most prominent, most prosperous CEO. She came to a standstill beside McKinney's vacant chair.

"What an odious little man," she said, not quite under her breath.

Delgatto took a long sip of coffee, then spoke over the rim of the cup. "I don't believe he's the simple . . . how do you say? . . . 'cowpoke' he would have us believe he is."

She stopped at the comment, then turned, giving Delgatto a long critical gaze. "What has led you to this rather impertinent observation?"

Delgatto placed his cup gently in its saucer, then templed his fingers, careful not to place his elbows on the table. This woman smacked of propriety and manners and could either be a formidable foe or staunch ally, depending on her first impression of him.

He cleared his throat and spoke in a low tone. "Mr. McKinney mentioned he'd been to Paris and knew I did not sound like my French compatriots. Yet he doesn't have the obvious air of a seasoned traveler. Plus, when I mentioned that I had matriculated elsewhere, he required no definition of the word, betraying an unusually extensive vocabulary. Finally, no self-respecting Southerner would use the word *y'all* in reference to the second person singular. It's strictly used as a plural."

The woman's face cracked with what was probably a rare smile. "Excellent." She held out a gloved hand. "Theodora Biddle. Of the Philadelphia Biddles."

Delgatto lifted her hand to his lips, placing a continental kiss on the back of her dark glove. "Monsieur Robert Georges Galludat . . . from a lamentably small village in the south of France." He offered her a pained smile. "I would stand. However . . ." He gestured weakly at the protruding wheels of his chair.

"Good manners. I like that." She held her hand toward the chair vacated by McKinney. "May I sit?"

"By all means." He made a concerted effort from his seated position to pull the other chair out for her, but she clucked away his gesture and seated herself without help. "So are you here for Dr. Ziegler's miracle cure?"

Her lip curled slightly when she said the doctor's name, and Delgatto made a split-second decision based on her obvious distaste for the man. "I cannot, in good faith, believe all his claims. They are . . . what is the expression? Too good to be true?"

She nodded with so much energy that her hat slid back and forth on her head. "My thoughts exactly. His so-called mental cures are nothing more than smoke and mirrors combined with an unhealthy dose of bunkum. I find him highly . . . distasteful. However, the hot springs and mud baths are particularly invigorating on their own, and I highly recommend them." She leaned forward and lowered her voice. "They've done wonders for my old bones. If my sister, Birdie, and I didn't come here every year, I daresay neither of us would be as mobile as we are today." She glanced unabashed at his wheelchair. "May I inquire as to the nature of your infirmity?"

A small flash of panic quickened his heartbeat before he managed to suppress the emotion. He had to remember, to believe no one could pull a better scam than he, in the past, present, or future.

He adopted a suitably sad expression. "A riding accident. A small girl darted in front of me on the road to my villa, and rather than run her down, I managed to"—he almost said *steer* as in *car*—"pull my horse back, but he reared, I fell . . ." He allowed his voice to drift off as if it were too painful to recall.

Unfortunately, Mrs. Biddle didn't pick up on the right cue. She pressed on. "So you have no use of your legs? No feeling?"

He spotted the ornate diamond hat pin tucked away beneath the feathers of her hat. One part of him yearned to examine the pin, perhaps pocketing it for a far better cause than holding Mrs. Biddle's hat in place. But the more prudent part of him saw the pin as a way to puncture his alibi. One jab with the pin and his lies about paralyzed legs would be exploded like a balloon filled with hot air.

"Actually, I do have some feeling in my legs. Perhaps too much feeling, as I am always in some sort of pain. My doctors believe the mud baths here might help rejuvenate, reactivate my nerves and restore part of my prior strength."

"Then how fortuitous that we've met." She leaned forward again, this time dropping her voicc to a whisper. "There are people around here who prey on unfortunate, unhealthy souls like yourself. And I don't merely mean that so-called Dr. Ziegler." She made a pointed effort of craning and glaring past Delgatto's shoulder at someone across the dining room. She straightened quickly. "Not now."

The waitress appeared, carrying a tray loaded with several steaming dishes. After serving Delgatto, she pursed her lips at the empty place setting. "Sir, do you know if Mr. McKinney is planning to return to the table?"

"I don't believe so. I'm afraid he left quite suddenly."

"Oh." She reshouldered the tray containing McKinney's breakfast. "Is there anything else—"

"One moment, young lady," Mrs. Biddle interrupted, gesturing toward her own part of the table. "No use letting good food go to waste. You may serve Mr. McKinney's meal to me, but make sure the charge goes to him." She stripped off her gloves. "Some people simply have no manners—to order food and not consume it. I cannot abide such wasteful actions."

"Yes, ma'am."

Once the young woman set out the various plates and left, Mrs. Biddle picked up her fork as well as the conversation. "Now, as I was saying, there are unscrupulous people here who prey on the weak and infirm." She paused to take a bite, chew, then swallow. "And your promise of good health makes you even more susceptible to their machinations."

"How so?"

Mrs. Biddle stiffened. "See those two ladies in the corner? The young one in blue and the older one, her mother, in brown?"

Delgatto noticed the two women in question in furious conversation at a corner table. They were obviously mother and daughter, both blond, big-boned, and looking as if mere food couldn't slake their hunger. "Yes. I see them."

"Those are two of the worst around here. That's Ermeline Molderhoffen and her daughter, Gertrude.

The Molderhoffens are facing severe financial difficulties, and both mother and daughter are out to strike it rich by finding wealthy husbands."

Mrs. Biddle glanced below the level of the table, ostensibly at his legs. "And an obviously rich but infirm young man might be a fine catch for them." The woman colored slightly. "Especially an attractive young man." The color faded as quickly as it arose, and she continued. "Should you let her, Gertrude will attend to you slavishly in hopes that any recovery you might achieve could be credited to her obsequious efforts. She will then trap you into marriage and expect you to use your fortunes to bail out the entire Molderhoffen clan from their financial failures. You'll then inherit an enormous family of drunkards, ne'er-do-wells, and gamblers who will proceed to deplete your coffers as quickly as they emptied theirs."

She leveled a steely stare at him. "There are many crooks out there, Mr. Galludat, waiting to pounce on the unprepared or weak, ready to steal them blind and do it while offering an attractive, if not beguiling smile. Don't become a victim, Mr. Galludat."

He contemplated the steam rising from his coffee. "I appreciate the warning, Mrs. Biddle." He studied the rippled patterns his breath left on the liquid surface. "I truly do."

And don't worry, I won't be the victim. I'll be the one doing the stealing.

Four

"You, my darling. You're the reason why I can now do this." The handsome French count was no longer seated in his wheelchair. He was standing and holding out his arms to her.

"You have inspired me to new heights. My love for you has given me back my legs, my health. In return, please allow me to take you away from such unnecessary drudgery."

Emily realized she was wearing a rag-like version of her usually spotless maid's uniform.

"Come with me, and we will live in my mansion in France, where a legion of servants shall serve you. I'll fill your days with beauty and culture and your nights with lavish attention and the most sensual pleasures you've ever dreamed of experiencing." He took an unwavering step toward her, arms outstretched.

"My love for you has healed my legs. But only your love for me will heal my heart."

Emily could say nothing.

"Speechless, my dear?" His smiled was almost wicked. "Then all you have to do to answer me and signal your love is to knock on the door."

Emily raised her hand but could find no door. Where

was it? She had to knock. She had to signal her acceptance of his love and to let him know she shared his feelings.

The door! Where was the door?

"Please, my darling," he pleaded. "Tell me you love me. Don't let me languish here, unsure of your feelings. Tell me you love me. . . ."

She dropped to her knees and began to pound the floor, hoping it would be a worthy substitute.

Knock, knock, knock . . .

Emily woke with a start, not recognizing her grand surroundings. As her fuzzed brain cleared, she realized she was still staying in the Royal Suite and that someone was knocking on her door with great insistence and perhaps even greater impatience.

She pushed aside the book she'd been reading before she fell asleep, a rather torrid story of an injured sheikh and the woman who nursed him back to health. The book had certainly fueled her rather odd but pleasant dream, but the reality of her dilemma chased away any lingering remnants of the dream.

She stared at the door with some trepidation. As far as she knew, the Major wasn't aware she was still in town, much less staying at The Chesterfield, surrounded by such luxurious appointments. If the rattling at the door meant she'd been discovered, then she'd need to think of a story that would prevent Miss Sparrow's generosity from turning into a liability.

Emily pulled her robe over her nightclothes and crept toward the door.

Should she say "Who is it?" and attempt to disguise her voice? If truth be known, she wasn't much of a mimic. What if the Major saw through any attempt she made to sound like someone who truly belonged in such decadent quarters?

But before she could reach the knob, it began to rotate.

She caught her breath, then heard a hoarse whisper in the hallway.

"Emily, it's me, Cornelia. Let me in before *he* wanders up her and sees me."

Releasing her pent-up breath with a relieved "whoosh," Emily unlocked the door, allowing her friend to tumble into the room.

Cornelia shot her a smile of theatrical disapproval as she struggled under the weight of her large parcel. "You have turned into a very deep sleeper since you've become M'Lady of Leisure." She shoved the bundle in Emily's direction as if to offer half of its weight. Emily dutifully complied, taking her end of the paper-wrapped parcel.

"So what's in the—"

"Wait." With her free hand, Cornelia motioned for silence. "Listen."

They could both hear the quiet tap of the Major's boots as he turned the corner, stepping off the thick carpet and onto the highly polished wooden floor. Then he started down the long corridor, pausing at every room, as if testing each door's security.

Emily gestured with a furious nod at the unthrown lock. But how could they lock it in time? Surely he'd hear the noise and be alerted that an unwanted resident had taken roost in The Chesterfield's finest suite. How would they avoid being discovered? Certainly if he heard them lock the door, he would fling it open right then and there and discover their subterfuge.

Cornelia could explain her presence. As a maid, she could simply say she was doing a little maintenance cleaning, having traded duties with the maid under whose responsibilities the suite fell. But Emily would have no such convenient excuse. She wasn't supposed to be in the hotel, much less in its finest suite.

She tried to shove the parcel back toward Cornelia so she'd be free to hide, but at the exact same time, Cornelia tried to force the parcel into her arms. Bigger and stronger, Cornelia won the battle, and Emily staggered under the item's unwieldy bulk.

Cornelia shifted toward the door and began to nod in rhythm to the Major's boots. The taps paused and Emily entertained a vivid image of the Major checking another door or perhaps examining the hall table for errant dust.

Lord protect any hall maid who left a speck of dust on a single piece of furniture.

Then the taps started again, indicating his approach.

How many doors were there between the hall table and this room? She racked her brain, but couldn't remember.

Step, step, step . . .

The taps grew louder.

Step, step—click.

Cornelia threw the bolt in perfect rhythm with the Major's boots, thus disguising her actions in the cadence of his footsteps. However, the danger wasn't over yet. Emily began to teeter under the overwhelming weight of the parcel, unable to say anything to alert Cornelia to her dilemma. Any sound that would warn Cornelia might still draw the Major's unwanted attention. Emily bit her lip as the package grew heavier and her knees weaker.

Luckily, Cornelia turned to share a silent look of triumph and recognized what dangers of discovery still faced them. Reaching down, she snagged the end of the parcel, which was dipping precariously to the floor. Emily regained the balance she had been losing.

They made faces at each other and waited in pained silence until the Major's heel taps stopped at their door, tested the knob, found it sufficiently secure, then moved on. They listened to his footsteps fade away. A few moments later, they both heard him hit the telltale creaky tread of the first step of the staircase.

Once she determined they were safe, Cornelia said a word that proper Southern girls simply didn't say in public or private.

"Cornelia!" Emily chided.

Cornelia made a gesture to the door. "I can't help it. That man vexes me to all ends. I have a mind to bring a curse on him."

"He's not a mean man," Emily offered in weak defense. "Just a strict one."

"A strict one who needs to learn a lesson or two." Cornelia and Emily shifted together and dropped the bundle onto the bed. Her friend continued with a rather evil laugh. "And I know just the right curse for a man like him. My Nanny May taught it to me." She made an elaborate swirling gesture with both hands toward the door.

Emily cringed in anticipation of a hex filled with a forecast of doom, gloom, and general mayhem. Cornelia was a very good friend, but her continuous need to hex people made Emily quite uncomfortable.

Then again, Cornelia's hexes never seemed to work very well.

Her friend spoke in a dramatic, solemn voice. "Major Payne—"

Emily tried not to giggle at the hotel's oldest joke concerning The Chesterfield's most major pain.

"—may you fall in love with a woman who will make your life as miserable as you have made ours."

It seemed a suitable curse, perhaps even a justified one, containing none of the usual elements of rampant warts, excessive hair loss, or uncontrollable flatulence. Emily had no problem adding a quiet, "So be it," to Cornelia's proclamation.

After a moment of silence, they both released nervous giggles.

"Banish him from your mind." Cornelia brushed away the memory with a sweep of her hand. "I've brought you a present from Maria." She turned to the bundle wrapped in muslin and tied with string.

Emily scanned the package, trying to determine its contents from its lumpy outline. "Another dress? But I have so many already, thanks to her."

"And Lady Arkling," Cornelia prompted.

"Even her." Emily released a sigh. "But don't you see? I'm afraid to go out and wear any of them because I'm afraid I'll run into the Major."

"He's a man." Cornelia made a rude noise. "He wouldn't notice. They never do. But what's even worse"—she made a face—"is that he's more than a man. He's an overbearing manager who sees you only as a servant. He's never been interested in your face, only the perfection of your uniform and the thoroughness of your dusting. That's why he tends to address us by title rather than name."

She cleared her throat and barked, "Maid!" in a perfect imitation of the man. " 'One of the Cat twins has made a mess on the second floor east landing. Clean it up. Now.' "

They both laughed, remembering the two small terrors, a set of four-year-old twins, whom the staff had christened "Cat-astrophe" and "Cat-aclismic."

"The Major calls us 'Maid' because he doesn't know, nor does he wish to learn, our names," Cornelia proclaimed.

"He knows mine," Emily said darkly.

"But only associated with a maid's uniform. Take away the uniform, and you're a perfect stranger to him."

"I don't believe that. He recognized me in town once when I wasn't wearing a uniform. He was no more cordial then."

Cornelia shrugged. "Then perhaps a bit more of a change is in order." She reached up and pulled at one of Emily's combs that helped keep the sides of her hair tucked into a neat bun. "If we make a change in your hair and add a bit of makeup, he'd never mistake you for the 'lowly' hotel maid who was supposed to go home after reaching the end of her contract."

Emily shook her head. "I'm afraid there's little you can do to change my looks. I look like myself and no other."

Cornelia's eyes twinkled. "When I'm through with you, you won't recognize your own reflection."

Emily eyed the large bundle. "If it takes that many hair implements and pots of rouge to make me look like a different person, then I'm afraid we'll be trying to complete a fool's errand."

Cornelia dismissed Emily's fears with a careless wave, then reached into her own apron pocket and pulled out a small drawstring bag which she dropped to the bed. "This will handle your cosmetic needs. And this"—she turned to the larger bundle "—is a present from Maria and from me." She untied the string and the paper opened to reveal layers of pink netting and shimmery white material.

Emily's heart took an extra beat at the whimsical beauty of the fabric alone. "What is it?"

Cornelia smiled. "Maria suggested that if we were to fully play out the Cinderella aspects of your transition from lowly maid tending the hearth to the princess of the kingdom of Chesterfield, then you needed a suitable costume for the Christmas ball."

"C-Christmas ball? But I'm not going to that. I couldn't."

Cornelia's eyes sparkled as she dumped out the contents of her drawstring bag onto the bed. "Oh yes, you can. And you shall."

Delgatto waited until Franz closed the door before jumping out of the wheelchair. He rubbed his aching rear and tried to massage back some feeling into one of his legs that had fallen asleep. Whoever had designed this contraption had spared no thought for the poor patient's comfort.

Talk about lousy suspension and the lack of any cushioning.

As he stretched out, trying to work out the kinks in his back, he noticed the invitation propped on the bedside table. *Ah, yes, the infamous Chesterfield Christmas ball.*

His mind wandered back to the news story he'd memorized as a part of his royal education. Although he'd taken his life's mission quite seriously—to recover the Heart and help his family regain its rightful honor—in some ways, the stories had been just history to him. The theft of the Heart was a mystery that time had somewhat obscured. Some of what he knew about the Heart of Saharanpur was family hearsay, which he knew was sometimes tainted by time or faulty memory. He'd learned firsthand from his Great Uncle Benedicto how wishfulness sometimes unseated accuracy as memories aged.

Of course, Delgatto listened and acknowledged the stories of old, but he dedicated most of his attention to more accurate accounts of the necklace, like those found in the old yellowed newspaper clippings his grandmother had provided him.

They were words he knew by heart.

He picked up the invitation and ran a finger along its deckled edge. History would try to repeat itself at the ball. The Heart of Saharanpur would decorate the neck of some lovely lady in costume. That much would be the same. But instead of it disappearing into the ether, never to be seen again, Delgatto would find it, take it, and use it to restore his family's honor and perhaps even a bit of their glory as well.

He stared at the word *masquerade.*

But there was one small problem. How did he come up with a suitable costume without any of the staff knowing and therefore being able to identify the man in it? He allowed himself a rather satisfied smile.

Where there's a will . . .

* * *

It took a full day for Delgatto to gather what he needed. He stole bits and pieces from here and there across the resort. He appropriated a brocade pillow from the billiard room, slipping it beneath his seat. In case anyone saw him, he could explain away his theft as temporary because of the wooden seat's discomfort. Anyone who had spent more than a moment sitting in one would concur wholeheartedly.

He entertained a group of children by doing a bit of sleight of hand with a deck of cards someone had left in the lobby. His big finale was to demonstrate his ability to pull a tablecloth from the table in the Great Hall without disturbing a vase of flowers. The children and even some of their parents all oohed and aahed over his success, and no one noticed that the tablecloth wasn't returned to the table but slipped under his lap blanket instead.

Once he deposited his ill-gotten gains back in his room, he called for Franz and asked to be taken to the bathhouse for a bath and massage.

Rather than use the wheelchair, Franz enlisted the help of yet another burly man (whom Delgatto felt compelled to name Hans) and the two of them used an "invalid chair"—not much more than a chair suspended between two horizontal poles—to manage the many sets of stairs that formed the pathway from the resort to the bathhouse. Delgatto felt like an Eastern potentate as the two men lifted the chair and trotted to the bathhouse via an outdoor footpath.

He shivered as he glanced back at the hotel, whole and intact here in the past, but nothing more than a broken, burned shell in his own time. He'd never thought about what the building might have looked like before tragedy struck. He glanced at the imposing brick building and tried not to sigh.

What a grand lady to have been lost.

As they continued to the bathhouse, he searched his memories, trying to recall exactly what had finally happened to the building.

Fire? Lightning?

General neglect?

Or had modern technology simply rendered the old girl useless in comparison to twenty-first century hotels complete with glass elevators, modems in every room, and built-in Jacuzzis?

Had she ended her life in a bang or did her whimper include a slow steady slide to oblivion via Magic Fingers vibrating beds and hourly rates?

God, he hoped not.

She'd deserved a more stately ending, more of a bang than a wham, bam, thank you ma'am.

His thoughts slammed back to the past as Franz and Hans deposited him in a dressing room. There he was given a long black swimsuit that almost made him laugh out loud.

No Speedos need apply, he thought as he tugged on the outfit. A minute or two later, the huge attendant—they didn't seem to come in any other size—entered the room and picked Delgatto up as if he were a small child and carried him through a back door and into a small bath.

There, the man plunged him into water so hot it could have cooked a lobster in three minutes. After two and a half minutes, the burning sensation had either subsided or his pain sensors had been cooked.

The bath attendant reappeared, dragged him out

of the water, and then deposited him back into the dressing room. There he was stretched out on a thin mattress placed on what looked like an old army cot. The attendant covered him in blankets and said in stilted English that he'd be staying there for a while to sweat the impurities out of his body.

"I check you in one hour, sir," the man said, his stilted language and jungle man muscles reminding Delgatto of Johnny Weissmuller on a bad day. "You need anything, you call out."

"Ungawa," Delgatto replied. The man gave him an odd look, then left.

Evidently he didn't speak Tarzan.

After the door closed, Delgatto counted to twenty before struggling out from beneath the six layers of flannel blankets that the man had piled on him. He crept toward the door leading to the bath. Earlier, he'd noticed that one bath area served two dressing rooms. Listening intently, he heard a familiar, reassuring sound in the other room.

He stuck his head around the corner and spotted a huge mound of blankets that were rising and falling in rhythm to the loud snores emanating from within.

Delgatto tiptoed around the sleeping man and examined the clothing neatly hung on hooks on the wall.

Buckskins.

McKinney.

Delgatto smiled to himself and plucked the large black cowboy hat from the wall where it hung next to the clothes.

He examined the material, then tried on the hat.

Perfect fit. He took it off and spun it around his forefinger.

It'd be the perfect cap to a perfect disguise.

Emily continued to hide in her room for the rest of the day, refusing Cornelia's offer to disguise her sufficiently to enter polite society as something other than a misplaced maid. She had a duty to protect Miss Sparrow's faith in her and not jeopardize the woman's position by being careless with her generosity.

But going to the ball . . . that was a different situation.

Any mask she'd wear would afford her a true sense of freedom, allowing her to be whoever she wanted for one magical night.

But until the ball, Emily was happy feasting on the treats that Rupert, Cornelia, and a host of other closemouthed friends sneaked up to her suite. Best of all, the suite included an entire bookcase, which provided sufficient entertainment to keep Emily happy as she lounged in the bed, eating grapes and reading tales of impossible feats, fantastical exploits, improbable wars and, of course, storybook romances to last a lifetime.

She was deep into her third book of the day when she heard Cornelia's special knock. Bounding from the bed, Emily left behind the tale of adventure to let her friend into the room.

Cornelia looked at the rumpled cover and the stack of books at the foot of the bed. "Reading again?"

Emily picked up her current tale. "It's been heavenly." She spun in a circle, indicating the room. "Is this how the rich people live? Lying around in bed, eating what they want, reading what they want?"

Cornelia sniffed. "Before Daddy lost his money, I don't recall reading being my favorite entertainment." She examined the bookcase. "In fact, I seriously doubt any of those books have been read in years." She ran a critical finger across their spines, then stared at the invisible grime on her finger. "Judging how often I have to dust them, I doubt anyone ever touches them, much less reads them."

"Well, if I were rich, that's all I'd do." Emily clutched her book to her chest. "Read, read, read."

Cornelia picked up one of the books Emily had left in a stack on the bedside table. "Fairy tales?" She offered Emily a sly grin. "Those are for children. Why read about them when you can live one?" She nodded to the costume which hung in prominence in the open wardrobe. "Shall we start getting you ready for your adventure, Cinderella?"

Emily glanced at the pink and white outfit and swallowed hard. "I suppose so."

"Then let the magic begin!"

Cornelia primped and curled, painted and powdered, but doggedly refused to allow Emily to see the results in the hand mirror.

"Not until I'm through," she exclaimed, moving the mirror out of Emily's reach.

Even after she stepped back and pronounced Emily "a living work of art," Cornelia still refused to let her see herself, going as far as throwing a sheet over the mirror standing in the corner of the bedroom.

"Not yet," she ordered. "Not until we're completely through with everything."

With Cornelia's help, Emily began to dress, starting with the specially designed petticoat. She stepped into the garment, which consisted of multiple rows of fine netting that cinched at her waist. The costume's skirt fit over the petticoat and was made of pink silk embroidered with small white roses and tiny green leaves. The top part of the costume consisted of a white silk overblouse with large flowing sleeves and a high ruffled collar.

Once Emily donned the blouse, Cornelia buttoned the row of tiny rosebud-shaped buttons.

"You know that Maria's husband carved all these himself."

"I'll feel terrible if I lose one."

Cornelia grinned. "If you're going to lose something, try a slipper instead of a button. That's the way Cinderella found her prince." She held out the most stunning piece of the costume. "And here's the best for last."

Emily held her breath as she examined the vest, mesmerized by both its intricate design and its practical structure. For all intents and purposes, the embroidered vest appeared to have sprouted a pair of white fairy wings that sparkled with gold flecks when they caught the light.

Upon closer examination, Emily realized Maria had caught up bits of gold glitter between the layers of gauzy material that made up the wings.

"It's . . . unbelievable," Emily said, running her forefinger down the edge of one wing.

Cornelia nodded. "Makes you believe in fairies, it does. Especially Christmas ones."

"I need a Christmas fairy. Or at least an angel." Emily gently pulled on the winged vest Cornelia held up for her. The tight-fitting bodice helped keep the wings in place so they didn't sag from the top.

Cornelia stepped back to admire the outfit. "You do look quite fairy-like." She pursed her lips and tapped her cheek in critical contemplation. "But you're missing one thing." She continued to tap. "And I'm not sure what it is."

Emily performed a small pirouette, letting the generous skirt swirl around her legs. "Can't you let me see what I look like? I have a feeling I know what this looks like."

"Not yet," Cornelia replied.

"But I have everything a fairy princess needs," Emily pleaded. She fingered a curl by her face. "Beautiful hair, an expertly painted face, a truly enchanting outfit . . ."

Cornelia's look of furrowed concentration melted into a smile. She snapped her fingers. "I know exactly what we're missing." She turned to the discarded paper that had protected the costume and searched through its folds. Finally, Cornelia discovered an overlooked package which she took entirely too much time to open.

"What is it?" Emily craned to see over her friend's shoulder.

"Have patience! It's tangled." Cornelia gestured toward the covered mirror. "Take down the sheet. You have my permission to admire yourself. I think you're going to be pleased."

Emily pulled down the fabric that covered the mirror and was taken aback by the fanciful reflection she saw there.

Her heart wedged in her throat as she stared at the unfamiliar image, one that, in her estimation, bore little if any resemblance to her.

The woman in the mirror was a magical creature, beautiful, ethereal . . . everything Emily wasn't. She rubbed her eyes as if they were deceiving her.

That's me?

The concept seemed as foreign and exotic as the person who preened in the mirror. When she smiled at the figure in the mirror, the figure smiled back. But when she spoke, her voice sounded far from beautiful.

"I look like . . . that?" she croaked.

Cornelia looked up and smiled. "Stunning, aren't you?" She abandoned her task and turned her attention to Emily's wings, fluffing them out and giving them minute adjustments.

Emily stared at her own image for almost a full minute until acute embarrassment set in and she turned away. No one should have that much depth or breadth of interest in herself.

But that was the point. She didn't feel as if she was looking at herself.

"And here are the finishing touches, Your Royal Highness." Cornelia nestled a golden crown in the curls at the top of Emily's head, then handed her a long stick which ended in a gilt star. "Or should I say Your Royal Fairy Highness."

Emily surrendered, allowing herself to gaze at her own reflection for as long as she wanted. "I can't believe it's me." She turned slowly, trying to catch a better view of the wings.

Cornelia shifted next to her and studied the reflection with far less rapture. She balanced her fists on her hips. "I still think there's something missing."

Emily released a sigh to reflect her utter satisfaction. "No, it's perfect! I look nothing like myself."

Her friend folded her arms and shook her head. "Don't be so sure. I still see my friend Emily when I look in the mirror at you." Cornelia's sigh reflected far less satisfaction and much more resignation. "Maria was right. She said I couldn't make you look different enough." Cornelia rustled through the discarded wrappings and then turned around, holding something made of feathers. "So she made a mask for you."

The feathered mask was white with gold along the edges and had been formed to look like a miniature set of wings, similar to those of her costume.

Emily held the mask in place as her friend tied the gold-colored ribbons behind her head.

"That's better, but it still needs something. Some jewelry, perhaps. I have Grandmama's cameo, but it's blue. You need something gold."

"Or green?" A shiver danced up Emily's spine. "I have the perfect necklace. . . ."

Five

Delgatto wheeled himself into the ballroom, which was already half full of people in a variety of costumes—some elaborate, some with nothing more involved than a simple black mask and regular party clothes.

A small orchestra commanded the stage, filling the air with a slightly familiar song that squatted on the edge of Delgatto's mind. He could remember as a child hearing his grandmother hum the tune as she embroidered, her needle flashing in rhythm to the lively notes. It was an infectious melody, one that spoke to him of home and love and family. It took all the control he had to fight the urge to tap his foot against the wheelchair in time with the music.

It was almost painful to watch the couples as they danced, knowing he couldn't jump up and join them.

"Monsieur Galludat!"

Delgatto scanned the room and found Major Payne hailing him from a large refreshment table covered in tempting foods. Delgatto propelled himself toward the man.

Payne nodded at the wheelchair. "Good to see you traveling under your own steam, sir."

"I prefer the independent life when possible."

Payne released a rare burst of laughter, a bit too loud and forced. "I don't blame you at all." The man pointed toward the end of the table to a large glass bowl filled with something pink and frothy. "May I offer you some punch?"

Delgatto noticed that Payne himself had something darker and foamless in his punch cup, perhaps accounting for his unnaturally pleasant demeanor.

"I think I'd rather have a bit of what you're having, Major."

The man blushed slightly and emitted another volley of slightly loud laughter. "Good show, old man. Good show. Certainly. Just don't tell everybody where you got it." The Major retrieved a clean glass punch cup and poured out an inch of amber liquid from a silver flask, which he produced from the folds of his costume. "Here you go."

"Thanks." Delgatto took a tentative sip of some of the smoothest Scotch he'd had in years. After he caught his breath, he added, "Your punch really packs a punch." Once the Scotch finished etching the perfect pathway down his throat, Delgatto gave the Major's costume a critical once-over.

"So . . . interesting outfit, Major."

The man wore a toga—not just some bedsheet affair, but an authentic-looking toga that would have done Julius Caesar proud, and an authentic-looking pair of dusty sandals with leather laces that wove around his hairy legs and tied just below the knee. In addition, a lethal-looking dagger hung from a gold cord at the Major's waist.

"An armed Julius Caesar?" Delgatto took another

appreciative sip. "I don't recall reading about that in my history book."

The Major patted the jeweled hilt of his weapon. "If Caesar had been equipped like this, I daresay the name of Brutus would have gone down in history only because of his failure to complete his mission."

Delgatto lifted his glass in mock salute. "Right along with that of General George Armstrong Custer."

Payne stiffened perceptibly and slipped his silver flask back into the folds of his toga.

Oops. Sore point. Probably knew Custer. Maybe you went to grade school together or something like that. Delgatto sighed to himself. *Oh, well, I didn't want any more, anyway.* After all, he did need to keep his wits about him. One drink would be sufficient to steel his nerves without deadening them.

Major Payne almost scowled as he gave Delgatto's costume an almost scathing glance. "And what . . . er . . . who exactly might you be?"

Delgatto adjusted his coat as best as he could while sitting in the chair. "Thanks to your young Rupert, who helped arrange for my costume, I'm one of your country's more famous statesmen, Benjamin Franklin, sometimes referred to in my country as *le Grand Père.*"

Payne furrowed his brow as he stumbled through a translation. "The big father?"

Delgatto offered a shrug and a smile. "It isn't a literal translation. In the American vernacular, it's 'the father of our country.' "

The wrinkles in Payne's forehead deepened. "But the father of our country is George Washington."

"Oh, I wasn't talking about your country. I was

talking about ours. More than one French schoolchild can trace his lineage back to a visiting American dignitary named Benjamin Franklin."

"How dare you impugn . . ." The Major swallowed the rest of his words as he made a determined show of containing his anger. He glanced pointedly over Delgatto's head, pretended to spot someone signaling for his attention, and mumbled an excuse to leave.

"That wasn't particularly kind."

The first thing Delgatto noticed when he turned around was a gold bracelet shaped like a snake and wound tightly around an arm so large that the bracelet created a spiral furrow in the flesh. The arm ended in a hand large enough to palm a basketball, but said hand was busy transferring the contents of a silver tray onto her own crowded plate of hors d'oeuvres.

Cleopatra shot him a toothy smile. "But since the Major is such an odious little man, I forgive you."

Delgatto ducked his head in a modified mock bow. "Thank you, My Queen."

Cleo gave him an appraising stare which made the hackles on the back of his neck not only rise, but also look for cover.

"I don't believe we've met." She held out her enormous hand, sporting a non-Egyptian-looking diamond engagement ring. He gave the stone a passing glance.

Paste.

And not particularly good paste at that.

"I'm Mrs.—"

Delgatto held up his hand to stop her. "Please—don't. This should be a night for revelry as well as mystery." He adjusted his own mask. "We wear these for a reason. An air of mystery can be very . . . enticing, don't you think?"

A fine blush spread up the rolls of her exposed flesh. "Oh my goodness, yes, indeed." She swallowed hard. "Enticing, indeed." She stared openly at his legs. "I suppose you're here for the cure. Is it working?" she blurted, adding a contrite, "If I may ask?"

He shrugged. "I haven't been here long enough to chart its effect, but I have complete confidence it will be able to restore that which I've lost."

"That which you've lost . . ." she echoed in a whisper. A moment later, she shook herself and cleared her throat. "Ah, yes. Well then, there is someone I'd like you to meet. She's my dau . . . er . . . a delightful young lady I met tonight. I have a feeling you two would find each other fascinating company. Stay right here!"

Cleo hiked up her voluminous skirts and plowed a path through the milling crowd. "Stay!" she commanded as if he were a misbehaving dog.

Delgatto knew his only course of action was escape, but he needed to do it in a more public fashion. He needed witnesses who saw him at the ball, then saw him leave as well. Sneaking off to avoid meeting Cleo's offspring wouldn't give him an adequate alibi, should he need one.

What he really needed was to cause a mild but memorable scene.

He waited patiently until Cleo came back, towing Marie Antoinette with her.

"I'd like to introduce my . . . er . . . friend, Marie Antoinette."

Marie bent forward to hold out her hand, but was

forced to lean back as her enormous wig began to slide forward. Trying again, she managed to hold out her hand without losing her head. "Enchanted, I'm sure," she said in a very nasal voice.

He took the proffered hand and kissed it. "Ah, a fellow countryman." He made a big show of looking around. "May I dare to hope your royal escort is not here tonight?"

She looked puzzled for a moment, then the light slowly dawned. She giggled—no, make that snorted—her reply. "You're funny."

"And hungry as well. May I offer the two of you some refreshments?"

Instead of scanning the table laden with food, Marie Antoinette eyed him with a look that reminded him of a hungry hawk spotting an injured field mouse. "That would be lovely." She looked as if she was ready to sit down and be served, but her mother slammed an elbow into her ribs. Cleo gave her daughter a frantic nod toward the table, which evidently jump-started Marie's good manners. "But, please, allow me to serve you."

"Then why don't we do this together." The moment he said the words, he realized his mistake.

She repeated the word *together,* managing to infuse it with enough sexual content to make herself blush.

The Major's smooth Scotch started an unwanted mambo in Delgatto's stomach. Even worse, Marie A. commandeered his wheelchair, running him up to and into the table.

"Oops." She giggled and pulled him back a couple of inches.

There, he selected from the hors d'oeuvres within

reach, piling an indiscriminate assortment of food on two plates.

While the mother and daughter team stood there, sharing looks of subterfuge and triumph, Delgatto deftly slipped the end of the tablecloth in the last link of Cleo's chain belt, which was looped loosely at her nonexistent waist.

"Shall we find a quieter corner?" He handed them the plates, then led the way, positioning himself in the lead position. His plan fell into place like well-organized dominoes.

Rather than check why her belt suddenly wanted to trail behind her, Cleo kept her matchmaking glances on Delgatto and her daughter, and gave her belt a sharp pull without looking. The tablecloth followed, dumping to the floor half of the food, as well as the silver punch bowl.

The bowl, being almost empty, bounced with a large metallic clang, creating more sound than damage. The noise startled the partygoers and drew their attention just in time to see Marie Antoinette screech in an unattractive high-pitched voice and back into her mother, who then ran into Delgatto's wheelchair.

Although the blow wasn't hard enough to knock him over, Delgatto was ready to take full advantage of the contact and threw his weight to one side, making the chair fall over. He made sure to land in a gangly sprawl, drawing even more attention to himself.

Help came from all sides except for his two screaming, crying escorts. Someone righted his chair, and Delgatto made a grand show of not letting anyone help him and crawling back up into the chair on his own. He made sure his mask came off in the process. There needed to be no questions as to who Benjamin "Wheelchair" Franklin was.

The Major intervened, taking control of the situation with a calm but firm manner. He ordered Marie and Cleo to a neutral corner, where they continued to cry hysterically and blame each other for the accident. He made a quick assessment of Delgatto's "injuries" and called for Franz, who appeared like a well-trained dog to take Delgatto back to his room.

The last domino fell perfectly.

Long ago, Delgatto had learned the turning-pale-on-command trick from a Madame LaRouche, a medium who supported herself in Dublin fleecing the living by conversing with the dead. So as Franz pushed him out, taking the most direct path, which just happened to bisect the ballroom, everyone in attendance saw poor Monsieur Galludat sitting slumped in his chair, eyes closed, face white as the proverbial sheet.

The perfect alibi.

Franz offered to help him undress and get in bed, but Delgatto declined, saying he was merely tired, not injured, and then a bunch of tommyrot about being independent and learning how to care for himself. Franz bought the explanation and left him alone.

As soon as the door closed, Delgatto counted to twenty, then jumped from the chair and stripped off his soiled costume. Benjamin Franklin would not be making a reappearance at the ball.

Neither would Monsieur Galludat.

He opened the armoire, reached into its darkest corner, and pulled out his secondary outfit. With his identity safely hidden behind the second costume and the mask, he'd be free to join in the festivities, dance, drink, eat—and, of course, find and steal the Heart of Saharanpur.

He closed his eyes, imagining the emerald, its weight resting in his hand. Just the thought of success made his palm itch. And who wouldn't savor the chase, staring down all that lovely décolletage?

After being bested by The Kid, Delgatto had entertained serious doubts that the King of Thieves would ever surface again.

A familiar sense of excitement began coursing through his veins.

The king was back.

Long live the king, baby.

When Emily entered, the ballroom didn't come to a standstill as Cornelia had prophesied. The music didn't stop. The dancers didn't freeze. But Emily still felt like the belle of the ball as several young men noticed her and started making their way through the crowd toward her. Soon, she had a slate of costumed admirers who were battling for a chance to dance with her, bringing her refreshments, paying her compliments, making her the center of their attention.

It was more than a dream come true. She'd never dared dream anything like this would happen to her, even in her finest and most self-involved daydreams.

After four rousing dances, she retired to a corner to catch her breath. Sitting at a small round table, she nursed one of the three punches she'd been served by her most dutiful admirers, whom she'd christened Tom, Dick, and Harry. They jockeyed like adolescents for her attention, bragging about their abilities and fortunes.

"Well, that's nothing," one young man dressed as a court jester said in response to another's wild boast. "I can perform not two but *three* back flips in a row."

"That's nothing." The second young man had abandoned his elaborate dog mask on the table, revealing a shock of red hair and a freckled face. "I can do that while holding a cup of punch and not spill a drop."

"Now, boys . . ." Emily stepped between the warring factions. "This isn't the right place to demonstrate such gymnastic feats."

"Let's go outside!" the third lad announced.

"No, it's snowing."

"Then let's go to—"

"Why don't you hold your competition in the Grand Foyer?" declared a deep voice from behind Emily.

"Great idea! There's plenty of room there." The three boys skidded away toward the exit, their attentions centered on their contest of skill and not on Emily, to her great relief.

But she still had to contend with this remaining suitor. She turned around to thank him and perhaps persuade him to tag after the other boys. But when she saw him step out of the shadows, her breath caught in her throat.

He wore black.

And he was no boy.

Emily wasn't sure whether he was supposed to be a highwayman or a buccaneer or what. Quite frankly, it didn't matter to her. What she saw stirred a part of her where her dreams, her imagination, and her womanly desire intersected.

He was magnificent.

Smiling, he doffed his black tricorn hat, revealing dark curly hair that spilled over the edges of the black mask that hid his identity. "The brigands have been dispatched, my lady," he said in a thoroughly American voice.

"Th-thank you," she stuttered like a schoolgirl.

He whipped his cape back, revealing a burgundy brocade vest that covered what appeared to be a flowing white shirt. His tight-fitting black breeches and boots clung to muscular legs. He reached out for her hand, and in the guise of kissing it, pulled her closer.

"In my lady's service," he whispered in a voice that sent shivers up her spine. He kissed her neck, and she found herself arching to meet him, savoring the contact of his body pressed against hers.

"Until we meet again." He melted back into the shadows and disappeared.

"Wait!" Emily stopped herself. What was she doing? He was a perfect stranger!

Then a small voice inside of her whispered, *Perfect, indeed.*

She clutched her throat, feeling her pulse, which still throbbed where his lips had grazed her skin in such a brazen but delicious action. Her heart suddenly skipped a beat.

My necklace!

She patted the neck of her costume, searching for the missing chain and pendant. *Please, tell me the chain didn't break! Tell me it hasn't fallen off!*

To her relief, she discovered the necklace had slipped itself beneath the vest and was merely hidden from view. She breathed a sigh of relief as she pulled the emerald from its hiding place and situated it in its position of honor.

Her thoughts turned back to the highwayman, and she released another sigh, this one betraying a part of her she wasn't quite ready to recognize.

Whoever you are . . . I wish you'd come back.

Delgatto had tried not to stare too openly at the woman in the fairy princess costume. He didn't have time to admire the eye candy. A surreptitious glance during their embrace had assured him she wasn't wearing the Heart of Saharanpur, so it was on to the next likely candidate.

For the first time that evening, he considered taking a break, maybe asking the princess to dance or some such thing. Then his sense of duty flooded back, filling the temporary gap in his attention span.

The news article from the future had given no details about the woman in the past who'd been wearing the necklace, so Delgatto's only recourse was to check out every woman in the place from eight to eighty—or eight hundred, as the case might be with some of the old biddies propped in the corner, tapping their canes to the music.

So far, the suave and debonair masked-man routine was working well. A stolen kiss here and a purloined hug there, and he was making pretty good headway in his search to see around the neck and down the cleavage of every female in the place.

Some sights were better than others.

And although the fairy princess's high-necked outfit didn't allow him any real view of where no man had probably gone before, he'd found her the most appealing of all the women he'd seen so far.

And he wasn't quite sure why.

Forget the fairy, he told himself as he selected his next conquest, a hatchet-faced woman dressed as the Queen of Hearts. After enduring two point three minutes with her, he couldn't bring himself to kiss her and instead employed the old "Oh my, there's a piece of lint on your shoulder" ploy to get close enough to inspect her. Seeing nothing of interest whatsoever, he pushed on to the next knot of women, evidently a group of four friends who had all dressed in bird masks—red, blue, pink, and yellow. He expected them to erupt in high-pitched giggles, but they were cool, perhaps even wary of a handsome masked stranger making their acquaintance with such deliberation. Such suspicions required a different story.

"Ladies." He motioned them closer and lowered his voice. "Are you familiar with the United States Department of Internal Defense?"

The obvious leader of the group was a tall gangly woman, perfectly personified by her pink flamingo feathers. She stared at him with a dubious gaze. "No, I don't believe we've ever heard of such an organization."

"I'd be surprised if you had," he confided. "We do try to keep a low profile."

Cardinal, a tall blond, eyed his tight pants in open admiration. "By low profile, do you mean not calling attention to one's self?"

"If so"—Blue Jay made great sport of scanning him from the tip of his boots to the top of his hat—"you're failing."

Delgatto shrugged. "When in Rome . . ."

The brunette Canary shook her head in disgust. "Please! Let's not mention the Major and his toga. It's not a sight I want to commit to memory."

Delgatto remembered the Major's hairy legs emerging from his toga and nodded in total agreement. "I'm not working with or through the Major. This is an independent, nonmilitary investigation. We suspect that one or more foreign operatives may be posing as guests and attempting to steal the personal effects of one of the hotel's real guests." He leaned forward. "I could use the help of a few observant civilians . . . like the four of you."

Their suspicions started to fade to curiosity. Blue Jay looked almost hooked. "To do what?"

"Keep your eyes open, report any suspicious behavior or activities." He paused, then added the sure clincher. "In defense of your country, of course."

The four women huddled together, sharing hurried whispers. Finally, Flamingo stepped back, allowing him into their small circle. It afforded him the perfect chance to examine them for telltale chains ending in very expensive gems.

"We'd be glad to help you. To help our country," Flamingo declared with patriotic resolution. "If we find anything, how should we contact you?"

He tapped his mask with his gloved forefinger. "My identity must remain a secret. So if you see anything or anybody suspicious, leave me a message beneath the cushion of the chair closest to the front door in the Grand Foyer." He made a pretense of seeing someone across the room. "Just sign it with a drawing of a feather so I'll know it's from you. Now, if you ladies will excuse me . . ."Delgatto tipped his hat and worked his way back into the shadows.

He continued to work his way through the room, methodically searching for the Heart. Although there were other riches that could be plundered, he did nothing other than take note of who possessed what valuable and its relative worth. Once he found and reclaimed the Heart, he'd have to fund his escape. If he stole judiciously from the various attendees, he could gather a suitable nest egg without leaving any one person particularly bereft. Then he could cool his heels for six months, return to the hotel in June, and let Miss Sparrow do what hocus-pocus she had to perform to send him back.

In some ways, the elaborate costumes made it easier to keep track of the coming and going of female guests. He kept a mental list of which women he'd examined and could dismiss based on the unique details of their costumes. As he worked the room, he kept an eye on the main door and noted who came and went.

Two hours into the ball, he'd reached a point where he'd surreptitiously examined the neck of every female in attendance. He wasn't sure whether he should breathe a sigh of relief because his plan of action seemed to be effective or kick himself because he hadn't found the Heart yet.

Whoever wrote that article had spotted the necklace. Why hadn't he done so as well?

He froze, then smacked himself in the head with his gloved palm. *You idiot.* It was all suddenly so clear to him. *Find the reporter!*

But the best way to find the reporter was to ask someone who probably knew every person in attendance, and Delgatto didn't want to chance a run-in with the Major, the very person who might realize that the Masked Highwayman was nothing more than a gate-crasher.

So Delgatto went to the next best person.

He found Rupert standing in the doorway, tapping his foot in time with the lively music.

"Nice party," Delgatto remarked, joining him at the door. He added a slight Southern twang to his voice, something the young man might remember if later asked questions about the Masked Highwayman.

"Seems to be, sir," Rupert said with a sigh. The clear message was: *How would I know? I'm stuck out here and can't come in.* He snapped out of his reverie and to attention. "Is there something I can do for you, sir?"

Delgatto waved away his question. "Nothing at all. I just came out here to get away from the crowd for a bit and thought I'd join you here. You've picked a great vantage point for viewing the room."

Rupert relaxed a bit. "Yes, sir." He gave Delgatto a quick but polite once-over. "Nice costume, sir."

"Thanks."

They stood there in relative silence, bathed in the sounds of the revelry spilling from the ballroom. After a measured moment, Delgatto spoke. "Maybe you *can* help me. I understand that your local newspaper is covering this event. Would you happen to know which person in there is their reporter?"

Rupert nodded eagerly. "Absolutely, sir. He's not here yet, but when he comes, you'll have no problem finding him. He'll be dressed in an outfit made entirely out of newspapers. Name's John Dunlop."

"Dunlop. Thanks."

The young man shot him a snappy salute. "Have a good time tonight, sir."

Delgatto scanned the ballroom. No new arrivals meant he could relax his guard, albeit only slightly. He thought about the various women he'd encountered during the evening and there was no contest as to which one had piqued his interest.

He spotted the fairy princess on the dance floor, being steered around in awkward circles by the Major. The man almost looked as if he were marching rather than dancing.

Her mask couldn't disguise her obvious discomfort. If any maiden needed rescuing, she did.

And he was all too ready to oblige.

She spotted him before the Major did, and hope flared in her eyes. As Delgatto approached, she actually mouthed the word, "Please," in anticipation of his actions.

He tapped the man on his toga shoulder. "May I cut in?"

The Major postured for a moment, remembered his place—not quite on the same elevation as the guests—then reluctantly released his hold on her. Delgatto stepped in to assume the man's place, and held her out at approximately the same arm's length distance, evidently meeting the man's approval. They both waited until they were several steps away from the Major before Delgatto pulled her closer and she whispered her thanks.

"This is the second time you've rescued me and I appreciate both times very much. Thank you."

"You're welcome. I thought you looked a bit . . . Payne'd."

She giggled at his pun. "It's not that the Major's a bad dancer. I mean, he didn't step on my feet. But I didn't feel . . . comfortable with him."

"And you do with me?"

She remained silent, but he noticed she made no effort to pull from their relatively close embrace.

"I'm sorry," he added with the proper note of contrition. "That was rude of me. Allow me to say that I hope you feel more comfortable with me."

If truth be known, she was causing him increasing discomfort of the most personal kind. Although he had no time for any sort of dalliance, if he was going to put the moves on anyone that night, it would be her. Beneath that mask, he suspected, was a beautiful face. And beneath that well-fitted costume, he was assured she had a body to die for.

"I do."

Her quiet words caught him off guard. "Pardon?"

"I do feel comfortable with you. Safe."

They were innocuous words, delivered in total innocence, with no double entendre, no winks, not even a knowing twinkle in her eye.

And they shook him to his core.

Safe? With him? He was a crook. Nothing was safe with him. Not women's jewels. Not women's hearts.

All he wanted was one Heart.

Then why did he want to stop in the middle of their dance and kiss her? To assure himself that this was nothing more than a simple, sexual attraction? That's what he ought to do. Stop dancing, kiss her, and then walk away and get back to work.

They stopped in the middle of the floor.

But theirs was no simple kiss.

As their lips met, they became the center of the

universe, with all the other dancers revolving around them in a blur of color. The music faded, drummed out of Delgatto's ears by the rush of blood from a rapidly beating heart.

Her heart or his?

He couldn't quite tell. His arms were wrapped around her, pressing her against him. The world continued to spin around them, unaware of the quiet moment of first passion they were sharing.

She broke off first, turning away and burying her face in his shoulder. "I shouldn't be doing this. I have no right."

He reached up and used his hand to gently lift her face into view. "You have every right."

She tried to smile. "No, I don't. I'm not supposed to be here."

Delgatto offered his own smile. "Neither am I."

"No." When she shook her head, her light brown curls bounced. "I'm really not supposed to be here." When she looked up, he could see enchanting green eyes hiding beneath her mask. "Please forgive me," she whispered.

She tried to step away, but he grabbed her hand. "Wait!" He watched a tear slide down her cheek, having escaped the mask that hid her identity.

"I'm sorry," she mouthed.

He stared at her, hoping to memorize every detail, knowing instinctively that this was going to be one of his greatest failures, letting her slip from his life.

He watched the tear fall from her cheek to her neck and form an uneven wet splotch on her blouse, right next to the Heart of Saharanpur.

Six

Delgatto's breath frozen in his throat.

The Heart of Saharanpur . . .

He'd seen only one picture of it. Only one painting of the Heart existed in the world, and it was kept under lock and key in a Russian museum. The gem had been immortalized in an ancestral portrait in which the ignorant artist had paid more attention to the queen wearing the necklace rather than the jewel itself. But Delgatto knew the stone as well as if he'd looked at it every day of his life.

The emerald dared to twinkle with something akin to insolence, as if mocking him. Here sat a king's ransom hung around the neck of a fairy princess.

A royal thief's dream come true.

He stretched out his hand, overwhelmed by the desire to touch the stone, possess the stone. But someone jostled his elbow.

"Here she is!"

The three young men he'd finessed earlier were now swarming them, effectively blocking him from his lifelong quest.

The tallest of the three spoke quickly to the princess. "The costume contest is about to start, Your Highness, and we believe you'll win."

Delgatto had two choices: either grab the necklace and run, or bide his time and choose a more opportune moment to take it. And despite his standing as a well-respected professional thief, his most basic nature wanted instant gratification and a chance to admire the gem's exquisite color as he cradled it in the palm of his very own hand.

Right then and right there.

But he couldn't allow a lifetime of desperation to make him act in a rash manner.

He also couldn't let a bunch of turn-of-the-century college frat boys separate him from said lifelong quest. Although not outclassed, he was certainly outnumbered. And judging by the less than friendly scowls the frats were shooting him, they'd already decided their primary mission was to drive a wedge between him and his fairy princess.

It took all the self-control he could muster to reach for her hand instead of the Heart. "It seems I must bid you *adieu* for the moment and leave you in these"—he coughed—"capable hands." He looked into eyes that took his breath away almost as thoroughly as had the sight of the stone. He leaned forward and whispered, "Meet me at the Spring Pavilion. At midnight."

After a heart-stopping delay, she gave him a small nod before being swept away by her group of admirers. But not all of the young men accompanied her. Two of them stayed behind, one standing on either side of him. They locked their arms in his and pulled him toward the nearest exit.

The last thing Delgatto wanted to do was draw unnecessary attention to himself in the ballroom, so he obliged his companions and accompanied them to an unoccupied hallway. He knew full well what they intended to do and was ready for the first punch with a countering move.

What he didn't anticipate was a third assailant waiting for them in the shadows. Delgatto managed to keep two attackers at bay, giving as good as he took, but the third man hung back, waiting for a propitious time to strike.

And when he did, it was lights out.

The young man in the court jester's outfit held Emily's hand a bit too possessively for her likes as he led her toward the costume judging area.

"I'm sure you'll win," he chattered nervously. "Then you'll truly be the Queen of the Ball." He tugged her toward the cluster of people standing by a makeshift stage. "And I'd be pleased to be your Royal Jester," he added, punctuating his remark with a bow.

Although lowly maids like her were never invited to attend The Chesterfield's famous Christmas ball, Emily had listened to tales of those who had either served at the function or had sneaked in for a few purloined moments. She'd spotted Rupert at the door at least twice, watching the proceedings.

The one thing she knew about the ball was that the winners of the costume contest were the first to unmask at midnight.

And she definitely would not be removing her mask in public tonight!

Emily glanced at an approaching group of dowagers who were also making a beeline for the contest sign-up table. As lovely and inventive as her fairy costume was, it couldn't compare to the obviously expensive and highly elaborate outfits the approaching ladies wore. However, her court jester escort continued to push her toward the table ahead of the oncoming group. She reluctantly took her place in line to register and receive a paper number to pin to her costume.

"Pardon me," one older woman sniffed as she shouldered Emily out of the way. The woman wore a Queen of Hearts outfit and had the off-with-her-head attitude to match.

The court jester bristled. "Wait your turn, lady."

The woman stiffened. "Why, I never!"

"Well you ought to." He let out a derisive snort of laughter. "It might give you something to do rather than run roughshod over innocent bystanders." He turned his back to her and nudged Emily back into her rightful place in line.

"What an insolent young man." The woman's voice rose. "I've never been so insulted in my life."

He whirled around and shook a gloved finger in the woman's face. "That's because you don't listen. People have been insulting you for years—you just don't listen carefully enough."

All Emily wanted to do was slink away, distancing herself from the rude woman as well as her own unwanted escort. The whole point of attending the ball was to quietly enjoy herself. But her beautiful gown had attracted more attention than she had expected. Her thoughts stopped at the memory of her highwayman and she shivered.

Some of the attention she had liked very much.

"What seems to be the problem?" a deep voice boomed.

Emily closed her eyes. And then there was the most unwanted attention of all . . .

The Major strode toward them, his laurel wreath knocked slightly askew, his dagger bouncing against his hairy leg. He attempted to click his heels, as was his usual military manner, but his sandals failed to make sufficient noise. He tried once more, then gave up, choosing instead to dip his head toward the dowager in acknowledgment. "May I be of some assistance, ma'am?"

She pointed one bejeweled sausage finger at the court jester. "This young man is being very rude. I want him removed at once."

"Nonsense," the jester snarled. "She tried to push her way into line, ahead of everyone else."

"I did no such thing." She used the same pudgy finger to tap the jester in the shoulder, pushing him hard enough so that he stumbled backward into Emily, knocking her off balance.

She braced herself against the table as a flare of pain shot up from her newly trod toes. To her surprise, her escort paid no attention to the fact he'd just stomped on her foot. Instead, he tightened his hands into fists and faced the Queen of Hearts.

"Listen, you old battle-ax . . ."

Fiery indignation bloomed across the woman's wide face. "Why you—"

He cut her off with a fierce scowl. "It never changes, does it? Just because you have money, you think you can—"

"Quiet!"

The Major might have been short in stature, but he made up for his lack of height with an abundance of voice. It was an attribute that guests seldom realized but something the staff lived with every day.

Especially at morning muster.

To Emily's utmost surprise, the Major stepped between both the jester and the queen, not stopping to address them, but instead, facing Emily.

"Are you injured, miss?" he asked with what Emily realized was genuine concern. "Do you need medical attention?"

She probed her foot, determining her injuries were slight, if any. "Thank you. I'll be fine."

"Are you sure?" He held out a hairy arm. "I'd be glad to escort you myself to the clinic and have Dr.—"

"No," Emily said quickly, hoping no one thought her objections odd. "No, thank you," she added. Early in her tenure as a maid, she'd tripped on a loose rug and had been subjected once to the doctor's rather odd ministrations. She'd vowed from that day on never to get sick or injured again, less she have to take his so-called treatments or bear his damp-palmed touch.

The court jester finally noticed what he'd done. Rather than apologize to Emily, he whirled to face the dowager. "See what you made me do? You made me step on her foot." He turned to the Major. "You saw her. She pushed me."

"I did nothing of the sort," the lady shouted. "All I did was inform you what a boorish, inconsiderate, ill-mannered . . ."

The Major raised one hand in hopes of halting her tirade. "Please, madam, I don't think this is the place—"

As the argument escalated, Emily chose that moment to step, or at least limp, away. The last thing she needed was this sort of unwanted and, in her opinion, unnecessary attention. As a hotel maid, she'd learned out of necessity how to deal with rude, demanding patrons without allowing them to make her feel insignificant. And to let it dissolve into name calling? Unforgivable! Too bad neither the dowager nor the jester had ever spent any time working as a servant and learned such important lessons.

As she slipped between the patrons who'd gathered to watch the fracas, she adjusted her mask, less they get a glimpse of her true identity. What would they do, what would they say if they knew the maid who had folded their undergarments and made their beds was attending their party as an uninvited guest?

I shouldn't have come, she repeated to herself as she worked her way toward the nearest door. In the distance, she thought she saw a caped figure in the hallway. Her heart quickened. Her highwayman?

She moved with more haste toward the exit, trying to negotiate an expedient pathway between the partygoers who hadn't been attracted by the imbroglio. As the crowd shifted, she momentarily lost sight of the highwayman and sped up to compensate. As she emerged into the hallway, she saw the trailing corner of a cape as the costumed man disappeared around the corner.

Emily ran as fast as possible, hampered somewhat by her now throbbing toes. She rounded the corner and skidded to a halt. The hallway was empty. No costumed men. No highwayman.

It was as if he had been a ghost.

But his very real words echoed in her ear: *"Meet me at the Spring Pavilion at midnight."*

* * *

Delgatto woke up in the dark. A thin sliver of light near his feet suggested he was behind a door, perhaps in a closet. Pushing away something that felt suspiciously like a broom, he fumbled for the doorknob, which pulled loose in his hand. He fought the urge to throw the knob, figuring it would most likely bounce off a wall and smack him in the face.

Instead, he patted the hidden pocket in his cape, pleased to discover his attackers hadn't rolled him before stuffing him in the janitor's closet. He pulled out the set of picks he'd modified from various bits of hairpins, bedsprings, and needles he'd pilfered when putting together his costume.

The lock had been designed only to keep out the curious, not protect a fortune in cleaning supplies. It took him no more than one flick of the wrist to free himself, but he stepped cautiously into the hallway, trying to adjust his eyes to the sudden change in lighting. It wouldn't do to be jumped and stuffed back into the blasted thing. Luckily, no frat boys were hanging around for a second attack.

He rubbed the sore spot on the back of his head. How long had he been out? His stomach did a small tango as he remembered his rather important appointment.

Midnight! Please don't let it be midnight.

His stomach switched to the rumba. *Or after midnight.*

He squinted at his wrist, half expecting to find his watch. He allowed himself a few choice curse words as he stumbled down the hallway, furiously plotting the most direct way to his rendezvous with destiny, fortune, family honor . . .

He skidded through the lobby, hearing a clock chime the hour. He counted as he made his way through the other costumed revelers.

One, two, three, four . . .

He spotted one of his attackers. Rather than confront the man, Delgatto ducked behind a rather large woman dressed as a peacock, using her to shield his progress to the door.

Five, six, seven, eight . . .

He made it to the front door. Rather than go down the stairs to the driveway, he stayed on the porch, weaving in and out of the partygoers. The crowd noise began to overpower the chimes.

Nine.

He spotted another of his attackers at the end of the porch. This time, the young man spotted him. Even worse, the young man waved to someone behind Delgatto.

Ten.

Delgatto turned around and saw the first attacker. They began to move toward him, hemming him in.

Eleven.

Left no other recourse, Delgatto chose his only avenue of escape. He leaped to the porch railing, balanced on the thin iron rail for a moment, then executed a flip, aiming his trajectory so that he cleared the shrubbery. Thanks to his two years as an acrobat in a traveling European circus, he landed with a neat tuck and roll.

As he flipped up to his feet, he thought he heard the faint start of the twelfth chime, but it was drowned out by the roar of applause from the crowd, who must have thought he was part of the hotel's entertainment. He paused long enough to give them a quick bow before speeding off to the gazebo, where he hoped and prayed his fairy princess waited with the Heart of Saharanpur.

He approached the area cautiously, half expecting the third attacker to step out of the shadows. Something bothered him about their need for retribution. All he'd done was encourage them to conduct their competition elsewhere.

No harm, no foul.

Certainly no scam or setup. Yet their response had been more aggressive than the situation warranted.

He circled the wooden gazebo, wondering what he'd find waiting for him. His heart's desire? Or just some juvenile undesirables?

A cloud of steam hung in the center of the gazebo, partially obscuring his view of the area. He could hear nothing but the soothing gurgle of the hot spring that the gazebo circled.

"Your Majesty?" he called out softly.

There was no answer.

"Queen Mab?"

Still no answer. Maybe she didn't realize he was addressing her. They hadn't exactly exchanged names or anything.

"Hey, Tinkerbell . . ."

Only the bubbling spring answered him.

His heart wedged itself in his throat, threatening to cut off his air completely. Still wary of a second attack, he approached the gazebo with every sense tuned to the max. He climbed the stairs, two at a time.

"Olly, olly oxen free . . ."

The gazebo was empty, save for a piece of paper pinned under a smooth rock to one of the benches. Delgatto snagged the paper on the fly, then jumped the gazebo railing and headed for the shadows. He wasn't going to hang around there and read it out in the open. The note could be a fake, designed to distract him into playing sitting duck.

Safely tucked in the bushes, he found there was just enough light to read the carefully inked words.

Dear Sir,

I'm afraid "sir" sounds terribly impersonal, but since I don't know your name, it'll have to do. I debated quite seriously the merits of meeting you as you requested, listening to both my heart and my head.

As you might have guessed, my head won. I'm not who or what you think I am. But I will forever cherish the memory of tonight and thoughts of what could have been.

Thank you,
Your Fairy Princess

The paper pleated unevenly between his clenched fingers. He was too angry to speak. The Heart of Saharanpur had been within his grasp, and instead of romancing it out from beneath its owner, he'd had to play it safe.

He let loose a string of curses that made him feel marginally better. He'd failed in his first attempt to retrieve the Heart. At least he could take some solace in the fact he'd seen it, knew it really existed.

Even better, he knew it was here and in the possession of one of the Chesterfield's more enchanting guests.

He released his breath.

Now . . . if I can only figure out who in the hell she is.

Emily sat at the writing desk, staring at the pages strewn across it. The note had been far harder to write than she'd ever imagined. She'd started and discarded at least five different versions of her note.

At first, she thought of herself as brazen merely for anticipating a relationship that, in reality, consisted of one complicated kiss and no more. But the more she wrote, the more the potential had become something she couldn't ignore.

She leaned back in the desk chair and closed her eyes. She'd seen, even known charming men before. Handsome ones, too. She'd even been kissed once or twice.

But never had she experienced a kiss like his. It was as if during it, she'd heard a lifetime of promises in the flash of that one brief moment.

But who was making those promises?

This total stranger?

Or was she merely putting words in his mouth as he placed his lips against hers? Had she been caught up in the intoxication of the moment to give him motives and actions that weren't really his?

She stood up and began to march around the room, trying to push away her fantastical thoughts and surrender to the rhythm of logic.

It was just a kiss, she thought in cadence to her steps.

It doesn't mean a thing. She repeated the thought as she made a circuit around the large room, the words and her steps quickening. *It was just a kiss, a kiss, yes, it doesn't mean a thing, a thing . . .*

By the third repetition, she'd made a complete circuit of the room and she took the extra steps to steer around the desk and stand by the bed.

As a child, she'd been taught she could literally drum ill thoughts or untruths out of her head by repeating their antithesis until they became more familiar and comfortable than the lies.

But this time, it wasn't working.

She launched herself at the large bed and, once the mattress reverberations stopped, buried her face into the nearest pillow.

"It wasn't just a kiss," she told the crisp white material. "And it does mean something. . . ."

Dreams punctuated Emily's sleep.

She dreamed that The Chesterfield wasn't a resort hotel, but a castle; and she was Cinderella at the royal ball. When the clock bells began to toll midnight, she made her escape, dutifully leaving behind her slipper for the prince to find. She reached her carriage when the clock struck twelve. To her surprise, her transport failed to revert to a pumpkin. Climbing in, she discovered the carriage had been commandeered by none other than the highwayman.

"I've been waiting for you," he said in a throaty growl.

He reached down, lifted her foot, and removed the remaining slipper. Her skin burned despite his gentle touch.

"Now the prince will have a matching pair," he explained as he tossed the shoe out the window. He turned his attention back to her, first removing her crown and then untying and pulling free the strings that held her wings in place.

"So you won't be tempted to fly away . . ."

His smile was wicked, but not half as wicked as the thoughts that filled her imagination.

He motioned for her to turn around. In her dream, it seemed a perfectly normal request that she followed without question. The highwayman began to toy with the tiny row of rose-shaped buttons that started at her neck and plunged far below her waist. With each successful unbuttoning, he celebrated by kissing her newly exposed skin.

As he worked his way down, her emotions and desires built like a whirlwind, picking up speed with each soft brush of his lips against her fevered skin. It was a heavenly feeling, being caused by a devilish man, and she knew she must resist such a glorious sin.

But she couldn't.

"Who are you?" she managed to say between gasps caused by his exquisite torture. "Who are you?"

His voice changed to a high falsetto. "It's me, Miss Sparrow."

Emily shook with a start, bolting upright in bed. She heard the woman's voice again. "Miss Drewitt, you must let me in, quickly!"

All Emily's sluggish mind wanted to do was to close her eyes and try to recapture the delicious sensations she'd left behind in her dreams. But she couldn't put aside the instinct to obey her former supervisor and gracious benefactress.

Emily padded across the Persian rug to the door and unlocked it. Miss Sparrow slipped through an impossibly thin opening and shut the door firmly behind her. "We have a big problem, Miss Drewitt."

Emily tried not to yawn as she stretched. "What, Miss Sparrow?"

"The Major is headed this way. Rupert is going to try to stall him as long as possible, but we can't count on gaining too much time."

The shocking news succeeded in restoring Emily's full faculties. "Coming here? But why? Did I do something wrong?"

Miss Sparrow offered her a thin-lipped smile. "You've done nothing at all wrong. It's just that we've learned that Mr. VanderMeer's cousin is scheduled to arrive on the noon train. He'll be staying in this suite."

"Today?"

"Unfortunately." Miss Sparrow scanned the room with a practiced eye. "We must get you and your belongings out of here before the Major arrives. He decided he needed to oversee the cleaning process personally." The woman marched over to the bed and began straightening out the sheets that Emily had tangled in her throes of dream-passion. Emily began to empty out the wardrobe, retrieving first her sewing basket, then stuffing it as well as articles of clothing indiscriminately into her carpetbag. As she ducked beneath a table to retrieve an errant shoe, she asked, "Why was there so little notice?"

Miss Sparrow punched the pillow a bit violently. "Edna Jean Barund was at the telegraph office several days ago to pick up a telegram she was expecting. Silas, the operator, had just received one for Major Payne, and Edna Jean offered to carry it back. Unfortunately, she stuffed it into her apron pocket and promptly forgot about it. She found it minutes ago." The woman's face darkened. "Three days late."

Emily grimaced. Although she had never been fond of the terminally grumpy woman, Emily could imagine the volcanic proportions of the Major's rage. She shivered at the thought and doubled her efforts. If the Major was on a rampage, the last place Emily wanted to be was in his path.

Or anywhere in the general vicinity.

A stern male voice echoed from the hallway. "Young man, will you cease and desist this interference?"

"Quick!" Miss Sparrow skidded over to Emily's position and grabbed her by the arm. She pointed to the butler's door. "Go out there and get dressed! Then come back to the suite by the front door."

"Huh?" Emily snagged her carpetbag with her trailing hand before Miss Sparrow could tug her off her feet and push her toward the door.

"Your uniform. Put it on!"

Emily ran toward the door, trying to keep her open bag from spilling over. Miss Sparrow followed behind, picking up the trailing clothes. Emily slipped out the butler's door and turned around in time to get hit in the face with the remainder of her clothing.

"Hurry," Miss Sparrow said through clenched teeth.

The door slammed closed and a moment later, the Major's roar filled the room. Emily picked up only a few words, but she fully understood the gist of what he was saying.

". . . two hours, forty-six minutes to clean . . .

fresh drapes . . . flowers . . . mattress . . . pig-sty . . ."

Emily gathered her scattered belongings, shoved them into her bag, and then tiptoed down the servants' hallway. There was no private place to change clothes, but she found a shadowy corner partially hidden behind an extra chest of drawers being stored there. To her relief, no one stumbled onto her hiding place as she changed into her maid's outfit. Once dressed, she left her bag in the bottom drawer of the chest and took a roundabout route before emerging in the guest hallway that led to the suite.

As she raised her hand to knock on the door, an odd thought hit her. *But why am I doing this? I don't work here anymore.*

Miss Sparrow flung the door open and grabbed Emily by the same arm she'd used to push her away. "Here's our replacement, Major Payne. I told you I could find a suitable replacement for Miss Barund." She winked at Emily. "We were very lucky to catch Miss Drewitt before she headed home."

The Major stepped into view. "Ah, yes. Drewitt. At least we don't have to train you. Your duty is to return this suite to its usual pristine condition. Not only did the former maid responsible for its upkeep shirk her duties, she failed to give me some very important information." He leveled Emily with a stony stare. "I trust you won't let me down and dishonor yourself like Barund did."

"N-no, sir. I won't. I promise."

"Good." He turned to Miss Sparrow. "I'll leave this in your capable hands. Mr. VanderMeer's nephew will be on the noon train. I want this room spick-and-span-new by the first train whistle."

"Yes, sir," they responded in chorus. As soon as the door closed behind the Major, Emily and Miss Sparrow turned and faced each other.

"I have my job back!" Emily exclaimed.

Miss Sparrow nodded, gracing her with a rare grin. "Who says you can't find the good in a bad situation? Although Edna Jean's incompetence has caused several problems, not to mention the abrupt elimination of your lodgings, her departure also gives you a new position and place to live." The woman glanced around. "However, your new room will bear little resemblance to this."

Emily pulled a dust cloth from the tin bucket of supplies at Miss Sparrow's feet. "Too much luxury is like too much sugar," she declared. "After a while, you lose the taste for it." She pulled on her best smile. "My new room may be less luxurious, but it'll be far easier to keep clean."

Miss Sparrow nodded. "That's a good way to think about this situation."

Emily began to polish the hall table a bit too enthusiastically. It was the only thing she'd allowed herself to think. Anything else, and she'd break out in tears . . . and everybody knew salt water wasn't good for furniture.

Seven

Delgatto stayed up into the wee hours, berating himself for his stupidity, his gullibility, and his total lack of skill as a Royal Thief. Even worse, his head ached as if someone had been playing timpani with his temples.

And speaking of drums, he knew he ought to be drummed out of the thieves guild. Out of his family. Out of this world, the next one, and anything that came after that.

What a dumbass mistake to make, he thought as he finally found a comfortable position in bed.

But a fitful night's sleep helped him gain a bit more perspective. His dreams were not fantasies of finding the Heart of Saharanpur in a wrapped box beneath the Christmas tree. Instead, his dreams, as usual, were a methodical planning tool, the part of his brain that stayed up while the conscious body slept, plotting his next steps toward the recovery of the emerald.

By the time he awoke, he'd mentally run through a dozen scenarios and settled on the one that had the best chance of succeeding.

The first step, literally, occurred at breakfast. As Franz pushed him toward the dining room, Delgatto greeted each person he passed with a hearty "Happy Christmas." To his surprise, their responses were equally as enthusiastic, if not more genuine. Breakfast was a vast buffet, the dishes reflecting the typical holiday fare from more than a dozen countries. He directed Franz to heap a wide selection and ambitious amount of food on his plate and then escort him to an empty table.

There were more families than he'd expected. He'd not seen that many kids running amuck through the hotel. Of course, with Major Payne roaming the hallways . . .

He counted at least a dozen small children eating breakfast, all dressed in their finest clothes: starched lace collars, elaborate hair ribbons, velvet suits. One particular boy looked absolutely miserable, tugging at a collar which had probably fit a week ago, but that he'd outgrown by that morning. Delgatto felt a familiar and sympathetic ache in his shin bones, having gone through a couple of painful growth spurts himself during those years.

The kid would be a great foil. Plus, he'd probably be thrilled to get out of the snug blue velvet suit as soon as possible.

Next, Delgatto needed an unimpeachable witness. A child didn't count. He needed an adult, preferably one whose powers of observation wouldn't be questioned. He watched Mrs. Biddle enter the dining room and he practically stood as he waved, trying to get her attention.

Calm down, he chastised himself. *Don't overplay your hand. You know better than that.*

Mrs. Biddle acknowledged him with one curt nod of her steel-gray bun and proceeded to the buffet, where she filled her plate. As she approached the table, she sidestepped one small girl who had broken away from her parents in order to investigate the Christmas tree in the corner of the room.

"Children," Mrs. Biddle said with something akin to a sneer.

"You don't like children?"

She sat down and arranged her napkin and utensils. "I can appreciate properly disciplined ones, but those are becoming fewer and far between. Things have changed since when I was a child. We were taught respect for our elders and instilled with a sense of propriety and manners. Not like the children of today. Most of them are being allowed to run wild without sufficient supervision."

How many times had he heard the same complaints made in his own time period? Evidently, every older generation was cocksure the younger one was going to the dogs.

Some things never changed.

He adopted his brightest smile. "It's Christmas. We can let the little heathens . . . er . . . darlings have one day of unmitigated joy, I suppose."

She sampled her eggs cautiously. "I must say you're in a good mood."

It's time . . .

"I feel glorious. I haven't felt this way in years, not even before the accident."

"Why the sudden change?" Her gray eyebrows pinched toward each other. "Don't tell me you've allowed Dr. Ziegler to talk you into some questionable procedures. Or that you've started taking his special black draught. That elixir is nothing more than pure grain alcohol with some coloring in it."

"Absolutely not. You cautioned me that he was—how do you say it?—a quack, and I've taken your warnings to heart." He flexed his arms as if to demonstrate his new strength. "It's the hot springs and the mud baths. They've made me feel like a new man."

She graced him with a benevolent smile. "I told you so."

He attacked his breakfast with artificial gusto. He'd much rather have a cup of Starbucks and a low-fat toaster pastry than this huge collection of fat and cholesterol. He could hear his arteries screaming in protest. Or was that merely the blood singing through his veins in anticipation of his next move?

Adrenaline had a way of clearing out the cobwebs in one's mind as well as one's arteries.

He paused between forkfuls. "Did you attend the ball last night?"

She stiffened. "No, I don't enjoy such frivolities. When people wear masks, they're tempted to take liberties they shouldn't."

"But it wasn't like that at all. You should have gone! It was magnificent. All those costumes, all those people having a wonderful time, dancing, laughing . . ." He leaned forward in conspiracy. "There was this one woman in a fairy costume who looked as if she'd stepped right out of the pages of a storybook! She was dazzling!" He paused and gazed across the room in an almost dreamlike state. "I've never seen anyone quite like her!"

Mrs. Biddle issued a small chuckle. "You sound smitten. Did you go up to her? Talk to her?"

He ducked his head. "I was too shy. How could I tell her that one look upon her beauty, one fleeting moment in her presence had done me more good than a dozen doctors?"

"Men," his companion said with a harrumph. "What good is mooning in the wings over a woman? You should have gone up to her, spoken to her. You should have at least introduced yourself to her."

He sighed and nodded. "You're right. And now I don't even know who she is because I had to leave before the unmasking."

She must have taken pity on him, because her usually rigid face softened. "I know most of the guests here. What did she look like?"

"It's hard to describe. She wore an elaborate mask that covered much of her face, disguising her identity. Average height and weight, I'd say. Brown curly hair." He pretended to mull over a mental image. "She wore some kind of necklace, maybe a family heirloom—a large green stone on a gold chain."

Mrs. Biddle shook her head. "Doesn't sound particularly familiar. The necklace, that is. However, her physical description could fit a dozen women around here, young and old."

He pushed away his plate, unable to endure the pretense of hearty eating any longer. "How can I find her? To thank her?"

"For what?"

"For this . . ." He rolled back a few feet from the table, turned his chair so he was facing the Christmas tree, and, after giving the woman a calculatingly shaky smile, he began to push himself upright. Finally, he stood in front of his wheelchair, at first unsteadily, then gaining more balance.

"Why, Mr. Galludat, that's wonderful!"

He shot her a determined but excited smile. "It gets better."

He pivoted and took one lurching, off-balance step, followed by another one, this time slightly more controlled. With each successive step, he grew stronger and steadier and the room became quiet. Soft gasps and hushed whispers filled the silence.

As he reached the tree, he knew he needed a big finish. He'd thought about falling to get the room's attention, but judging by the sounds and the few faces he could see, he already had them in the palm of his hand. He had sympathy now and needed to mix in a little sentimentality.

He spotted the little girl who had abandoned breakfast to examine the blown glass ornaments adorning the tree. Someone had also decorated the tree with white candy canes, but evidently small hands had stripped the candy from all the branches within their limited reach.

Making slow, steady progress toward the tree, Delgatto reached up, plucked a candy cane from a high bough, and then, with deliberate stiffness, bent over, handed it to the child, and patted her benignly on the head.

"Happy Christmas, little one," he said, making sure his voice broke in mid-sentence.

Rather than be in awe of what a magnificent medical miracle had been wrought on this, Christmas Day, that a poor tortured soul had been released from the shackles of his disabilities, the little girl snatched the proffered cane, wiped her nose on her sleeve, shoved the candy in her mouth, and mumbled, "More."

"Try 'thank you'," he said under his breath, not breaking his beatific smile.

Applause erupted around the room, and a crowd of well-wishers surged toward him. Delgatto took the opportunity, babbling excitedly about his Christmas miracle and making sure he loudly placed the inspiration of such a miraculous recovery on the lovely shoulders of the beautiful woman who'd dressed as a fairy at the ball.

He called the crowd to attention.

"I know this is an unusual request, but I feel I owe quite a debt of gratitude to the woman who inspired my recovery. If she is indeed in the room, I wish she would identify herself. Or if any of you know who she is, please point her out to me. It is imperative I let her know what a pivotal role she has played in my life and my future."

To his surprise, no one claimed to have been the fairy, nor did they know who had worn the costume. He didn't try to disguise his real disappointment.

Someone slapped an arm around his back. "Don't worry, son. We'll help you find the little filly." Horace McKinney shot him a toothy smile. "Right folks?"

A chorus of well-wishers replied with promises of help. Then the crowd suddenly parted, a swathe cut through them by Mrs. Biddle pushing Delgatto's wheelchair. Judging by the looks of the people's faces, she steered without concern about their toes.

"Here," she commanded. "You don't want to overdo your first day on your feet. Sit."

He hesitated, not wanting to finish quite yet.

But McKinney damned near pushed him into the chair. "You heard the lady, son."

Delgatto complied. As they rolled back to the table, the crowd and their congratulations waned. Evidently, even Christmas miracles didn't warrant more than the typical fifteen minutes of fame. But that didn't bother him. He'd received the right response from a sufficient number of eyewitnesses to continue his plan.

It was simple, really. In the future, people exercised for hours on the Stairmaster; here in the past, he'd put in his hours on the stairs themselves, calling it "therapy" as he struggled to publicly reactivate long-disused muscles. And when people got used to the sight of him on the stairs, they wouldn't think twice when he added a new regimen of walking down the hotel's long hallway

All for exercise, you see.

And no one in the world would suspect poor Count Galludat was deliberately widening his walking range so he'd have the freedom to break into the room of every female guest at The Chesterfield, should the need arise.

He almost rubbed his hands in greedy glee. One of those guest rooms contained the Fairy Princess and her royal necklace and he was going to find both of them.

Too bad he could only keep one.

Miss Sparrow dismissed Emily as soon as she gathered the regular girls who always cleaned the Tower suites. They knew where all the dust bunnies hid and several tricks about moving some of the larger pieces without leaving unsightly scrapes on the floor.

Emily ended up with Cornelia's hallway and Cornelia inherited Edna Jean's area of responsibility.

Emily was secretly glad not to be reminded of her former living arrangements. She'd assumed the new hallway could be no worse than the rooms she'd cleaned in the past.

She was wrong.

This group of invalid hall rooms had very special guests with equally special needs. That meant it took extra special care to clean their rooms. The guest in the first room evidently had taken a mud bath but not bathed sufficiently in the bathhouse, choosing instead to leave dark telltale footprints across the room and a dark ring in the bathtub. She cracked open the door to the hallway, expecting to see matching marks on the carpet outside, ones she would have to get on her hands and knees to scrub, but luckily there were none.

No mystery there. The guest must have been transported by chair back to his room. Emily started examining the furniture and drapes, discovering smudges where the guest had braced himself as he walked to the bathroom.

She couldn't blame the guest, then. The real guilt lay squarely on the massive shoulders of the guest's assigned attendant, who should have assisted his charge in showering both at the bathhouse and in the room. She made a mental note to mention it to Miss Sparrow who would, in turn, talk to the head of the attendants.

After an hour of scrubbing, cleaning, dusting, sweeping, and sheet changing, Emily balanced her hands on her hips and scanned the room, admiring her handiwork. She tried to savor the sense of accomplishment, but the memory of her time spent in luxury tickled the back of her mind. Those had been very precious days she had spent lounging around the elegant suite.

Her mouth suddenly started watering for strawberries, and she remembered she'd just started a new book from the suite's private library and now would never know how it ended.

She trudged to the next room, finding it devilishly hard to build the enthusiasm needed to clean up behind a very large woman who'd evidently had a hissy fit and broken two water glasses by hurling them across the room. After carefully picking up the shards of glass, Emily began the delicate process of cleaning the strong alcoholic smell from the wallpaper.

Unable to remove all the signs of the woman's rage, Emily managed to shove the dresser over several inches to cover the offending stain. She pulled her notebook from her apron and made a notation about the stain with the date. Major Payne insisted on written records to substantiate all room damage and the last thing Emily wanted to do was give the Major an excuse to get rid of her, especially her first day back to work.

Before she entered the third room, she stopped at the door to pray another disaster wasn't awaiting her. She knocked and, receiving no answer, used her passkey to enter.

The room was dark. In order to see, she had to stumble to the window without tripping over unseen obstacles and throw back the heavy drapes that blocked out all light. The strong sun blinded her for a moment. After her eyes cleared, she turned around, fearing to see what inventive mess awaited her.

The room was perfect.

The bed was made. The towels were folded and on the rack. Dishes on the food tray had been wiped clean and stacked neatly, something few guests ever did. She gaped at the unexpected sight and allowed herself a smile.

"Thank you," she whispered. "A Christmas present at last."

Despite the room's seeming perfection, there was still work to be done—towels and sheets to be exchanged, furniture to be dusted.

But knowing at least one guest had such consideration renewed her flagging energies. She began to hum as she dropped the clean linens on the bed and walked into the bathroom in order to clean and polish its fixtures. As she collected the used towels, she heard the main door close.

"Sir?" she called out, knowing most guests didn't want to be surprised by an unexpected person popping out at them.

There was no answer. She stepped out with her armload of towels and practically dropped them as she saw the man kneeling on the floor beside the bed. His abandoned wheelchair sat behind him, suggesting he had fallen out.

"Sir, are you all right?" she said, rushing toward him.

He flinched, raised up, and hit his head on the edge of the bed frame. He sprawled spread-eagled on the carpet, cradling his head in his hands.

"Don't move, sir." Emily dropped the towels where she stood. "I'll go get help!"

"No," he commanded in a surprisingly strong voice. "I'm all right. Just a little rattled."

To her amazement, he rolled over with relative ease to a sitting position, still pressing his palm against his injured head. She didn't expect such mobility in an invalid.

"You startled me," they said simultaneously. They both laughed, hers nervous and his slightly pained.

He shifted to push himself up to his knees, but lost his balance. Emily responded in an instant, bracing him, trying to help him to the bed. Somehow they got tangled, and her efforts ended up making them both fall to the bed in a provocative heap, with Emily on the bottom.

"You startled me again," he offered, his lips only inches away from her cheek.

"I'm s-sorry," she stuttered. They were in a most unseemly position, one that made her feel uneasy in some very odd ways. Although she ignored her lack of size in most cases, figuring that determination could make up for shortness in stature, for a moment, she felt particularly small.

And vulnerable.

He stared at her. "Do I know you?" He shot her a devastating grin which made her toes curl. "And if we haven't met, I think this constitutes a formal introduction."

She found it increasingly hard to speak and tried to convince herself it was merely because of his weight pressing into her. Not his presence alone . . .

"T-train," she managed to gasp. "M-met at train."

"Ah, yes, the train. Now I remember. You woke me. When I first saw you, I thought you were an angel." His gaze danced lightly over her face. "And now I fully see why I made such an understandable mistake."

As much as Emily somewhat enjoyed the odd feelings he was stirring in her, she knew their unseemly position could be instant grounds for her dismissal. "Please," she hissed between her gritted teeth. "Let me try to slide out. If anyone sees us . . ."

"If anyone sees us, I'll explain how you jumped to my rescue when you thought I'd been injured." He locked his arms straight, suddenly freeing her from the pressure of his weight. She slid out of his awkward embrace, lost her balance, and landed on the floor.

He flipped around to a seated position on the bed, extending his hand toward her. "Now it's my turn. Are you all right?"

She refused his hand, figuring that they'd end up in another tangle on the bed, and she might not survive a second close call. "Fine, sir," she said, struggling to her feet. "It's you . . . um . . . your health that concerns me. Did you fall from your chair? Should I go fetch the doctor?"

He withdrew his helping hand and rubbed the back of his head instead. "I'm fine . . . and I didn't fall. I was looking for my shoes under the bed." A new light entered his eyes. "I need my shoes now. Something wonderful has happened." He stood up, grabbed the crutches nearby and demonstrated a few hesitant steps. "They're calling it a Christmas miracle. I tend to agree."

"Miracle indeed, sir. Congratulations. As I told you when we met, the hot springs can work wonders."

"It wasn't the hot springs. It was a woman. A beautiful woman at the costume ball last night. She . . . inspired me. And look at me now." He executed a perfect turn.

Emily's smile had genuine origins, but deep inside, she allowed herself to entertain a bit of disappointment. How marvelous it would be to inspire such a man back to good health and obvious happiness. But it couldn't have been her. First, she wasn't the type to inspire any man to any feats, miraculous or not. And second, she didn't remember seeing any of the costumed revelers sitting in their wheeled chairs.

"That's wonderful, sir. Would you prefer I come back later to finish your room?"

He looked around, wearing a confused look. "Why are you working? It's Christmas. You should be home with your family, celebrating."

Emily tried to maintain her smile. "The Chesterfield offers its guests complete service every day of the year." Her smile faltered a bit. "And I guess you could say that right now, The Chesterfield and its staff are my family."

"Then this guest declines your services. The least I can do is offer you a day off from cleaning up behind the likes of me. Take the time you would have spent in here doing something else, like taking it easy. Sit down, put your feet up, and drink a cup of coffee." He reached into his pocket and pulled out a coin which he slipped deftly into her pocket. "Consider it a Christmas present from me."

"But, sir—"

"No buts." He reached toward the foot of the bed and straightened the stack of clean linens sitting there. "I'm perfectly capable of making my own bed."

"But—"

He raised his forefinger to his lips to silence her. His eyes twinkled. "Merry Christmas, Miss . . ."

"Emily. Emily Drewitt."

"Merry Christmas, Miss Drewitt. Now get out of here and go enjoy yourself."

The door closed firmly behind Emily and she stood in the hallway, clutching the soiled linens. She slipped her hand into her apron pocket and pulled out the twenty-dollar gold piece. Only once before had she ever received a gratuity like that, and it had been accompanied by some very improper suggestions of how she could repay her benefactor. She had dropped the coin into the water glass on the bedside stand, which also contained the man's teeth, and run out.

Emily held the coin tightly in the palm of her hand. There had been no obvious strings attached to this gift. No lascivious suggestions. No indecent proposals. She started down the hallway, then stopped.

Then why did she feel . . . awkward accepting it?

She pivoted and returned to the door, where her knocks rang with an ominous tone.

The door opened, and the man's face lit with another smile. "Emily! Hi again. Did you leave something behind?"

She held out her hand, the coin catching the light and winking insolently. "I need to leave this. I can't accept this, sir."

He wrapped his warm hand around hers, gently curling her fingers around the coin again. "Yes, you can. It's a present. From me to you."

"B-but I can't accept that much."

"Sure you can. Once, long ago, my mother worked as a maid, and she told me stories about all the things she had to do. She was underappreciated, underpaid, and always overworked. So let me at least offer you a small token." He paused for a reverential moment. "For *ma mère's* sake."

"Your m-mother . . ." Emily repeated, finding herself suddenly lost in his dark, handsome gaze.

"Say 'Merry Christmas,' Emily," he prompted.

"Merry Christmas," she dutifully repeated.

As he closed the door, he added, "And let me know if you see any Christmas creatures with wings. There's one certain Christmas angel I'm desperate to meet."

Eight

Delgatto closed the door behind him, berating himself for the close call. He hadn't had time to rid himself of the entire highwayman's costume and had hidden it under the bed instead, waiting for the opportune time. After all, he didn't want anyone to make a connection between a crippled count and the very mobile highwayman.

How the hell was he supposed to know the maid would be there?

At least she'd fallen for his charming stranger routine. His stomach suddenly twisted with an unfamiliar emotion. It took him a moment to identify it: honest guilt.

If truth be known, he wasn't being charming merely to distract her from his real mission. He'd been attracted to her, pure and simple. He remembered her with all too much clarity from the train.

At first, he'd thought she was an angel. Considering his rather devilish nature, it seemed like a good offset, good to balance evil.

But now, as in the rest of his career, he didn't have time to pursue any sort of natural pairing, no personal relationships with a maid, a madam or a matron.

Come to think of it . . .

The key—pardon the pun—attraction of a maid was access to her passkey, something he'd found infinitely useful in the future. Then again, that was . . . or at least would be . . . the days of electronic card locks one couldn't easily pick without a slew of electronic gadgets. He glanced at the polished wooden door and its simple and ineffective lock.

Who needs a passkey?

Something else twisted in his gut, this time a pang rather than a pain.

Me, if it means getting a chance to be close to her.

Delgatto shook his head as if able to shake away such counterproductive thoughts.

Bad boy. Let's get our mind out of the gutter, OK, Delgatto?

What he needed to do was concentrate on exactly how he was going to rid himself of the costume without anyone knowing.

His decision?

Do it one piece at a time, and in different places. If he played his cards right, no one would be able to trace any of the highwayman's costume back to the recovering count out for a stroll. He reached under the bed and retrieved the bundle, separating out the brocade vest and securing the rest back in its hiding place. Folding the vest into the smallest possible bundle, he slipped it into the pocket of his heavy coat where it barely made a bulge.

It was high time for the count to venture outside for a bracing blast of winter air. For a moment, he had a mental image of himself as another count—in this case, Dracula—swooping down on the unsuspecting Emily Drewitt, paying particular attention to her very lovely neck.

Get a grip, man.

There was a time for everything, and this was the right time to start ridding himself of the costume.

His belabored trip to the front foyer was filled with Christmas greetings and congratulations for his newfound abilities. Only one person seemed less than enthused about his miraculous recovery.

The Major.

Perhaps it was the man's usual nature to be suspicious of everybody and about everything. But when he approached Delgatto, he wore something beyond his usual aloof look. His words bordered on mockery. "I see congratulations are indeed in order, Monsieur Galludat. I'd heard word of your Christmas miracle, and I see the gossip was true. You're walking."

"It's marvelous, isn't it?" Delgatto exclaimed with just the right tinge of excitement. "And I owe it all to The Chesterfield."

The Major cracked the smallest and coldest of smiles. "That's not what I heard. Someone said you were crediting your . . . miracle to one of our guests." His expression said, *And if you do, you're either the biggest fool in these parts or have a scam going.*

Delgatto shrugged, nearly losing his balance on the crutches. "What can I say? I'm French, and we're notorious for being hopeless romantics. I will admit that a beautiful young woman may have helped me gird my strength, but in reality, it was the restorative powers of the hot springs and those *magnifique* mud baths that caused me to regain that strength in the first place. As to the beautiful young woman dressed in white with angel wings and wearing a feathered mask, she's merely the one who inspired me to reach this new plateau."

He paused for a moment. "You wouldn't happen to know who she was, would you? I'd like to thank her for providing me such sterling motivation."

"I know who you're talking about"—the Major blushed slightly—"but I never saw her unmasked. I'm afraid I don't know who she was, either."

Aha! So the Major had noticed her, too. Probably every man in the place had. But Delgatto found it oddly disconcerting to learn the Major had a heart buried deep within his stiff personality and even worse, that they might have the same taste in women.

Delgatto pressed on. "If you do learn who she is, would you let me know? I'd like a chance to express my thanks in person."

"Certainly." The blush faded quickly and the Major turned back into his usual self, a stiff, efficient manager. But his sense of distrust melted away as well. "Then let me wish you a Happy Christmas as well as give you my congratulations for your first steps on a road of recovery."

"Thank you, Major Payne."

"Should I call a carriage for you?" The Major nodded at Delgatto's coat.

"No, thank you. I'm merely stepping outside for a breath of fresh air." *And to get rid of some of the evidence.*

"Then I'll let you be on your way. Good evening, sir." The military man pivoted sharply and headed off in the opposite direction, most probably to accost some other poor, innocent schmuck.

The doorman wore a smile as wide as the door he opened. By the time Delgatto reached the first chair on the covered porch, a dozen people had greeted him and half of them made highly encouraging remarks about his newfound abilities. It almost made him sad to be fooling them. Then again, no one would be hurt by his actions. All he intended to do was track down his family's possession and restore it to their ownership.

Their *rightful* ownership.

He managed to clump down the portico stairs just awkwardly enough to look inexperienced with the crutches as well as with his new sense of mobility, but possessing enough control that no one tried to help him. At the bottom of the stairs, he found a large barrel filled with ash.

The bellboy named Rupert was trudging up the driveway, evidently returning from one of the outlying buildings. He greeted Delgatto with a hearty hello.

"I heard you were back on your feet, Mr. Galludat. Congratulations. A Christmas miracle, indeed."

"Thanks, Rupert. Do you have a minute?"

The young man snapped a salute. "Yes, sir. What can I do for you, sir?" He looked poised, as if ready to dash off on whatever mission Count Galludat might require of him.

"Relax. I have only a few questions. It's more a matter of satisfying idle curiosity." He pointed to the ash-filled barrel. "What is the purpose of this barrel?"

Rupert rubbed his hands together briskly and blew on them. "Normally, during winter, the grooms and the doorman keep a fire in here so they can warm their hands while they attend to the carriages. And see this little trap door?" The young man used the toe of his boot to indicate an opening at the bottom of the barrel.

"You can open that and get out the ashes. We use them to spread on the driveway when it gets icy. It helps the wheels get more traction." He paused, then smiled. "I thought of that myself."

"Ingenious."

"Thank you, sir. Anything else pique your curiosity? I'm your man with all the answers. If I don't know it, I'll make it up." He laughed. "Sorry, sir. I get a little slaphappy at Christmas."

Delgatto shrugged. "No more questions that I know of, but I'll make sure to ask you, should any occur to me. You do seem to have your finger on the pulse of whatever goes on around here."

The young man beamed. "Indeed I do, sir. You never know when you'll learn something new from a guest or figure out a better, more profitable way to do something. I do try to keep my ears open and my mouth shut."

"Smart lad."

Someone called Rupert's name and he made a face. "It's Mrs. Biddle again." He leaned closer in obvious conspiracy. "That woman frightens me. I'd better go see what she wants."

"Sure. Oh . . . by the way, last night at the Christmas ball, there was a woman, a young one, dressed like an angel or a fairy—something with wings. Would you happened to know who that was?"

Rupert shook his head. "No, sir. I'm sorry. I don't."

Mrs. Biddle repeated his name, this time with more insistence.

He grimaced. "Sorry, sir. I'd better go see what she wants. Bye, *Mon-shur* G." He dashed up the stairs.

Delgatto remained at the barrel, pretending to admire the scenery, but actually scoping out the people in the general vicinity. To his relief, Mrs. Biddle raised her voice, garnering the attention of everyone within listening range. While everyone was distracted, he slipped the vest into the barrel, making sure it was hidden beneath charred sticks and not visible to the casual observer. He patted his jacket for a match but found none.

What he'd give for a butane lighter.

Lacking that, he prayed that one of the staff would find a need to start a fire very soon. Until then, the vest was at least in a better hiding place, one that couldn't be tracked to him.

He brushed off his hands and started the long, theatrical mounting of the stairs.

Can you say "genius"?

Later that day, he began his stair-exercise routine after submitting himself to a long soak in the mud bath. In all honesty, the baths did seem to have some beneficial effects. After his long soak, he felt unusually limber, and it was hard not to reflect that with a renewed spring in his step. It wouldn't do for him to recuperate too quickly.

He stood at the foot of the grand staircase and began to climb it. He had proceeded up six steps when he heard a familiar voice call his name.

"Monsieur Galludat?"

He turned. "Yes, Major Payne?"

The Major caught him in a steel-trap glare. "I need to talk to you." His face darkened. "Now."

Delgatto had no option but to follow the man. To refuse would have caused more of a spectacle, more attention than Delgatto wanted at the moment. As he hobbled behind the man on the long trek to the office, he felt like a recalcitrant schoolboy being hauled by a teacher to face corporal punishment at the hands of the Headmaster de Sade.

Had Emily the maid complained about him? Told about how the two of them had fallen onto his bed? The memory of her almost made him smile. Then he remember where he was going. If he only knew why.

Once they reached the office, the Major closed the door for privacy and stalked around his desk. He sat, folded his hands on the desk blotter, and leaned forward.

"Who are you?"

Delgatto decided cool indignation would be the appropriate response. "What do you mean, 'Who are you?' I'm Robert Georges Galludat from France."

The man shook his head. "Try again." He reached down and pulled out the brocade vest Delgatto had fashioned from a purloined cushion. He arranged it on the desk, smoothing the wrinkles from the fabric. "One of the attendants saw you throwing this away. He didn't understand the ramifications of it, but I certainly do. I'm a very observant man. I recognize the material from a costume I saw at the Christmas ball." His eyes glazed over with a frigid look. "When you were wearing this vest, you needed no wheelchair, no crutches. So I ask again. Who are you?"

A dozen explanations exploded in Delgatto's

head. A scam artist always had one or two pet tricks up his proverbial sleeve, but most of Delgatto's hinged on technology that wouldn't exist for another hundred years. So he winged it, dropping the count's nondescript European accent and speaking in a decidedly American one.

"Sir, I'll have to ask for your confidence in this matter."

The Major looked unimpressed. "That depends on what sort of confidence trick you're trying to pull." He reached below the level of the desk and returned, depositing a pistol on the desk. He wasted no time making threats. Delgatto had no qualms that the man would shoot.

He had to think and think fast. Inspiration hit.

Delgatto cleared his throat. "My name is East, sir. James East." He stood up straighter, abandoning his prop crutches. If he was going to make the Major believe this "Wild, Wild East" scenario, he had to play every angle. "And I work for a special detail of the Secret Service under the direct supervision of the president."

"President Harrison?"

Thanks, I couldn't remember who was President. "Yes, sir. I was sent here undercover to conduct an inspection of The Chesterfield and its staff."

"Why?"

Why, indeed. A presidential vacation? A let's-play-hide-the-cigar assignation? It had to be good, and it couldn't be anything close to the truth. If the Major knew he was looking for a priceless jewel, greed might get the better of the man. It had to be something the Major couldn't directly profit from.

Inspiration hit again.

"The president is going to be entering some delicate negotiations with a country I'm not at liberty to name. The . . . foreign negotiators are willing to meet on American soil, but not in Washington. They don't want us to have a home-field advantage, so to speak. So I've been sent to determine what level of protection and comfort we could find should The Chesterfield be chosen as the location for this very important meeting."

Major Payne looked like he was warming to the scam. He hadn't tumbled completely, but to Delgatto's relief, he returned the gun to the drawer. "But why pose as an invalid?"

"I can't really tell you much." The stalling technique bought a second or two. "However, one of the participants would benefit as much personally from The Chesterfield's hot springs as his country would from a successful negotiation with the U.S." He held out his two open palms. "Two birds, one stone . . ."

"When is this supposed to occur?"

The smart scam artist knew when to have all the answers and when to play dumb. Delgatto played his hand.

"I'm not at liberty to say, sir."

"What about our guests who already have reservations?"

He shrugged. "Decisions like that are made on a level far above me. I'm here merely at the president's request to determine if the building and its grounds could be made secure enough for such an important and pivotal visit." He leaned forward in obvious conspiracy. "Certainly, many of your guests are—shall we say—high profile and would be amenable to postponing their vacations as a personal favor to the president. Those who might not be so inclined out of sheer patriotism would be handsomely recompensed for the interruption in their plans."

"At the government's cost," the Major prompted.

"Absolutely." Delgatto stood at attention. "We can count of your cooperation and silence concerning this matter, can't we?"

For one long moment, Delgatto wondered if the hook had been set deep enough to haul the Major in. The man scratched his chin in contemplation for several seconds. Then, to Delgatto's relief, the Major stood, stuck out his hand, and said, "Absolutely. I'll do anything I can for my commander-in-chief."

They shook hands, and Delgatto heaved an artful sigh. "I'll have to inform my immediate superior that I had to break confidence to brief you. However, he's going to be very impressed that you penetrated my disguise. It speaks well of your security measures."

The little man puffed up like a preening peacock. "I take pride in doing my job well." He paused. "Is there any other assistance, information, anything else you need?"

Delgatto pretended to contemplate the request. "All I can ask is that you deflect or defuse any attention or concerns that might be given me by the staff or guests."

"Certainly."

"Thank you. Your country appreciates your cooperation."

The Major stood and saluted smartly. Delgatto acknowledged the gesture with a casual imitation. He reclaimed his crutches, made a grand show of adopting his former identity, and moved awkwardly toward the door. He stopped and turned around. While he was spinning the world's biggest yarn, he might add a little embroidery for his own sake.

"One last thing . . ."

"Yes?"

"You may see me in close proximity to one of the hotel's female guests or staff member. If it is an employee, I'd appreciate it if you don't reprimand her and will allow me to conduct that part of the investigation unhampered."

"One of our employees? I don't understand."

"I can't go into much detail, but I'm looking for a woman who may have family connections that could possible aid the negotiations." *Ah yes, the Master Manipulator strikes again.*

The Major looked perplexed. "I don't understand."

"Someone with ties to the old country."

"Oh . . . I see. Well, I'll turn a blind eye to any seeming improprieties as long as you can assure me nothing of an actual improper nature is occurring."

"Absolutely. Thank you, sir."

After the door closed behind him, he tried not to smile.

This is much too easy.

Nine

Delgatto waited until after lunch before starting his new stair-mastering exercise regime. As he struggled up each step, slowly and somewhat dramatically, he garnered a variety of responses, from verbal encouragement to hostile stares from his fellow guests. But it didn't matter what people thought as long as they noticed and eventually accepted the man who used the stairs as his therapy. After a while, his presence would slip under their radar and he'd be free to pilfer, pillage, and plunder as he saw fit.

But best of all, he'd have an excellent vantage point to observe the guests and figure out which of the hotel's female guests were single or attached and in what rooms they were staying. Once he identified the likely prospects, he'd establish any pattern of behavior they had—whether they took daily walks, preferred a specific time to eat, went to bed early . . . or alone. He'd watch for anything that would help him determine the best time to break into and search their rooms for the Heart of Saharanpur. By early evening, he'd found several likely suspects, including Mrs. Molderhoffen and her two daughters. He'd already pegged the Molderhoffen momma as the pudgy Cleopatra and one of the daughters as

Marie "let them eat cake" Antoinette. But no one had any details on the younger girl. Was it a classic Cinderella tale with the younger, pretty daughter sneaking into the ball against momma's wishes?

There was only one way to find out.

Struggling back to his room, he closed the door, tossed his crutches aside, called for the maid, and waited in his wheelchair. A few moments later, there was a soft knock.

"It's the maid, sir. You called for me?"

"Come in."

The ever delightful and quite delicious Emily Drewitt peered through the opening of the door. "Yes, sir? Do you need your bed turned down?"

To her credit, the girl didn't even blush at the word. And yet, he'd already betrayed his interest in her with an extra heartbeat at the first sight of her. "No, thank you. But I do need to speak to you."

She stepped into the room, still clutching the doorknob. "Sir?"

"All the way inside, please. And close the door."

She looked dubious, as if propriety frowned on such action.

"I'm over here," he said, indicating his wheelchair. Then he pointed to the corner of the room. "And the crutches are over there."

She misunderstood his comment. "Shall I fetch them for you, sir?"

He shook his head. "No, no . . ." He sighed. "Just close the door, please. I need to speak to you about something."

After a long moment's introspection, she followed his orders, stepping just far enough into the room so that she could close the door.

"Do you clean the Molderhoffens' rooms?"

A delicate wrinkle formed along her brow. "The Molderhoffens?"

"Loud lady who always wears flashy flower-print dresses and a hat with a droopy daisy. Her daughter is tall, skinny, bucktoothed. Wears two big sausage curls on either side of her face as if they had a chance in . . . Hades of covering up her gigantic ears."

Emily covered her mouth to stifle her laughter, having instantly recognized the pair from his eerily accurate description. Then she reddened and regained her composure. "I'm sorry, sir. That was rude of me."

"No, it's not. They're not people—they're caricatures. Badly drawn cartoons of real folks like you and me."

She relaxed slightly. "I don't clean their rooms, sir, but I believe my friend Cornelia does."

"Could you arrange for Cornelia to come here?"

She regained her look of distrust. "I don't believe so, sir. It's not proper, nor should we be answering any of your questions about another guest. If you don't mind, sir . . ." She began to inch toward the door.

"Wait a minute."

Now she looked even more alarmed, as if she was ready to bolt. But it wasn't fear that lit her eyes, it was determination. He suddenly realized no one bossed this lady around. No one. He had but one possible chance of appealing to her and regaining her cooperation.

He stood and took a fluid step toward her, betraying his so-called infirmities by using no crutches. "There's something I must tell you." He paused for drama, but instead of capturing her attention, he found himself captivated instead by her. She was small in stature, but he had a distinct feeling the petite frame was misleading.

What was the saying about good things coming in small packages?

He reached up and snagged her hand, his fingers easily circling her wrist. He could feel the blood pounding through her veins.

Inside, she possessed the ferocity of a lion.

He cleared his throat. It was time to break character . . . with another character.

"My name's not Galludat. I'm not French."

Emily stared at the man who no longer spoke in smooth European tones, but in a decidedly American accent. Her stomach flared in pained warning.

"And you're not crippled," she added, wrenching her hand from his control and reaching for the doorknob.

"No, I'm not." Instead of advancing on her, he stuffed his hands in his pockets and slouched, evidently trying to look less threatening. "Emily, I'm sorry I've lied to you, but it's been for a very good reason."

She stiffened. "So you say."

He reached down, retrieved his crutches, leaned one against the bed and held the other out to her. "You'll feel better if you have a weapon at hand. Then, once you're armed, you can hear me out, right?"

She thought about his logic and found it strangely reassuring. Snatching the proffered crutch from him, she held it tightly, trying to divine the optimal way to hold it for maximum protection. Should she hold it out front like a billiard stick so she could poke him should he advance? Or back like a baseball bat, so she could swing in case of danger?

He continued, heedless of her quandary. "Have you ever heard of the Secret Service?"

The term was vaguely familiar and it took her a moment to remember the story of Mr. Moscowitz the butcher and the bad money. "There were some men who came to our neighborhood, looking for a counterfeiter who had been handing out fake money. I believe they were from the Secret Service."

"Then you know it's a government agency with authority and everything." He paused to mesmerize her with his dark stare. "I'm a Secret Service agent, Emily," he said in a low voice. "My real name is East. James East. And I've been sent here to investigate the hotel for a possible presidential visit. We've had word that there might be a faction already in place here that is so violently opposed to the president's policies that they might bring physical harm to him. I'm investigating the rumors of such a faction and their possible leaders."

She swallowed hard. The Chesterfield? The bastion of the patriotic? Unthinkable. "And you think the two Molderhoffen ladies might be a part of the . . ." She couldn't bring herself to say the word.

"Conspiracy," he supplied. "It's entirely possible. And then again it might be merely an evil rumor, being spread to distract me from the real culprits. It's up to me to investigate and make that determination." His look of concern faded into an attractive smile.

A *very* attractive smile.

"Could you contact your friend and find out what you can about the Molderhoffens and their habits?"

Such adventure and intrigue, Emily thought. *And in our very hotel!* She didn't know whether to shiver in delight or tremble in fear. If someone was willing to harm President Harrison, then no one was truly safe.

Emily glanced at Mr. East's warm, inviting smile and shivered, this time with neither delight nor fear, but another emotion.

He leaned forward and took her hand. Her skin burned at his touch.

"So? Will you?"

For a moment, she'd forgotten the question and was entertaining several other questions she might answer with an emphatic Yes. Then she recalled their conversation. She gulped. "Yes, sir, Mr. East."

His smile widened. "Call me James. I'll be here, waiting for details."

"Details," she echoed weakly.

"Find out about their habits. When do they get up? When do they like to eat?" He paused, then added, "When do they go to bed and with whom?"

Emily felt a wave of heat infuse her neck and face. To her surprise, she looked up and discovered he was blushing as well. It was an unusual sight to see—a man blushing—but a refreshing one, she had to admit.

"Yes, sir," she whispered. "I'll find out what I can."

He ran his finger around his collar to loosen it. "And make sure you say nothing to your friend about who wants this information and why. The only people who know my true identity are you and the Major."

The Major! If Major Payne thought Emily was even

in the same room with a guest like Mr. East, holding a prolonged conversation, much less one that had her blushing every few minutes, she'd hold The Chesterfield record for shortest length of employment. Luckily, Mr. East seemed to read her mind.

"If you're worried about the Major, don't be. He knows what I'm doing and has OK'd me taking one of the staff in my confidence and asking them to help me." Mr. East paused to seize her with another fathomless gaze. "I chose you."

I chose you. . . .

The words continued to echo in her ears even after Emily escaped from the suffocating heat of the room and ran off on her official errand.

She found Cornelia in the linen closet on her floor, stacking clean sheets and towels. Emily had planned to use her most artful abilities to ferret out as much information about the Molderhoffens as she could. But once she got started, she realized how much she hated lying to Cornelia.

So instead, she bent the truth.

"There's a very handsome man asking questions about the Molderhoffens. I think he's sweet on the daughter."

Cornelia snapped a towel in Emily's direction. "That cow?"

Emily shrugged. "To each his own. Can you tell me about them? The daughters and the mother?"

Fifteen minutes later, Emily walked away with a new appreciation for her friend, for whom no detail was too insignificant or unnoticeable. But as Emily neared Mr. East's room, her sense of amazement faded and the kernel of excitement resurfaced.

She knocked on his door. "Maid, sir." Inside, she

heard a muffled, "Come in." Using her passkey, she let herself into the room, willing her hands not to shake. Was it actually the sense of intrigue that excited her so, or the man who presented the intrigue?

Mr. East, who had been standing between the open doors of the armoire, stepped into view. His white shirt gaped open, revealing crisp dark curls across his muscled chest. She gaped at the sight for several seconds before she pivoted in horror at her breach of manners and propriety.

"I'm sorry, sir," she managed to say in a strangled voice. Her heart was thundering in her chest and her brain was entertaining some very improper thoughts that left her just a bit weak-kneed.

His voice held a tone of amusement. "That's quite all right, Miss Drewitt. I apologize for embarrassing you."

"N-no apologies needed, sir." She swallowed hard and began to stare at the door. "I spoke with my friend, as you asked."

"And she said?"

Emily paused, not quite sure where to start in the long litany of facts and rumors Cornelia had supplied.

"It's safe to turn around now."

Emily complied and watched him finish buttoning his shirt. "Start with their background. Who are they? Where are they from?"

She made her report, trying to be as thorough as Cornelia. But it was hard to maintain her composure as new emotions swam around her.

She had been in the company of a handsome man before. One of the stable lads had become quite sweet on her the previous year, and he was a strapping young man, very handsome and very attentive.

Emily fully understood the rising flow of passion and yearning, but never at this level of emotion and with someone so entirely inappropriate. Despite Mr. East's subterfuge, he was still technically a guest, which meant she was to have no personal connection to him whatsoever.

But here she was, sitting in one of the chairs by the window, talking to him as if he were someone of her own low station like a simple stable lad.

After her recitation, Mr. East graced her with a warm smile. "This is great information. Your friend has quite an eye for detail. We could use someone with her talent for observation in the Secret Service."

"No doubt she would love an opportunity to snoop and gossip for her government."

"No amateur snooping, please. Leave that to us professionals. She should stick with gossiping." He leaned forward in his seat and grasped her hand in his warm one. "Emily, I have another favor to ask of you."

She was proud of her ability to speak without choking. "Yes, sir?"

"I need to search their rooms tonight—to look for notes from possible conspirators, criminal plans, lists of foreign confederates, that sort of thing. And I'll need someone to play watchdog for me so they don't walk in on my investigation. Will you help?"

"Yes," she whispered. "I'll help you."

"Good!" He bounded to his feet, helping her up as well. He retained his grasp on her hands, his fingers intertwined in hers. As they approached the door, he lifted her hand to his mouth for a quick kiss. "Thank you, Emily. You don't know how much it means to me to get your cooperation. If the ladies always eat at eight sharp, then that'll be the opportune time for us to strike. Meet me at the stairs closest to their room at seven-fifty, OK?"

She nodded and made a rather stammered response before she allowed him to push her out of the room.

Weak-kneed and out of breath, she leaned against the wall outside his door. Hearing approaching voices, she snatched the dust cloth from her apron pocket and began to dust the mirror hanging in the alcove near the door.

As the guests passed by, paying no attention to a lowly hotel maid as she cleaned an already spotless mirror, Emily was painfully aware of a distinct sensation in her hand at the exact place where his lips had touched her skin.

She stopped and stared at the back of her hand, almost expecting to see a fiery imprint to match the sensation emanating from it.

A handsome government spy and his partner.

It sounded eerily like one of the books she'd read while in the Tower suite. But in that book, the two fell in love amidst the peril.

Emily drew a deep breath and tried to forget the wild extremes of the day—waking up in the penthouse suite, becoming a maid again around mid morning, and, by lunch time, becoming a partner to a government spy.

She sighed.

Intrigue aside, she still had six more rooms to clean.

Ten

Delgatto tried not to think about Emily for the rest of the day. She might be a pleasant distraction, but he didn't need anything to dilute his attention from his main goal of finding and stealing back the Heart of Saharanpur.

The image of the emerald kept flashing through his mind, teasing him, making him itch with desire. However, more than once, the jewel became mixed up with Emily, and his desire for the stone magnified into his desire for the woman.

Ridiculous, he told himself.

A simple transfer of affection. The emerald was his goal, his future, his mistress.

And even if Emily happened to be the perfect woman, his one true soul mate in the world, his duties to his family superseded any needs to himself. That had been drummed into his head from his childhood on. Every course he took, every skill he mastered, he did for the sake of his family's royal heritage. Like his father and grandfather before him, he honed his thieving skills for the one chance to regain the stone and reclaim their honor.

No woman, no matter how beautiful, how desirable, how delicious . . .

An unquenchable pain of longing extended from the center of his body, radiating outward.

No woman, no matter how beautiful, how desirable . . .

The pain, the longing built in his pants until it was almost overwhelming.

No woman . . .

Damn!

A cold bath didn't work quite as well as a cold shower, but Delgatto figured it was his only recourse.

But as the water cooled down his libido, it chilled his thoughts as well. What would failure mean? What if the woman with the Heart slipped away? What if he didn't find her?

Would he be stuck in the past? Would he return to his same fruitless future—a future without the Heart of Saharanpur?

No family honor. No reclaimed glory.

No love.

No Emily?

The old familiar pain rose again. This time, he tried to ignore it. When a cold shower didn't work, the next best thing was physical labor.

Although the effort of climbing stairs wouldn't really tax his energies, the effort of acting as if it was a long, laborious task would provide some of the distraction he so desperately needed at the moment.

So he dressed, picked up his crutches, and headed out.

This time, the curious stares were fewer and the long demands of Christmas had reduced the number of "Attaboy!" encouragements to the bare minimum. Couples were too busy with themselves to notice him. Parents were hustling cranky children up the stairs to their rooms. Most of the children had a death grip on some sort of newly cherished gift. The few kids who didn't have a new toy in hand were busy scoping out the other children's presents.

Delgatto watched as one little boy deftly picked the pocket of another child, stealing a candy cane. When the child looked up and realized he'd been observed, he shrugged and, with equal skill, replaced the candy.

You got a future as a thief, kiddo. Except you're never supposed to give it back.

The rest of his exercise was almost uneventful. One old biddy gave him the evil eye because she evidently thought he was monopolizing the railing. But another gaggle of old women, led by Mrs. Biddle, put the evil-eyed woman in her place with a few choice retorts.

As she passed by, Mrs. Biddle remarked, "It appears as if your abilities are definitely returning, Mr. Galludat. Just make sure you don't overdo the first day, or you'll be paying a mighty stiff price for your efforts." She cracked a rare smile. "Stiff price." She turned to her companions. "I believe I have made a jest."

They cackled in delayed laughter and wandered down the stairs toward the dining room.

A few moments later, two of the three Molderhoffens appeared. Gertrude was coming down the same side of the stairs Delgatto had claimed as his own. When she reached him, she smiled her coquettish, bucktoothed grin and stepped around him, making sure to brush against him slightly as she passed by.

She probably meant it as a provocative gesture, a tempting graze of her bare shoulder against him, but instead, she damned near knocked him off his two good feet. Had he been as feeble as he portrayed, she would have knocked him into tomorrow . . . or at least down the stairs.

Worse of all, the stench of her perfume was almost more than he could manage. Although he tried to stifle it, he sneezed.

At the sound, she whirled around. "Pardon? Did you say something? To me?" She wore the same wistful look as a child anticipating the first of many Christmas presents.

He sneezed violently again and, unable to speak, made the most polite "no" gesture he could manage. Once she got out of scent range, his sneezing stopped.

"I'm so terribly sorry. I do hope you get better," she purred.

"Thank you," he rasped.

The pair continued to ricochet down the stairs, accosting every man in their path. As soon as their attention was safely on to their next victim, Delgatto looked up to see Emily lurking in the shadows in the landing above him. He hurried his pace up the stairs. Thanks to Emily's maid friend, he knew the missing Molderhoffen daughter was in town, attending a lecture at the library. Just as well, too. He didn't need the distraction of knowing his fairy princess might be close at hand.

Once at the top of the landing, he made his way toward the Molderhoffens' rooms. As he passed by Emily, he didn't look toward her, but he whispered, "Be my lookout. If they come back, give me an early warning signal."

"What sort of signal?"

"Something loud enough for me to hear in the room."

She looked around and spied a metal tray on a serving cart in the hallway. After freeing the tray and wiping it clean, she tucked it under her arm. "I'll drop it if they come back."

"Good." He paused and added a "thanks" that made her blush.

If the truth be known, he was a bit warm under his collar, too.

Delgatto stood by the door, pulled out his homemade picks, and made short work of the lock. Anyone observing him would simply think he had the key and was entering his own quarters.

Once inside the dark room, he locked the door behind him and waited until his eyes grew more accustomed to the darkness. While he waited, he made a few modifications to his attire, buttoning his jacket to the neck, using a dark scarf to cover his white shirt collar, and pulling on a pair of dark gloves he'd lifted from a large-boned woman who had hands like a man. He'd tucked his mask from the Christmas ball in his pocket, knowing that should he be discovered, it might offer some protection of his identify during a getaway.

He'd learned long ago that anticipating failure wasn't necessarily inviting it.

He squinted as his sight sharpened somewhat. *What I'd give for a flashlight right now . . .* He made do instead with a purloined candle and started his search.

Ten minutes later, he'd tossed the room, discovering several things. The daughters were slobs. Moving in their room was like walking through a minefield.

Discarded hangers hid beneath piles of clothes, ready to trip the unsuspecting. Hair combs were stationed in strategic areas, their sharp points turned up to spear the unwary. Used glassware was scattered all around the bed within arm's length, like an early warning system.

The mother was not much better when it came to keeping things straight. A trail of clothes led from the armoire to the bed to the bathroom. Delgatto noted that the discards were actually rejects, all of which had split side seams. Evidently Mrs. Molderhoffen was enjoying the haute cuisine a bit too much and was growing out of her clothes, which had been abandoned in messy heaps on the floor.

And the worst part was knowing that both rooms were cleaned every morning and they enacted this much damage in twelve hours or less.

But the biggest discovery was that none of them owned any real jewelry, much less the Heart of Saharanpur. What few pieces they had were paste or gems of such poor quality they had no real value.

Delgatto sighed, then jumped as he heard a loud, metallic bang in the hallway.

Emily's signal.

Someone was coming.

He heard a curse outside and then, "Clumsy girl."

The lock began to rattle. He had only moments. He hid behind the heavy drapes, hoping to find the window unlocked. Looking down, he judged the drop to be twenty feet, something he could manage if he could get the right footing and preparation beforehand.

But time was a scarce commodity.

The door open. The lights flared.

"But, Mother," Gertrude whined.

"I don't care if you're hungry. I will not sit in that dining room with those . . . rude women. If they won't keep their nasty comments to themselves, then we will eat by ourselves. I'll have a tray sent up. Go tell that clumsy girl in the hallway we want two meals brought to the room immediately."

Gertrude complied, and Delgatto could hear Emily's response. She sounded nervous. He just hoped she didn't tip her hand. He could still get out of this mess.

Somehow.

Gertrude slammed the door, and judging by the creaking springs, threw herself on the bed. "I hate it here," she sobbed. "I want to meet a man. I want to get married. I want to get away from *her!*"

She sniffed and snorted. Then he heard the odd rustle of paper. She sniffed again and he heard her belabored words.

"Dear Diary, it's Christmas and I did not get the present I so longed for. I know it's Mother's fault. She runs off any man who dares to look at me. Even worse, she stops me from approaching the men who really interest me."

Yeah, like every guy in the place doesn't cringe and look for cover when you bat your eyes at them.

"There was this man at the ball dressed as a highwayman. I know he saw me and I know he was interested—he kept giving me these looks."

That was panic.

"But Mother wouldn't let me go to him, and I don't know who he was because of the mask. I've been looking for him among the guests, but so far, no luck."

Thank God.

"I'm sure he wanted to meet me, sweep me off my feet, and marry me."

What part of Disneyland do you live in, sister? Fantasyland?

"Mother thinks Lucretia is the 'pretty one' but all Lucy does is read books. She didn't even go to the ball. Instead, she stayed here and read. But Mother . . ."

She broke down in fresh sobs. Suddenly something hit the curtains and fell at his feet. In the light from the moon, he could see the earnest schoolgirl handwriting on the open pages stained with tears.

His disdain for her melted somewhat.

She wasn't more than a kid.

And kids had the right to dream and wish and hope . . . And not live in the shadow—the enormous shadow—of their parents' unfulfilled dreams.

Maybe he could kill two birds with one stone. He pulled on his mask, ran a hand through his hair to mess up the count's neat do, and took a deep breath.

"Don't be afraid," he said in a deep voice as he stepped around the curtain and into the room.

She gasped, but luckily didn't scream. "Who—who are you?" Reaching down, she pulled at the quilt as if she were partially unclothed and needed to cover herself. However, he could see she was fully dressed.

"What do you want with me?" she said through chattering teeth.

"Please." He held up a gloved hand. "I will not harm you." He took an artful pause. "I could never harm you."

She squinted. "I saw you at the ball. You were the . . ." her voice trailed off.

He nodded. "The highwayman. I saw you there and I wanted to talk to you, but fate wasn't kind." He cringed. He'd never be able to forget the buck-toothed Marie Antoinette.

"I never found a chance to speak to you alone, my Queen Marie Antoinette. Our chance to meet was . . . foiled by another queen."

"Mother," she growled as if describing something floating in the gutter. "Cleopatra," she spat, as if her mother should find that asp, and quick.

He made the mistake of shifting toward the bed, which she misinterpreted. But he couldn't tell whether she was afraid he was going to attack her or fearful he would not.

To dilute the meaning of the movement, he dropped to one knee. It was nonthreatening and also suggested more romance than sex. He could pretend to be infatuated with her, but the prospect of actually being with her was more than he could take.

"I couldn't let a day pass without trying to speak to you. There were so many things I wanted to say last night."

She was getting into the mood, discarding the protective coverlet and moving toward the edge of the bed and sitting primly. "And there were so many things I wanted to hear you say."

"I . . . I could love you," he started, then turned his head away. "But I have promised my love to another." He added a shuddering sigh. "For our families' sakes, I was forced to accept her hand, and we are to be married." He turned back toward Gertrude. "But when I saw you at the ball, I knew you were special—that if I were free to choose, I would choose you. But alas"—he almost raised his hand to bite his knuckle in the time-honored gesture of the melodrama hero—"I'm not allowed such freedom."

"You poor thing."

He tried not to smile. He'd transformed her "poor pitiful me" emotion into sympathy for someone else. It could become a healthy start to building some self-esteem.

"Yes, poor in spirit because I will never be allowed to follow my heart and see where it leads. We may have been magic together . . . but we'll never know."

"Never?" she asked in a strangled voice.

"You temptress, you. My heart knows what my body will never feel. But I'm a man of honor, and I can't pledge myself to you when I've promised my troth to another."

"Then why did you come?"

"To tell you what a powerful effect you had on me, so that we can both savor what might have been. I may be forced to offer my body, my spirit to another, but you shall remain in my heart. It truly is better to have loved and lost than never to have loved at all."

Even thieves steal from Tennyson.

He reached out, gently lifted her hand to his lips, and kissed it.

"Arrivedercci, mi amore."

A new light reflected in her eyes, one that relished the concept that *someone could love me.* She reached up and gently caressed his cheek. "But I don't even know your name." Her fingers hovered below his mask. "Or what you really look like."

He captured her hand and brought it to his lips again. "You know my name in your heart." He stood, inching toward the door. "Farewell, my sweet. I will remember you always."

There was a sudden knock at the door.

"They've found you!" Gertrude bounded out of bed. "You must hide!"

Delgatto figured the knock simply meant supper was served, but he'd allow her to play out this little fiction. "I must have been followed. I must leave. To save your reputation."

"And yours," she added in honest concern. "Under there," she pointed to the bed. "No, that's the first place they'd look. In there!" He allowed her to push him toward the bathroom door.

Once there, he realized there was no convenient window for escape. If he wanted to leave Gertrude with the perfect ending, he had to escape now. The only other passage was through her mother's room.

Maybe she was asleep.

Maybe he could simply run through the room and out the door before she could realize what was going on and stop him. It would take mere seconds to turn himself back into the count, who might even volunteer the direction the miscreant fled who had burst from her room.

Whatever he did, he couldn't stay there. If he wanted to leave Gertrude with a better sense of self and keep her from longing after him long after she should, he needed to disappear.

Now!

That meant a trip through the mother's room. He took a deep breath, flung open the door, and prepared to race across the room. But the sight of what he saw shocked him to a standstill.

Mrs. Molderhoffen preened in the mirror, dressed

in nothing but her undergarments—a lacy chemise and a set of pantaloons done up with scarlet ribbons. To top it off, she had a red feather boa draped around her neck, and she seemed to be dancing.

When she saw him reflected in the mirror, she opened her mouth to scream. Delgatto went with his instincts. He sprang to her side, slid an arm around her waist, pinning her arms down, and put one palm over her mouth.

"Don't scream," he commanded in a low voice. "I won't hurt you. Do you understand?"

She nodded.

"If I remove my hand, will you remain quiet?"

She nodded again.

He removed his hand, noticing the scarlet imprint of her lips on his glove.

Great. Bet that won't come out.

"Have you come to r-rob me?" She shuddered. "Or worse?"

He could feel her heart thundering through her chest. To his surprise, she leaned her head backward against his shoulder and spoke in a husky whisper. "Do with me what you must. Just . . . be gentle."

He stood there, having no clue what to do next. But she did. She pivoted around, breaking free of his grasp. Instead of laying him low with a knee in the groin, she threw her arms around him and began to pummel him with kisses.

The force of her momentum pushed them backward onto the bed, where they landed—he on the bottom, she on top. She continued to shower him with sloppy kisses while she fumbled with his clothes, specifically the waistband of his pants.

It took his sluggish brain a moment or two to realize what was happening. She was attacking him! His muffled words of protest sounded weak and ineffectual in his ears.

"No . . . stop . . . let me up . . . don't do that . . . don't grab . . . ouch! . . . that."

She paused to shoot him a grin which dripped with wicked hunger. "Oh, would you prefer to be on top?"

In one swift and almost effortless move, she bench-pressed him up a foot, then flipped both of them so she was now on the bottom with him straddling her. He would have been amazed at her strength if he wasn't already petrified by her behavior.

"Are you going to tie me up?" she asked breathlessly. "There are some silk scarves in the top drawer of my bedside table."

He swallowed hard. This was not a woman who had a priceless gem to protect.

No way, no how.

"Perhaps you should undress me first," she said, licking her lips and arching her back so that her enormous bosom quivered in his direction.

Delgatto couldn't help it. He panicked.

He jumped off the bed, landing on his butt on the floor. There, he began scrabbling backward like an upside-down spider, doing anything he could to get away from her. Flipping over to his hands and feet, he continued to crawl, trying to find enough balance to stand and run like hell.

She tackled him at the door, snagging his feet and dragging him back toward the bed, one meaty hand on each of his ankles.

"You're not getting out this easy," she said in a

commando voice. "You're going to ravish me, understand?"

He held onto the edge of the table nearest the door, but it offered him no anchor as it fell over, dumping her purse to the floor. The bag gaped open and he saw the shiny grip of a small derringer in the bag.

Good God, she's armed!

The revelation made him fight for purchase that much harder. The rug buckled beneath him.

"You're . . . coming . . . to . . . bed . . ." Mrs. Molderhoffen said between gasps for air, each word accompanying a new tug at this legs. She released one of his ankles and used her free hand to claw up his leg, evidently looking for a better handhold . . . perhaps the one particular handhold that might make him more responsive to her wishes.

His only solution was to fight back, violating one of his most basic and sacred tenets: never hit a lady. But then, Mrs. Molderhoffen wasn't acting much like a lady.

He flipped himself over and, now facing her, cocked his arm back and let his fist fly, only to have his punch intercepted by her big mitt of a hand.

Although he pushed with all his might, she held his arm at bay. "Maybe I'm the one who needs to do the tying."

She used her other hand to clip him on the chin, making stars explode in his head. He collapsed, feigning unconsciousness, hoping it would buy him a few moments to devise a quick plan.

They both heard a voice in the next room.

"Mother, I heard a noise. Are you all right?"

Mrs. Molderhoffen sang out in a sweet voice, "I'm fine, dear. I merely knocked over my purse."

"Shall I come in and help you pick it up?"

Delgatto sneaked a peep at his captor, who wore a panicked look. "No, dear. I've gotten it already. I think I shall retire early tonight. I'm feeling rather under the weather. Tell Lucretia not to bother me when she returns from town. She can tell us about the lecture in the morning."

"All right, Mother. If there's anything I can do to help, just let me know."

Delgatto realized Gertrude might be his only savior, his best bet for getting out of this predicament with his virtue left. He tried not to telegraph his plans, taking in an unnoticeably slow breath before getting ready to shout her name. He opened his eyes in time to see Mrs. Molderhoffen coming at him. Suddenly, he was pinned to the floor by her entire weight, blinded and with his air completely cut off. Belatedly, he realized that the woman had slammed into him, smothering his face with her enormous cleavage.

He began to claw for freedom, trying to extricate himself from the mountain of flesh. If he ever got out of this even remotely intact, the memory of her mammaries would fuel his nightmares for years to come.

Somehow, he managed to find her long braid of hair, evidently dislodged by their struggles. Using it like a rope, he pulled her head back, causing her to yipe in pain and release him.

His qualms about hitting a lady had vanished completely and he landed a good blow on the side of her head which made her reel for a moment. While she recovered, he extricated himself from beneath her and made a lunge for the door. He almost reached it, but a large hand grabbed his shoulder and spun him around.

Her meaty fist caught him on the side of the head. This time he wasn't faking as he slid to the floor, fighting to stay conscious.

"Mother, I heard another noise." The voice emanated from the bathroom. "Are you sure you're all right?"

Mrs. Molderhoffen moved with surprising speed and agility to the bathroom door. Glancing back and assuring herself he was going nowhere, she stepped out of view into the connecting bathroom.

Delgatto knew this was his one and only chance. He forced himself to his feet, stars notwithstanding, stumbled toward the bathroom door, and slammed it shut. He grabbed a chair and stuck it beneath the doorknob.

It would slow her down for as long as she failed to realize she could exit through her daughter's door and enter her own room from the hallway. But Delgatto counted on it taking several seconds for her to recognize her options.

He stumbled toward the door leading to the hallway, ripping off his mask along the way. By the time he hit the door, Mrs. Molderhoffen was using her considerable weight to try to dislodge the chair.

Staggering into the bright hallway, he ripped off his scarf and began unbuttoning his jacket as he ran . . . or at least tried to run. He was still wobbly from Mrs. Molderhoffen's right hook.

"Sir!"

He pivoted, figuring someone had seen him exit the room and the jig was essentially up.

"Over here."

It was Emily, beckoning him to an open door. He stumbled in her direction, almost falling twice as waves of darkness spotted his vision. He made the last five feet on instinct alone and stumbled into her arms as he crossed the threshold.

She staggered under his weight, but managed to both hold him up and close the door behind him.

"I've got you," she said in a voice that promised protection—perhaps even something else.

He smiled. Then the world faded into a comforting black.

Eleven

Emily collapsed under his dead weight, but was able to lower him to the floor without injuring either him or herself. She reached up and turned the lock just moments before she heard a roar from the hallway.

"Where is he?" a woman screamed. "He's not finished yet."

Another less frantic voice joined hers. "Calm down, Mother. You've been dreaming."

"I've done nothing of the sort!" The woman's outraged voice echoed through the room. Emily realized the two women had stopped right outside the door.

The younger voice grew softer. "Come back into the room. Please. You don't want anyone to see you like this."

Emily could contain her curiosity no longer and pushed herself up from the floor high enough to peer through the keyhole. She saw something—someone—dressed in white lace and red ribbons standing by the door.

The revelation hit Emily like a wet sponge. *She's in her undergarments!*

She didn't know whether to laugh or be embarrassed for the woman. Then a thought struck her. What was Mr. East doing in that room with an undressed woman?

Perhaps he was the one who deserved the sympathy. An image flashed through Emily's mind as she imagined Mr. East walking into the room, stunned to discover a near naked woman lying in wait.

The absurdity of the concept almost wiped away Emily's worst fears. Somehow, she knew he wouldn't have tried to take advantage of a woman like Mrs. Molderhoffen.

A kernel of doubt slipped through her defenses.

Would he?

Emily left her charge on the floor and lit the gas lamp. She'd been lucky there was an empty room on the floor, despite the usual heavy holiday occupancy. The room had sustained damage from the previous occupant, a rich eccentric writer who had decided to plot his next book on the wallpaper. Then, angered by a rejection from a publisher, he'd taken his anger out on his current project, as well as the wall it was written on, by destroying it using whatever weapon had been handy—empty liquor bottles, chairs, etc. After the man checked out and the damage was discovered, the Major had spent a half hour in their next morning muster ranting about the maid who had not reported the first signs of trouble, therefore letting the problems mount.

Emily adjusted the lamp until the flame was low, giving her enough light to cause eerie shadows in the room, but not enough illumination to be seen beneath the doorway leading to the hall. She looked around at the cloth-draped furniture and the worktable dominating the center of the room. Lucky for them the carpenters had been given Christmas Day off.

Mr. East shifted, drawing her attention. "God, kill me now," he said with a groan. He pushed himself upright and groaned again.

Emily squatted beside him. "What happened, sir?"

He shook his head, then winced. "I'm not too sure. It's all fuzzy right now." He started to rise to his feet, and Emily steadied him. "I think she hit me." He rubbed a red mark on his face and tested his jaw by working it gingerly with his hand. "Ow. I know she hit me."

The kernel of guilt shifted in her chest, tightening around her throat. "I tried to warn you they were coming, sir. But they moved so fast . . ."

He dismissed her concern with a wave of his hand. "Oh, don't worry. I believe you. I learned firsthand exactly how fast she is." His face darkened. "And how strong."

Emily slipped beneath his arm to provide the balance he evidently lacked. Together they lurched toward a chair-shaped cloth lump. Emily reached down to pull off the material, revealing the broken chair beneath.

Mr. East began to lean more heavily against her, his strength evidently waning. If she didn't get him seated somewhere, they'd both land in a heap on the floor. Stumbling toward the bed, she managed to balance him long enough to tug at the canvas that protected the frame and mattress. One corner of the material hung on something behind the bed which had been shoved against the wall. She gave the canvas a sharp pull and it freed itself unexpectedly, causing her to lose her balance. They tumbled in a spin to the mattress, the protective cloth snapping around them like a shroud. And if the binding material wasn't bad enough, she landed beneath his dead weight.

After regaining her breath, she became aware of the very provocative nature of their position. But the more she struggled to free herself, the more entangled they became.

"Wake up, Mr. East," she hissed between her teeth. Any louder and she might alert the world outside to their unseemly position; any quieter and she might not rouse him. But it was hard not to panic.

He shifted, sighed, then opened one eye.

"Last time I was on the bottom." He shot her a slightly lopsided grin. "This is a vast improvement."

Panic began to clog her throat. "Please, sir. This isn't . . . proper."

His grin and his awareness of his surroundings seemed to grow at the same rate. "But it is mighty comfortable, wouldn't you say?"

She couldn't control herself. Her heart began to pound in her chest; her breath became harder to catch. If anyone walked in on them, she'd be horrified. The punishment for aiding and abetting an apparent criminal would be nothing compared to being caught in a compromising position with a man. The Major would understand her role in the "crime," since it wasn't really a crime at all, but if anyone found them like this, she'd be summarily dismissed and her reputation would be destroyed.

Panic welled up, making it hard to talk. "Please—do something—now!" She struggled to catch her breath and started thrashing against the horrible material that imprisoned her.

"Calm down, Emily," he ordered in a soft voice.

She was seized by only one thought, one instinct: an overwhelming desire for freedom.

"No, we can't . . . I must . . ." Thoughts swirled in her mind like a tornado, too fast to articulate. "Get out . . ."

"Emily," he warned. "Be quiet."

Quiet. Her logical mind seized on the need to be quiet, but the need to scream became overwhelming. She had to express her fears. She needed to scream. She must scream.

She closed her eyes and drew in a breath to scream. And he did the most remarkable thing.

He kissed her.

It was a total surprise, a shock to her system. But perhaps a shock was just what she needed. Suddenly her attention was diverted from their predicament and caught up instead in the sensation of his lips on hers. There was a sense of warm reassurance in his kiss, but as he lingered, deepening the kiss, it became more than mere reassurance. It was an intoxicating promise of what could be. As strong and as commanding as her fears had been, that energy was now being channeled into the pleasure of their intimate contact. Desire cut through the maelstrom that had dominated her brain just moments earlier, and all she could think of now was the delicious feelings the kiss was generating throughout her entire body.

He broke off the kiss as suddenly as he'd begun it.

"Better?"

She drew in a shuddering breath. "No. Do it again."

"Emily." His voice held a note of admonishment and amusement. "First things first."

She nodded. He was right. "Yes, sir," she said with a lingering sense of regret.

He stretched, then groaned. "I think I can get us out of this." He flexed his arms, which only served to tighten the canvas around her. Although she didn't cry out in pain, he noticed the grimace on her face.

"OK, so that won't work. Sorry. Maybe there's another way."

They tried to roll in order to unwrap themselves, but the material refused to untangle.

Her panic began to surface again. "What do we do now? If you can't force your way out and we can't—"

"Stop, Emily." He paused to capture her with a dark stare. "There's another way, but you'll have to be quiet—and still—in order for me to do it. OK?"

In the war raging between her sense of desperation and her attraction to and faith in him, he won. She drew in a breath of air, this time not as shaky as before. "Yes, sir."

"This is hard to explain, but just be patient."

He closed his eyes. For a moment, she thought he'd passed out. Every muscle had gone limp. Then he slowly opened his eyes, staring straight ahead as if she wasn't there. He continued to stare into the distance, his eyes growing more vacant at each passing second. Although his stare was empty, she had a feeling he was concentrating hard. His breathing became quick and shallow. Then she felt the muscles of his stomach begin to undulate.

It was an age-old motion, one that spoke to, called

to, the woman inside of her, but somehow, she knew his actions weren't a preamble to a coupling. He began to rotate one shoulder and then there was a small sound, almost a pop. Then, material loosened around them somewhat. He flexed the other shoulder and, at the same sound, the material grew almost slack. His undulating motions continued, and she realized he was making progress, literally slithering out of their wrap like a snake shedding its skin.

She tried to push away the feelings that were growing inside of her, to explain them away as an uncontrollable physical response to his inadvertently tantalizing movements. But she found it very hard not to surrender to the delicious feeling he was creating in the center of her body. As he inched out toward freedom, his body began a long, tortuous trip along hers. Her face slid from his cheek to his throat and then to his chest, where she could hear the incredibly slow beat of his heart.

He stopped his rhythmic motion once his arms were free from the material, and she almost cried out for him to continue. He stayed still for a few more moments, then flexed his arms with another volley of pops. The light entered his flat eyes as he seemed to snap out of whatever trance he'd been in.

Lifting off of her, he made quick work of unwrapping the material. Once freed, he rolled over, lying back down on the bed again.

Emily wanted to savor the warm currents that flowed through her body, but her curiosity also demanded satisfaction. "How did . . . *what* did you do?"

He grinned, then winced as he rubbed one shoulder and then the other. "It's a contortionist's trick.

You slightly dislocate your shoulders—which is relatively easy if you're double-jointed like me—then you're able to wiggle out of tight spots. I've been doing it all my life." He shifted uncomfortably. "Just not lately. Looks like I'm not quite as double-jointed as I used to be." He rotated one arm in a circle, and a small spasm of pain shot across his face.

"A con-contortionist?" She wasn't familiar with the word.

"Well, in this case, an escape artist, like Harry Houdini. That's how he escaped from straitjackets."

He said the name as though she ought to recognize it, but she didn't. "Houdini? Is he a friend of yours?"

He coughed, then flushed for some reason, perhaps betraying a friendship that had not gone well. "Uh . . . no, just a . . . performer I've heard of." He stood up quickly as if wanting to dodge any further conversation, but his reddened cheeks suddenly paled and he sagged back to the bed.

"Whoa, she really packed a wallop." He probed his jaw carefully. "I'm lucky she didn't break a bone."

She examined his skin, her fingers tingling in contact with his bristled jaw. "You're also lucky she didn't catch you."

He nodded. "You can say that again. Thanks. If it hadn't been for your quick thinking, she would have trapped me like a rat. And God knows what she would have done with me once she had me."

Emily found his comments confusing until she remembered the sight of the woman in her ribbon-festooned bloomers. Suddenly, she understood his reference and covered her uncontrollable gasp with her hand.

"She tried to . . . ?" The words wouldn't come. "To you?"

He nodded. "And she almost succeeded. I tell you, I was fearing for my life." He added a short bark of laughter. "And my virtue."

Emily blushed. She'd never considered the idea of a woman forcing her attentions on a man in quite such a manner. She stole a glance at Mr. East. At least Mrs. Molderhoffen had good taste in men.

A noise outside commanded their attention. A voice rose in the room next door. Delgatto motioned for Emily to join him, and they pressed their ears against the common wall.

". . . had a gun and demanded I disrobe. I refused, of course."

Delgatto glanced at Emily and drew a solemn cross over his heart. "Never happened," he whispered. "I promise. I don't use guns and I have never forced a woman to undress." He added to himself, *But after that kiss, I would have liked to undress you.*

To his relief, Emily nodded with enthusiasm. "She's just trying to protect herself."

He allowed his glance to linger on her a moment longer than was really necessary. *If only you could read my thoughts.*

Delgatto heard a voice and recognized the Major's stentorian tones. Evidently, Mrs. Molderhoffen had decided to call in the troops.

"We've had no reports of a gun-toting burglar roaming the halls of The Chesterfield. Your daughter said she believed you'd been dreaming—"

"I was not asleep!" Her adamant shout was so strong it almost shook the walls.

"Is anything missing?"

"Yes, my diamond engagement ring from the late Mr. Molderhoffen. It's very valuable, a family heirloom."

"When was the last time you saw it?"

"I took it off before the costume ball and put it here in my jewelry satchel. As soon as that ruffian left and I'd regained my senses, I searched for it and found it gone."

Delgatto shook his head. What a liar. She'd worn the ring to the ball with her Cleopatra costume. He'd noticed the diamond and instantly assessed it as a fake.

He glanced at Emily and shook his head. "The ring's hidden beneath her lingerie in the second drawer on the left. I saw it when I was searching through her things." He shuddered at the memory of the woman's hands on him.

"And you didn't secure your valuable in our safe as we request?"

They couldn't hear what the woman said next, but a few moments later, there was the bang of a door being slammed, the brisk heel-taps of the Major fading away down the hall, and the unmistakable sound of someone crying.

"Get a grip, you silly girl," the elder Molderhoffen told someone, presumably the younger Molderhoffen.

"B-b-but I sent him through your room because I thought you were asleep."

"You giddy chit. What he told you were lies. He didn't fall madly in love with you at the ball."

Emily looked at Delgatto, raising her eyebrow.

"I'll explain later," he whispered.

"—he did. He told me so. But his family is making him marry someone else. He just wanted me to know. See? Men do find me attractive. You don't have to keep trying to foist me on them. I'm totally capable of finding my own man."

"Stupid girl. Men like him don't fall head-over-heels in love with girls like you."

"He did." Gertrude seemed to be building up steam. "And another man will, too. I'm not the hopeless case you make me out to be, Mother."

The last words did Delgatto's heart good. Maybe the girl would untie some of the iron apron strings and get out from beneath her mother's enormous and controlling shadow.

Another noise in the hallway startled them. It was the Major again.

"—check all these rooms. If the guests are in, I'll speak to them. If they're not, we'll check the room to see if it looks as if it's been disturbed."

"Yes, sir." Cornelia's voice rang out clear.

They heard the Major knock on one door, but couldn't hear the questions he asked or the answers he received.

Emily pulled at Delgatto's sleeve. "What do we do now? If they catch us in here . . ."

Delgatto stood up, fighting the dizziness that made his vision swim. "Hide."

She glanced around. "Where?"

He tried to stand without swaying, but lost his balance and sat down hard on the bed.

"You hide under the bed," she offered. "I'll stay here and try to explain things to the Major."

Black spots began to fill his vision. "How can you explain you're hiding in a closed room? This isn't even your floor."

Inspiration hit as the room started to spin. "I have an idea." He grabbed the edge of the mattress, trying to keep himself upright. "Get both of those drop cloths and that broken chair," he commanded. "And put out that light." She blew out the lamp, fetched the materials, and brought them to the bed. "We're going to lie down on the bed and cover ourselves with the drop cloth. Then we load the other stuff on top of us. Anyone looking at the bed will think the carpenters simply tossed the chair and the extra drop cloth on them to get them out of their way."

The black spots began to fill in his vision. "Cover me and then slide in between me and the wall. Even if someone finds me, they might not find you." With fingers that didn't want to work well, he managed to tug his mask back into place. It might give him a brief moment of anonymity.

He sank to the bed, barely cognizant of the musty cloth that settled over his face. He roused somewhat when he felt Emily slide in next to him, wedging herself between him and the wall.

The last thing he heard before surrendering to the beckoning darkness was a loud voice calling out, "What's going on here?"

Twelve

Emily held her breath and tried not to shiver. She could just barely make out Mr. East in the shadows. He lay there, perfectly still. How could he remain so calm?

She heard the Major's voice. "What's going on here?"

Cornelia answered, "This is the room where Mr. Urie, that writer, went wild."

"Yes, yes, I remember now. Queer man, that Urie. Who would have thought a man that big would have such difficulty holding his liquor?"

Emily heard the jangle of keys.

"Have you had any additional troubles with your passkey at any of the other rooms?" the Major asked.

Cornelia stumbled on her answer. "Um . . . er . . . no, sir. No problems before. This is the first time. Do you think someone has tampered with the lock?"

No wonder it won't work. You don't have the passkey. I do. If she hadn't been so scared, Emily would have smiled at her friend's inventive answer. It was very astute of Cornelia to place the blame on a malfunctioning lock rather than admit she had no passkey. Had the Major realized it was gone, he would have summarily dismissed Cornelia, then most likely discovered Emily's unseemly hiding place and her companion.

She heard the Major's heel-taps as he stalked around the room. She tried not to shake; discovery might occur even yet.

"Help me look around and tell me if you see anything out of the ordinary. And make a note to contact the locksmith. I had a spot of trouble opening the door myself."

"Yes, sir."

Emily dared not cross her fingers for fear the movement would call attention to their hiding place.

"I'll check the bathroom. You check under that bed," the Major ordered.

They were the sweetest words Emily could imagine at that very moment. Someone rustled the covers and then there was the sudden rush of fresh cool air. She peeped out in time to see Cornelia register a look of surprise, dismay, and perhaps a slight amount of appreciation, having found a very handsome masked man lying asleep under the sheet. It was a full second later before she realized that Emily was tucked in beside him. Cornelia's look of shock faded into a surprised, knowing grin.

She winked.

Emily held up one finger, signaling for her friend to wait for one moment, then gently reached into the apron pocket which was unfortunately wedged beneath Mr. East's leg. After a panicked moment, she found the passkey and held it out to her friend.

Cornelia moved with a graceful movement to take the key and slide it into her own pocket. Winking again, she dropped the cloth back in place, and called out in a strong voice, "Everything looks fine over here, sir."

Emily took a deep breath of relief, trying to ignore the strong odors of paint, turpentine, and sawdust. To her horror, she sneezed.

"Gesundheit, Miss Furman."

"Thank you, sir." Cornelia added a theatrical sniff. "Must be the sawdust."

Emily heard her friend whisper, "What do you know? He knows my name."

The Major's voice sounded close. Too close. "What's that, Miss Furman?"

Cornelia must have turned sharply, because the bed suddenly rocked as something hit against it. "Uh . . . I said, 'It l-looks the same,' the same as it did this morning."

Thank heavens, the Major didn't seem to notice Cornelia's nervousness. "Then let's not waste my time with this room and continue to the next."

"Yes, sir."

Emily sent up a prayer of thanks to the heavens above for making the Major choose her very best friend to help him in his search. Cornelia might give Emily a private ribbing for having found her in bed with a man, but she'd never spread an evil rumor about the unfortunate and unavoidable situation.

As soon as the door closed and locked, Emily pulled back the covers to gasp for air.

"That was too close, Mr. East."

He offered no response.

She looked at him closely. His eyes were closed. His face was slack except for the slight swelling at the jaw below his mask.

The mask.

A shiver danced across her shoulders and down her arms. He had been her masked admirer at the ball. The highwayman. Why hadn't she figured that out before? She drew in a shuddery breath, remembering what delicious feelings he'd stirred in her at the ball. And the thrill of his hurried whisper, making an assignation with her. The lost sense of adventure, the regret she'd experienced when she'd decided not to meet him . . .

He had been breathtaking in that costume. Even now, dressed in his plain black outfit, he was equally impressive. But how could she explain her ruse? That she'd been posing as a member of the hotel's elite, dressed in finery that perhaps she'd had no right to wear, despite Cornelia's and Marie's insistence?

He was no Prince Charming and she was no Cinderella. And the sooner she put that notion out of her head, the better. If anything, she now had a new sense of disappointment with which to cope. Gertrude Molderhoffen could still look back upon her adventure and fully believe she had been the object of great and perhaps even noble affection.

Emily had merely been another of Mr. East's investigations. Had he planned to arrange a rendezvous with her and then search her quarters while she waited for him in the gazebo?

And she couldn't even be mad at him. He was merely doing his job.

But wouldn't it be nice to be able to pretend I'd been the belle of the ball?

She sighed, pulling herself back to their tenuous present.

"Mr. East?" She reached over and shook his arm, but he didn't respond. He just lay there. She shook him even harder and his head lolled to one side. For one horrific moment, she wondered if he was dead.

In a flash, her world, her sense of well-being was in danger, threatening to cave in on itself. Even if she barely even knew the man, there was something about him, something enticing, something intrinsically important about him. She'd always made a practice of listening to the little voice inside of her, following her own instincts when it came to assessing people. And at this moment, her instincts said that she should care a great deal about whether he lived or died.

A great deal, indeed.

She swallowed hard as she touched him again, this time with much more hesitancy. What would she do if she was indeed lying in bed next to a dead man?

Emily used her forefinger to gingerly touch his face.

It was warm.

She held her finger beneath his nose. Was he breathing?

Suddenly, a sigh racked his body. Her heart jumped and she snatched back her hand. Was this the death rattle she'd always heard about?

Her heart misfired again as he heaved a sleepy sigh and then rolled over, muttering something she couldn't understand.

Then he emitted a slight snore.

Asleep?

She didn't know whether to be elated or upset with him for making her contemplate the worst.

"You're asleep?" she repeated aloud. She punched him in the arm, having lost her reservation and trepidation. "How could you sleep at a time like this?" Her relief and anger mounted simultaneously. "I thought you were dead."

He roused slightly. "Whah? Huh?" He opened one eye. "Where am I?" He focused slowly on her. "Heaven. You're that angel. I remember you. Come back for me?"

She punched him in the arm again. "I'm no angel."

More alert, he rubbed at his arm. "So I'm learning. Ouch."

Emily shushed him, not sure if the Major was truly out of earshot.

Mr. East opened his eyes more fully. "Wait." He pointed at her as if his wits were starting to return. "Emily." He looked around the darkened room. "We were hiding." His slightly befuddled, bemused look dissolved instantly. He glanced around the room. "Are they gone?" he added in a low voice.

Emily nodded. "It was close. My friend Cornelia found us, but she won't tell. I slipped her the passkey back so she wouldn't get into trouble. The Major will never know it was gone."

Mr. East offered her a small smile. "Smart thinking." He stretched and winced as he pushed to a sitting position. Then he turned and offered Emily a hand she declined.

"What's wrong?" he asked. "We succeeded. I learned that Mrs. Molderhoffen is a sex-starved widow, her oldest daughter is a hopeless romantic and her younger daughter is a bookworm, but none is the woman I'm looking for." A wide grin split his face. "And thanks to your quick thinking, neither the Molderhoffens nor the Major caught me. I'd say this was a success, generally speaking."

"A success?" Emily felt a stone in the pit of her stomach. "Of course you think it was success. You got off scot-free. On the other hand, I'm never going to hear the end of it from my friend, Cornelia. She found me in bed with a man."

The next morning, Delgatto awoke somewhat stiff and sore. But he wasn't ready to admit that, at thirty-eight, he was starting to lose the top end of his speed and agility. He could still blame his misfortunes on odd turns of fate, on the incredible luck of others, and, in this case, on a big woman with a really good right hook.

Anyway, his physical ability was only one aspect of his range of skills. He could still spin a good story and get himself out of trouble.

Right, Mr. East?

At the breakfast buffet, the news of his miraculous restoration paled beside the rumors running rampant about Mrs. Molderhoffen's appearance in the hallway of her floor, ranting and raving in a reportedly drunken rage while scandalously dressed in nothing but her underwear. The scuttlebutt elevated the oldest daughter from her mother's pale and forgettable appendage to a put-upon caregiver.

People were actually sympathetic to the young woman, explaining her lack of social prowess now as her mother's fault, not her own. The four young ladies who had appeared at the ball dressed as birds, who Delgatto recognized sans feathers, evidently decided to take Gertrude under their wing, so to speak, and had invited her to sit with them at their otherwise closed table. Apparently, the younger daughter hadn't emerged from her books to notice anything was amiss.

Gertrude was the center of attention and was loving it.

And Delgatto was just as content to limp into the dining room on his crutches in near anonymity. He ordered a light breakfast, wondering if some of his slowness had been due to lack of conditioning and too rich a diet.

"Boy, you ain't going to grow up to be big and strong unless you eat like a man," intoned Horace McKinney from across the room. Delgatto froze in mid-bite until he realized the man was chastising a young boy who was toying with his oatmeal. The Texan ruffled the boy's hair, luckily not seeing the child's reaction to the contact. Delgatto smiled to himself. *I'd stick my tongue out at the man, too, if I were you.*

As McKinney made his way toward him, Delgatto's stomach sank. All he wanted was a quiet breakfast, to ponder and then identify his next most likely suspect.

McKinney pulled out the chair beside him, turned it around, and straddled it like horse. "Well, good morning, pardner."

Delgatto dipped his head. "And to you, sir."

"What's with this namby-pamby 'sir' business? I ain't your pa." Without waiting for a response, McKinney leaned closer, conspiracy lighting his eyes. "D'you hear about old Mrs. Molderhoffen? Went off her nut last night. Swore she'd caught a man in her room scrambling through her scanties. That broad has bats in the old belfry, eh?"

Delgatto pretended not to understand.

"Bats in the belfry," the man repeated, tapping his head. "You know . . . no one's in the Notre Dame but the hunchback, and he's not talking much."

Delgatto nodded. In some ways, the explanation made sense far beyond McKinney's intent. It gave Delgatto more ammunition to know that the man wasn't the self-made good old boy he made himself out to be.

And perhaps the blowhard was just what Delgatto needed to make sure no attention came in his direction. If he needed a fall guy, McKinney was the perfect person.

They finished their breakfast in relative peace, punctuated only occasionally by McKinney's desire to point out what he'd learned about some of The Chesterfield's more recent guest. He pointed out one stately looking woman.

"They say she's from one of the richest families in Scranton, Pennsylvania. Her people reportedly own a prosperous coal mine in town. But you'd never know it by the way she acts. She squeezes a nickel so hard you'd swear you could hear Miss Liberty scream."

Delgatto filed the man's impressions in the back of his head. As they always said, it took one to know one, and Delgatto found that especially true when identifying those on a lower rung of the evolutionary criminal ladder. It was easy for him to recognize the con man in McKinney. It should be just as logical that McKinney could recognize someone of a lower criminal phylum than himself.

And if this woman had some con artist tendencies, she could also be the thief who originally stole the Heart of Saharanpur from his family and had succumbed to the temptation to wear the necklace out in public at the ball.

Sometimes good thieves weren't necessarily smart thieves.

Delgatto placed his knife on the edge of his now empty breakfast plate. Perhaps he'd arrange to visit her room that night just to make sure.

During the morning muster, Cornelia kept giving Emily the eye, which alternately embarrassed and amused her. During the Major's most serious moment, discussing a maid's infraction, she found the laughter building up inside herself, and it hurt to contain it.

After being released from their muster, Cornelia grabbed her by the arm and hauled her over to an empty corner of the hallway.

"Tell me everything!"

Mr. East's parting words echoed in Emily's ears: *Don't tell your friend who I am. Don't try to lie, just explain that you can't talk about it now, but you can tell her later. Much later.*

Easier said than done, Mr. East.

Emily faced her friend, opened her mouth . . . and never got a word in edgewise. Cornelia, lacking the facts, had spun a magnificent tale which sounded vaguely similar to the plot of one of the books in the penthouse suite. Books, incidentally, Cornelia had sworn she'd never read.

". . . and that mask. Oh, Lordy, I thought I'd never seen anyone so dashing, so handsome, so . . exciting in my life." She fanned herself with a clean dust cloth. "Oh, my goodness gracious me."

"We—"

Cornelia cut her off sharply. "Stop. Truth be known, I don't want any details. You and I both know anything you can tell me will pale in comparison to what I can imagine. You're far too good a person to have fallen as far off the path as I might wish you have."

Emily's face grew tight and hot. "Cornelia!"

"Well, it's true, isn't it? What I can imagine far outstrips what you've actually done."

Emily offered a small shrug. "Maybe."

"Maybe nothing. Listen, my friend, you ought to take advantage of this situation to . . . widen your experiences. Learn a little more about how to enjoy life." She paused, then grinned. "I just have shivers when I think of it. A daring masked man."

"Ladies?"

It took only one censuring word from the Major to break up their tête-à-tête. They scurried onto their floors, where Emily found her attention wandering all that morning. And because she couldn't concentrate on her duties, she was forced to work twice as hard to get half as much done.

Her thoughts kept wandering back to the previous night's adventures, the alternating moments of her worst fear of discovery and the undeniable thrills of being in such close quarters with Mr. East.

And that kiss . . .

She closed her eyes and savored the memory of his lips pressed against hers, first with a sense of necessity and then melting from a sense of duty and protection into something far sweeter, far more enjoyable, far more personal.

She'd never been kissed so thoroughly in her life

and she couldn't help but wonder if she'd ever experience anything like that again.

She paused to stare into the mirror she'd been absentmindedly polishing for at least five minutes.

Get control of yourself, Emily, she admonished herself. *It was only a kiss.*

One magnificent, soul-capturing kiss that would become the standard against which all other kisses would be compared.

She sighed, trying to ignore the woman with the flushed face who stared back at her from the mirror.

Emily managed to pay more attention to the tasks at hand and continue her duties. It wasn't until she reached the middle of the hallway that she realized Mr. East's room was two away. This thought spurred her to pick up her speed, and she went from someone too lost in her daydreams to function to the most efficient, speediest housekeeper The Chesterfield had ever seen. She whipped through the room, almost running as she hung up clothes and picked up dirtied towels, returning the room to some sense of order and cleanliness that the occupant seemed unable to maintain.

The next room was even worse, as if some great conspiracy had been hatched to keep her out of Mr. East's room. The room's occupant evidently had an aversion to using the trash can and instead created a mound of his discards on every flat surface in the room. One sheet had a suspicious hole burned in it and the bedside table had a burn mark the size and shape of a cigar. The guest had tried to cover the mark with a glass ashtray which was strangely unused.

She sighed and wrote down the damage in her notebook, noting the day, the time, and the name of the registered guest. She'd learned that the Major didn't charge every guest with the damage inflicted during their stay. There seemed to be a hierarchy; the higher up the social chain, the less likely the guest would be approached to pay for the damages incurred. And in Emily's thinking, those were the people who were in the best position to pay and not suffer any ill financial consequences.

But should one of the staff have an honest accident and scratch a table, they were dunned immediately and their small salary became even smaller.

She looked around the room, surprised to see she had completed her job. Distracted by her mental rant about the sloppy and sometimes idle rich, she'd distracted herself from her next duty: cleaning Mr. East's room.

She knocked on the door rather timidly and held her breath in anticipation of a response.

There was no hearty "Come in."

He wasn't there.

She knocked louder this time, announcing herself as was her custom and then unlocked the door, all the while wondering if she should be relieved he wasn't in. How could she exchange everyday pleasantries with a man who had shimmied up her body—albeit out of necessity—and left her breathless with desire. She was almost appalled at her longing for him . . . er . . . for him to continue creating that silvery sensation inside of her again.

She walked across the room and threw open the curtains that muffled the window, letting the somewhat pale December sun stream into the room.

She turned toward the bed, allowing her imagination to place him there, shirtless, befuddled with sleep and tangled in the sheets. He would look up, see her, and then grin.

But the bed was empty. The sheets weren't tangled, but neatly arranged. And no smiling man waited for her, ready to lead her astray into a world of decadent passion.

Emily stared at the bed for a moment, willing the image to reappear, but her imagination refused, evidently rebuked by the part of her that laughed at her unworthiness for such thrilling affection.

Instead of stewing, she began to clean furiously, channeling her frustrations into the completion of her duties. But then she made the mistake of picking up his discarded shirt, folded neatly on the bench at the foot of the bed.

She couldn't help but notice its scent, something warm and inviting, something that instantly reminded her of him and the intoxicating closeness they'd shared in the bed. A sense of longing hit her squarely in the center of her body, radiating outward to make her loins ache and her arms and legs grow weak. She sat down with a plop on the bench, still clutching his shirt.

Why are you doing this to yourself, Emily?

An argument arose within her.

One side said it was unconscionable for her to harbor such desire for a guest.

Her other side retorted that he really wasn't a guest, but a government agent.

But what difference did that make? Like a guest, he would be there for a short while, then be on his way to his next duty.

There was no winning the debate. In either case, part of her would lose, and the side that won would still wonder if it was merely a case of rationalizing the matter.

She decided her best solution was to hurry up and get through. Then she could leave his room and try to sort out her thoughts in a more neutral place.

Once finished, she gathered her supplies in their bucket and headed for the door.

It swung open.

It was him.

The smile he gave her seemed strained. "Oh, hi. I didn't know you were here. I can come back later."

She opened her mouth to speak but no words came out. Instead, she picked up her pail and started for the door.

He raised his hand to stop her and even had the audacity to wink at her. "Could I ask you a favor? I could use another set of towels, if you don't mind."

She found her voice. "C-certainly, sir."

He held the door open wider, allowing her to escape, and then he ambled in on his crutches.

She paused to let an attendant and his wheeled-chair charge pass through the hallway, then stepped around them and stomped to the linen closet, where she selected another set of towels. She returned to Mr. East's closed door just as the attendant and his patient turned the corner.

She knocked a bit louder than necessary. "Maid service," she called in a flat voice.

The door opened wide enough for him to stick his head out and scan the hallway.

Then he suddenly grabbed her arm and pulled her into his room.

The moment the door closed behind them, he took her into his arms and kissed her. It was warm, gentle, almost chaste, containing none of the fire from the night before. Plus, it didn't last long enough to suit her.

But he did give her the same grin she'd imagined earlier.

"I just wanted to thank you for saving me last night. That was really quick thinking."

Emily stared at him. The dark tendrils which had fallen across his forehead the night before were now slicked back neatly. Last night's adventuresome government agent looked far too tame in the light of day.

There was only one thing to do.

She attacked him, pushing his crutches aside, wrapping her arms around him, and giving him a kiss that rocked him to the soles of his feet and back up again, centering its strongest sensations below the belt.

At first, he used his arms to steady them for fear her energetic actions were going to make them fall to the floor right then and there . . . which wasn't a bad idea, once he thought of it. After he established some sense of balance, he returned her affections, kiss for kiss, touch for touch.

It was fantastic and perhaps a little guilt-generating, too. After all, initially he'd planned merely to flirt with her in exchange for a little early reconnaissance on the female guests who fit the fairy's profile: single, rich, and in possession of a priceless royal necklace.

But halfway through last night's debacle, innocent flirting had changed into something with far more depth. It was much more than just his basic attraction to her.

Judging from her response, she considered it something far more important, too.

He lost himself for a few moments in the heady sensations of their kiss, the provocative thrill of their hands making tentative excursions into lands heretofore unknown. He discovered delicious evidence of small, firm breasts beneath the many layers of her maid's uniform. For a moment, he wondered what she'd look like dressed in the apron alone.

She broke away, gasping for breath. "I shouldn't . . ."

He picked her up and carried her to the bed. "Say that again."

She looked up at him, tears sparkling in her green eyes. "I c-c-c . . ."

She threw her arms around him, pulling him down to her, and gave him the longest, most soul-shattering kiss he'd ever experienced—and that included his youthful tryst with a countess whose name he was already forgetting.

He tugged at the apron strings that held the garment at her neck. Once freed, he moved the material away, revealing Emily's prim high-necked work dress. He unfastened the top button and kissed the exposed skin of her neck, causing her to shiver. He repeated the process, her shiver turning into a slightly stronger tremor. By the time he reached the soft "v" of her modest cleavage, she quivered in response and her hands began an exploration of their own, unfastening his vest, then tugging his shirt free of his pants. She reached for his shirt buttons, but he guided her hand down to his waistband, where he needed the most help.

She hesitated and withdrew her hand. It seemed to break the spell they were under. She trembled again, this time not out of desire, but some other emotion. Fear? Guilt?

She broke away, dropped her head and shook it. "I'm s-sorry. I—I can't do this . . ." Gently pushing him away, she sat up, her tears making damp circles on the apron top that had fallen loose to her waist.

"You don't have to do anything you don't want," he offered, trying to regain control over his own body. He was as hard as a bedpost and his body was screaming for a slow, tantalizing release. In the back of his head, he was cussing a blue streak. She was magnificent. Unique. The perfect woman . . .

. . . and she lives in the nineteenth century.

And he wasn't the sort of man to look for a little slap and tickle with the locals while visiting their fair land before returning to his own place—or, in this case, time—in the universe.

"You don't have to do anything . . . but allow me to apologize. I'm sorry. I was trying to take liberties that weren't mine to take."

"I . . . I'm the one who initiated this. I didn't mean to be a tease."

He wanted to pat her arm, offer her some sort of reassurance, but he didn't dare touch her for fear of frightening her or losing control himself. "You're not a tease. You merely stopped things before they got out of hand. I respect that." He stepped closer, unable not to. "And I do respect you."

While she covered her face with her hands, he

took advantage of the time to fix his pants and tuck in his shirt.

She drew in a shuddering breath, then opened her eyes and began to return her outfit to some semblance of order. She managed to button her top with her shaking hands, but the apron strings seemed beyond her ability.

"Allow me."

He gently turned her around, took the strings from her, and tied them into a semi-neat bow behind her neck. "Is that loose enough?"

She nodded, then broke into a fresh cascade of tears. He stepped around her, then pulled her against his chest. After a moment's hesitation, she leaned toward him, wrapped her arms around him, and heaved great sobs into his vest and shirt.

"I'm so sorry," she repeated.

"You have nothing to apologize for." Gingerly, he pushed her back until she was at arm's length and he could stoop down to look her directly in her teary eyes. "When it's the right time, you'll know it. And, God, I hope I'm the lucky guy you choose when it does happens."

"I'd have to love the man . . ." A dark red flush brought unnecessary color to her cheeks.

He offered her an encouraging smile. "As well you should."

She stopped crying, looked up, and caught him in a gaze both innocent and provocative.

He heard his own words echo in his heart . . . *and, God, I hope I'm the lucky guy you choose.*

Thirteen

Delgatto was useless the rest of the day as his mind and heart warred on the issue of one Emily Drewitt. His body's demand for satisfaction was only partially slaked by a cold bath. It also needed a dip in the hot springs and then a vigorous massage by a woman named Helgretta, who had to have been Franz's sister/aunt/mother/significant other.

As Helgretta the Horrible ground her elbow into the small of his back, he was finally able to think about Emily without various key body parts jumping to attention. It was against his creed to seduce a woman merely for gathering information about her or others. Were his actions a violation of rules that had served him well over the years, or had he actually found the right woman?

She was smart, beautiful, inventive, quick . . . beautiful. His mind lingered over a mental image of her face. Then his attention slid downward, letting his imagination fill in the gaps.

And he had a helluva goood imagination . . .

He blinked, belatedly realizing he probably wore the biggest, sappiest smile in known captivity.

Suddenly, Helgretta found it necessary to pull his

arm backward, damned near pulling it out of its socket as she continued to massage his back.

She grunted, then raised one hairy eyebrow in rare Teutonic praise. "You flexible. Very good." She said nothing else, but punctuated her admiration with a carnivorous smile.

His stomach soured—as did his thoughts.

Despite Emily's momentary outburst of passion, he knew she possessed high moral standards. If she ever learned the truth about his quest much less found out about his real profession, she'd go running off into the distance, screaming.

No, honest people like her didn't cotton to thieves, even royal ones with a legitimate mission.

The best thing he could do would be to reestablish a less personal relationship with her. After all, he didn't dare bring anyone else into the Secret Service Agent scam. As his grandmother always said, "Loose lips sink ships." So both Emily and the Major would have to remain his only sources of information about the other guests. Luckily, Emily's friend had seen only his masked identity.

If it works for Bruce Wayne, maybe it'll work for Count Galludat.

Helgretta continued to pummel and torture him for a while, then finally swaddled him like a child and left him on the cot to sweat out the impurities and hopefully not a few brain cells in the process.

After his treatment, he had to secretly marvel over how good he felt. Once he returned to his own time and place, he'd have to investigate similar treatments. His Houdini trick the night before had left him with a stiffness and a twinge in both shoulders, an unfortunate byproduct of his fooling himself into believing he had a thirty-something brain in a twenty-something body.

But Helgretta's House of Pain had eradicated his aches, and he had a hard time not reflecting the spring in his step as he hobbled back to the main building.

Rupert opened the door for him, adding a snappy salute. "You're looking particularly peppy today, Mr. Galludat. Helgretta or Olga?"

"Helgretta." Delgatto smiled. "Who would guess one could feel so . . . relaxed after enduring such a painful treatment?"

The young man nodded knowingly. "The more it hurts, the better you'll feel." A commotion at the front desk commanded their joint attention.

Mrs. Molderhoffen and her daughter stood by the desk amidst a pile of luggage. Molderhoffen the Elder was giving the Major a piece of her mind—a commodity already in short supply, in Delgatto's opinion.

To his credit, the Major was accepting the tongue-lashing without changing his relatively cool visage. He muttered soothing things which seemed to somewhat pacify the woman. Delgatto noticed Gertrude seemed less nervous than usual and stood serenely as she watched her mother put the Major and the staff through their paces. The younger daughter, Lucretia, was perched on the tallest trunk, her attention centered on her book and not her mother's commotion.

Several porters had begun to move the luggage outside and load it into the back of the passenger wagon.

"They're leaving?"

Rupert nodded. "Ahead of schedule. They had the

room booked for another two weeks. She's probably trying to talk the Major into a refund."

"Mission Impossible, eh?"

The young man cocked his head. "Mission impossible . . . I like that phrase."

You and Tom Cruise.

Although Mrs. Molderhoffen appeared as if she would self-destruct in five seconds, Gertrude didn't. She actually insinuated herself between her mother and the Major, taking over the conversation. Whatever solution she came up with seemed to suit both her mother and the Major. As Gertrude walked away, there was something different about her. She didn't walk hunched over in her mother's wake as usual, but led the way to the door, her mother in the secondary position, the younger one in a distant third.

Delgatto stepped aside as Rupert pulled open the door for the departing guests. "Hope you had a nice stay, miss and ma'am, and a pleasant trip home."

Gertrude graced him with a smile that almost made her look pretty. "Thank you, Rupert. We appreciate all you did to see to our comfort." She discreetly held out her hand, pressing a bill or two into his gloved palm.

He blushed. "Uh . . . thanks, miss." He tipped his head to the younger and then the elder, who merely scowled as she passed.

As the door closed behind them, Rupert emitted a soft whistle. "I don't know who we thank for that change. Helgretta's good, but not that good."

Delgatto decided to play along. "Change?"

The young man nodded. "Gertie barely spoke when they got here. Mrs. M. did all the talking—and yelling and demanding and matchmaking. She tried to push Gertie off on every eligible male in the place."

"Staff included?"

Rupert blushed. "No, thank heavens. Though for a while, I thought Mrs. M. was getting sweet on the Major." He shivered. "That would be a match made in heaven."

"Or hell."

The young man's blush deepened. "I wasn't going to say that, but . . ." He stared through the window at the two women who were being helped up into the wagon. "But something's happened to her. I'll have to put my ear to the grapevine and see if anybody has any clues as to the cause."

Delgatto stared at the young man's eager face. If anyone could ferret out information about the guests and the happenings at the hotel, it would be Rupert. But the young man was too bright. If Delgatto started asking pointed questions, Rupert's radar would go up and his strong curiosity would become more a liability than an asset.

Unless . . .

Unless Emily was the one asking the questions. Perhaps Delgatto could encourage her to utilize Rupert's widespread talents to help gather informations. If Delgatto could convince her to transfer some of her attention and perhaps affections to Rupert . . .

Something inside of him twisted in revolt.

He found himself unwilling, unable to complete the thought. He knew in his heart Emily wasn't that sort of woman. How did the old song go? Something about if you couldn't be with the one you love, love the one you were with.

Muscles that had been coaxed to stand down tightened up again. Just the thought of Emily and Rupert made Delgatto knot his hand in a fist.

If he so much as touched her, I'd kill him.

The strength of the concept almost made him gasp for breath.

Where did that come from?

All his career, he'd prided himself on his nonviolent way of approaching his craft. Stealing was a matter of finessing, not fighting. Outside of the Heart of Saharanpur, there was no treasure great enough to result in violence.

Until now.

Emily.

"Mr. Galludat? You all right? You look a little pale."

Delgatto shook himself back to the present and consciously unclenched his fist. "Guess I overdid it."

"Shall I call for an attendant with a chair?" the young man asked solicitously.

Delgatto waved away the offer, thanked the young man and then headed back to his room, where he planned to give himself another half hour to stew about his newfound sensibilities before forcing himself to return to his reconnaissance of his next suspect.

It didn't pay to ignore revelations, but it also didn't pay to let them overtake his attention. But a half hour later, his moments of contemplation hadn't eased the ache. He wanted her, pure and simple. But he couldn't have her. It wouldn't be fair to her or to him. No hit and run relationships, especially those that started in a century other than his own.

He used an artfully awkward gait to walk the hallway, having switched from the crutches to a cane. By time he reached the stairs, he had half convinced himself he could withstand the pressures of the heart to obey the dictates of his brain. But the glimpse of a maid in the distance evaporated his resolve like water droplets on a hot griddle.

When the woman turned around, he realized it wasn't Emily. But it merely proved he could talk and plan all he wanted to. The feelings wouldn't go away.

He'd just have to deal with them as best as possible.

Yeah . . . right.

All Emily wanted to do was stay in her room the rest of the day, but no maid was ever excused from her responsibilities due solely to a broken heart.

Worst of all, she couldn't lose herself in her duties. There was no task so difficult or time-consuming it would drive out the accusations that continuously circled in her mind.

She had behaved in a highly improper manner and had most likely shattered any chance of developing a decent relationship with Mr. East because of her ill-timed advance.

Who was she kidding?

What sort of relationship could exist between a dashing government agent and a lowly maid? Not even the tawdry literature she'd read while staying in the Tower suite had dared to suggest such a possibility. Such things happened only in children's fairy tales.

The sooner she put her wanton desires behind her and acknowledged her true position at the bottom rungs of The Chesterfield's social ladder, the sooner she could forgive herself and resume her life in anonymous servitude.

She looked down to discover she'd been scrubbing the same spot in the tub for the last few minutes. Tossing the brush into her cleaning bucket, she stood, stretching her cramped muscles.

Thank heavens, it was the last guest room on her floor, and she could limp back to her bare room, stretch out on her thin mattress, and pray she could go to sleep and escape the guilt that gnawed away at her sense of self-esteem.

She'd taken several steps into her room when she spotted two folded pieces of paper on the floor. Her hands shook as she bent over and picked them up.

Turning up the lamp, she seated herself at her desk and read the first one, a telegram from her parents:

DOING FINE STOP ALL WELL STOP HAVE BUYER STOP ARRIVING CHESTERFIELD NEW YEARS EVE STOP MAKE THE BEST DEAL POSSIBLE STOP COUNTING ON YOU STOP LOVE MOTHER AND FATHER

Emily thought about the necklace nestled beneath the loose bottom of her sewing basket. It had been in their family for years, and she hated parting with it. But if the money could be used to help her father's ailing business, then perhaps it was time to sell the necklace. It did her and her family no good hiding in a basket. At least she'd had a chance to wear it that once.

But how shocked would the buyer be to learn he

wasn't purchasing the necklace from a hotel guest, but one of its maids?

She sighed and tucked the telegram beneath her blotter, then turned her attention to the next piece of paper, this time a handwritten note. Her breath grew short as she read it:

E.

I hope that we can still work together. There's no one else I can trust. I need your help and value your judgment.

E.

It was signed with a drawing, a sketch of a compass with the pointer headed east.

Her hands continued to shake as she rolled up the paper and held it near the lamp's flame. It caught fire immediately, the ink turning briefly green as the paper charred and crumbled into flakes. As the flames began to work toward her fingertips, she blew out the fire and was left with a small corner of paper.

It was the piece with the compass drawing.

She examined it more carefully and realized that beneath the initials, N, S, and W, (the E had burned away) there were a second set of letters printed lightly at the compass points: V, L, O. She stared at the drawing for a full minute before she realized that with the missing "E," the letters might also spell L-O-V-E.

Her heart wedged itself in her throat.

What do I do now?

She tucked the scrap of paper beside the telegram beneath the blotter, then moved away from the desk as if the paper might call to her and make her entertain thoughts she shouldn't.

She shifted toward the door, her hand hovering over the knob. What she really wanted to do was sit down with Cornelia and sort out her thoughts, but she'd promised Mr. East she wouldn't mention anything to anybody about his mission.

Tears welled up in her eyes and she contemplated the possible benefits of a good hard cry.

But then she heard someone else doing just that.

Opening her door, she discovered a woebegone figure in the hallway, a maid, evidently a new one she hadn't met yet. The girl was tall and big-boned and probably strong as an ox, attributes the Major usually preferred. More than once he'd suggested Emily's small stature was a detriment when it came to handling her share of the housekeeping duties. Later, she learned he'd carefully orchestrated his complaints, realizing her reaction would be to prove him wrong. That way he managed to increase her workload without her complaints because she viewed it as a challenge, rather than an imposition.

Fool me once . . .

Emily had never made that mistake again.

But evidently this poor girl hadn't learned the basic lessons about surviving the Major.

"Are you all right?" Emily asked in a low voice. She never knew whether people wanted solace or silence.

"He's just so m-mean," the girl wailed between sobs.

Emily knew exactly who she was talking about, but asked the question, anyway. "He who?"

"That man . . . that 'Major' person."

Emily tried not to smile. The girl had no idea the Major affected almost every new maid that way. It was an employee's rite of passage to be accosted and dressed down by the Major. If he didn't send a maid away in tears at least once at the beginning of her tenure, something was wrong.

"Why don't you come in, and we'll talk. I'll teach you a couple of tricks about how to survive the Major. He's more bluster than bite. Sometimes." She paused and stuck out her hand. "I'm Emily. What's your name?"

The girl sniffed, wiped her hand on her wrinkled apron, then shook hands with Emily. "My name's Tiffany."

"That's an unusual name, but a pretty one. I don't think I've heard of a girl named Tiffany."

The girl's shoulders convulsed again. "Neither has the Major. He says I must use a more . . . appropriate name, something suitable for a maid." Her lips trembled. "He wants to call me Beulah." She made a face. "Can you imagine anything so hideous in all your life?"

"Would you like to come in and talk?" Emily pushed her door open wider. "Maybe we can come up with another name that will suit the Major. Something you like as well." She stepped aside to let the tall girl lumber into the room.

As Emily closed the door behind them, she sent up a small prayer of thanks. The best way to forget her own problems was to become fully embroiled in someone else's.

She drew a deep breath, plastered on her best smile and said, "Now, let's think about names that you can use. You know, Fanny sounds a lot like Tiffany. Maybe you can use that name instead."

The girl sniffed, appeared to be getting control of herself, then broke out in a fresh wave of howls. "But that's ugly, too."

Emily's smile faded a bit. Maybe this wasn't such a good idea.

Delgatto hung around the bottom of the grand staircase, watching the guests come and go and, more importantly, watching for the Major.

Mr. East had some more questions.

Once safely in the man's office with the door closed, Delgatto made a conscious change in posture, going from the recovering count to the stalwart government agent.

"I'm sorry to bother you, sir, but I need some help. My contact in Washington has received some disturbing information that suggests foreign operatives opposed to the negotiation talks may have already set up camp here. If so, I need to figure out how many people are involved."

The man placed his elbows on his desk and templed his fingers. "A conspiracy?"

"Possibly. Or it could merely be one disgruntled person whose bite is perhaps worse than her bite."

The Major didn't fail to pick up the clue Delgatto left dangling.

"Her? You believe it's a woman?"

"That's what the reports suggest. They've identified at least one woman who may be involved. The trouble is we don't have a description other than the usual—between twenty and forty, attractive."

The Major tapped his desk. "That describes a great deal of our guests."

Delgatto decided to narrow the field a bit. "Our operatives think she's working by herself at this point, so it's quite likely she's posing as a single woman."

"Hmm. That decreases the possibilities a great deal."

"Could I ask you to prepare a list of The Chesterfield's single female guests, giving me the background you may have on them—names, room numbers, whatever else?"

The man pulled out the top drawer on the side of his desk, revealing a neat file filled with cards. "Certainly. I can have that information for you in just a few moments. I keep individual information on file for each of our guests, any particular likes, dislikes, habits, etc. We find it a great help in anticipating their future visits or, in some rare cases, discouraging any subsequent reservations."

Delgatto hid his smile. *God, I bet you'd love a computer.*

The man flipped through his cards, reading them, then pulled out only three or four from the stack. "Here you go. These are our female guests who are here by themselves. We do have one group of women here together—four friends who are sharing two rooms. Shall I include them as well?"

"Better safe than sorry."

The Major smiled. "My sentiments, exactly. You just can't be too careful." He lowered his voice. "And these four? They might be equally as suspect. The staff has overheard them discussing some foolishness about a women's national council or some such organization that wants to give women the vote. Like I said, one or more of them might be a ringleader for discord."

"Women wanting to vote. What nonsense," Delgatto said with a remarkably straight face.

"My sentiments exactly." The Major bent down to transcribe the names and room numbers of the group of female malcontents as well as those of the other single women they'd identified.

Once finished, he blotted the paper, then folded it and handed it to Delgatto with a sharp salute. "In the service of my country, sir."

"Your country and your president thank you." Delgatto tucked the paper in his inner vest pocket, reclaimed his walking sticks, and left the Major to contemplate the downfall of a future America in the hands of women voters.

Crossing the foyer, he took another look at the list, memorizing the names and room numbers. Two were on the second floor, including the Scranton coal heiress McKinney had mentioned that morning. Three rooms, including the suite occupied by the suffragettes, whom he'd already identified as the Four Feathered Friends from the Christmas ball, were in the Tower.

Eliminating the four women, he decided to concentrate initially on the two women in the Tower suites, figuring that the fairy princess obviously came from money, judging by the expense of her costume and the nonsentimental monetary worth of the Heart of Saharanpur itself. And such a well-funded woman might stay in the more luxurious Tower suites.

But he still needed help.

He still needed Emily. In more than one way.

He thought about the note he'd slipped under her door. Had she found it yet?

He hoped so.

God, he hoped so. . . .

Fourteen

That night at dinner, Delgatto managed to seat himself close to the Scranton coal heiress, otherwise known as Juliana Brady. She was quiet, just on this side of mousy, and just as cheap as McKinney had suggested. She examined the menu prices and questioned the waitress about every dish, as if trying to determine if its ingredients warranted its price. To her credit, she kept her comments low key, not necessarily drawing attention to herself and her ever present sense of thrift. But he noticed, of course, and wondered if perhaps the family fortunes weren't quite all they were cracked up to be. Maybe she was trying to keep up appearances by staying in a Tower suite, but had to cut corners elsewhere.

He tried to imagine the woman dressed in the fairy outfit.

He squinted. *Maybe.*

Two young men came over to her table, and Delgatto overheard them inviting her to a party.

Go, he commanded under his breath. *And stay out long enough for me to case your room.*

She offered them an earnest smile and graciously declined the offer. Delgatto watched his plans go up in the proverbial puff of smoke.

Then she added, "Brother Callaghan has asked me to sing at both of his services tonight, as well as all next week." She gave them her most earnest smile, laying her hand on one young man's arm. "I know he'd love to see you there, as would I."

Hallelujah, Sister Juliana!

The two young men stammered their excuses and extricated themselves from her grasp as quickly as humanly possible. Evidently, they weren't churchgoing types.

She paid no mind to their rapid retreat and continued with her meal. Delgatto watched her do everything short of licking her plate clean. Waste not, want not, pay not. Yet somehow, as she hoovered her meal, she managed to remain prim-looking, eating it one precise bite at a time.

After she was through, she folded her napkin neatly, signed her check, and pushed away from the table. While she retrieved her coat and hat from the cloak closet, Delgatto managed to get up ahead of her. As she passed by, he artfully dropped one of his walking sticks. A well-mannered soul, she stooped to retrieve it. He made sure to collide with her.

With reflexes that would have made Fagin proud, he dipped into her string purse and removed her room key, all the while looking as if he was holding onto her for balance. He didn't even flinch when he ran into something unexpectedly sharp in her purse.

"Oh my goodness," she chided. "Are you all right?" She reached out and steadied him.

"*Merci,*" he said. "I am so sorry to have lost my balance. I didn't hurt you, did I?"

"No. Not at all. It's quite all right."

He bowed stiffly at the waist, then picked up her

hand and kissed it in his best suave and continental way. "I thank you for helping me maintain both my balance and my dignity."

She colored slightly. "You're quite welcome." She paused, taking a quick glance at his walking sticks. "You know, The Chesterfield is a marvelous place for recuperation, but it addresses only the needs of the body. Have you thought about addressing the needs of the soul? You may find that a great aid in your recovery."

"Indeed, I have. One of my brothers is a Roman Catholic priest and the other is a doctor. Between the two of them, my mind, body, and soul are all being well cared for." To forestall any talk of Protestant conversion, he kissed her hand again. "But thank you for being concerned about my spiritual well-being. It is greatly appreciated." The clock in the Grand Foyer began to chime, offering him a perfectly timed escape. "Oh, would you look at the time? I must retire to my room and begin my evening prayers. Would you excuse me?"

"Not at all." She indicated her coat and hat. "I must run myself or be late." She offered him a shy smile. "I'm making my singing debut at the church tonight. Until next time . . ."

"May your performance be enlightening to all those who hear it." Delgatto shot her his most charming smile, bowed again, then waited until she took a few steps away before turning and heading for the hallway that lead to his room. As he lumbered along, he kept his eye on a mirror that afforded him a good view of the front entrance. He kept an eye on her as she exited the building and kept watch until he was sure she was well on her way to church.

While he walked along slowly, he took the time to examine his hand, trying to determine what sort of sharp thing he'd run into while dipping into her purse. The three evenly spaced indentations suggested he'd come up against a fork.

In her purse?

He shrugged. Some people had very strange eating habits.

Pivoting, he headed for the stairs for one of the count's after-dinner exercises. His fellow guests paid him little attention other than to shift to the opposite side of the staircase, leaving him one handrail to himself.

After making his laborious trip to the top floor, he was rewarded by an empty hallway outside Juliana Brady's door. Under the guise of resting against the wall, he slipped the key into the lock and, making sure the coast was clear, entered the room.

In the darkness, he practically stumbled over a set of suitcases sitting near the door. She was leaving? But hadn't she said something about singing at the church all the next week?

He sighed. In any case, she'd made it easy for him if she'd packed everything up. All he had to do was go through her bags. And he was lucky, too. Had he waited a day, she and possibly the Heart of Saharanpur might have walked out of his life.

He unfastened the first bag and was greeted by her underwear—stiff, cotton things with about as much personality as she had. But beneath the last layer of clothes, he found a curious assortment of items—a silver-handled hairbrush engraved with the initial "W," two framed pictures which fit suspiciously similar sized spots in the slightly faded wallpaper over her bed, three towels with the hotel crest on them, a copper vase bearing the hotel crest, and a handful of costume jewelry, mostly odd pieces—single earrings, broken strings of beads, and the like.

In the second bag, there was only a perfunctory layer of clothes and more reclaimed goodies which either belonged to the hotel or, very likely, its other guests. Evidently, the woman would steal anything that wasn't tied down.

The last bag had a false bottom which was filled with silverware pilfered from the dining room. He counted the pieces and discovered she'd stolen service for twelve, including serving pieces. All it lacked was one fork, and Delgatto knew the exact whereabouts of that missing piece: her purse.

But that didn't matter. The most important point was that despite all the things she'd stolen or liberated, she evidently had never gotten her hands on the Heart of Saharanpur.

Delgatto allowed himself one really good curse word as he contemplated how easy it would have been to have simply stolen the Heart from her.

He eyed her loot, suddenly seeing a complication at hand. If she left without being discovered for the sneak thief she evidently was, then once the stuff was reported missing, the Major might start an investigation and even step up the hotel's security, making Delgatto's life even more complicated.

But if she doesn't get away with this . . .

He bent down to examine the seam running along the bottom of the large carpet bag.

I'm afraid you're going to suffer some equipment failure.

* * *

After several failed attempts, Emily finally got the newly christened "Fannie" out of her room. The nonanatomical spelling of the name turned out to be the sticking point. After the girl left, Emily found herself pacing, creating a path from door to window and back again, as if waiting for a shoe to drop—or in her case, a sign from the East.

She groaned at her own pun, then jumped at the sound of an unexpected knock on the door.

She sighed. Tiffany-turned-Fannie had returned twice already for reassurance. As Emily opened the door, she mentally prepared the final piece of advice she was going to offer the girl, but James East stood at her door.

Her mouth gaped open and her mind instantly filled with a thousand thoughts, the most pressing being: *What will the staff do or say if they see a guest standing at my door?*

Even worse: *What will the Major do?*

She scanned the hallway, thankful to realize there were no witnesses to this transgression. Then she grabbed Mr. East by the lapels and literally hauled him into her room, slamming the door shut behind him.

He grinned, and his expression almost knifed through her resolve.

"What are you doing here?" she managed to say without a telltale gasp.

"I need you . . ."

She swallowed hard, realizing how many different meanings the words had.

". . . to help me."

Something inside of her twanged in disappointment.

"I've discovered one of the hotel's guests is a sneak thief. She's evidently preparing to leave, perhaps even skip out on her bill."

Emily fought to concentrate on the problem at hand. "The Major will explode. What guest? And what has she stolen?"

"A Miss Juliana Brady, staying in a Tower suite. And she's stolen mostly odds and ends, some of it not worth much. The most valuable thing is a silver-handled hairbrush that quite probably belongs to another guest."

"Miss Woodrington. She's already reported it missing. For a while, one of the maids was under suspicion. But from what I've heard, she's no longer being blamed."

"Well, she didn't do it. This Brady woman did. Who knows? She may simply suffer from a case of kleptomania."

"From what?" Emily had never heard the word, but at first blush, it sounded both painful and contagious.

He smiled. "Kleptomania—it means she steals things without even thinking about it. It's like an uncontrollable urge to steal." He grew thoughtful. "But then again, I've never heard of a kleptomaniac stealing the exact service for twelve, one piece at a time. They're usually not that well-organized."

"I'm surprised Chef Sasha hasn't burst out of the kitchen, threatening to cut off the hands of whoever has been stealing his silverware. I've been told he counts it periodically."

"Judging by the fact her bags are packed and ready to go, I think she's making her move tonight."

"Then we need to inform the Major immediately."

Mr. East smiled. "I have an even better plan."

* * *

Emily stood the first watch, lurking in the shadows of the hall window curtains, keeping a close eye on the door to Miss Brady's Tower suite. Somewhere between one and two in the morning, the door opened and Miss Brady stepped out, bags in hand.

Emily pulled the string that hung down from the window to the corresponding window below, alerting Mr. East, who waited one floor down. After the woman started down the stairs, Emily abandoned her post for ones with progressively better views, but out of the woman's direct sight. Finally, the woman reached the top of the lobby stairs. She peered around the balustrade carefully and discovered the room was empty. A night manager sat in a chair behind the front counter, peacefully asleep.

She started down the stairs, tiptoeing unnecessarily on the carpet. As she approached the last few stairs, Mr. East stepped into view, right in front of the woman.

"Going somewhere, Miss Brady?"

She suppressed a small scream. The night manager shifted in his chair, snorted, but didn't wake up.

"You startled me," she offered in weak explanation.

"So I did. It's awfully late for a lady such as yourself to be headed out."

"It . . . it's an emergency." She took a minute to think. "I've received a wire. That's right, a wire from my father, who is terribly ill."

"That's terrible! I hope he gets better. Please, let me call a porter for you. You shouldn't be lugging that load by yourself."

Her voice betrayed her panic. "Oh, that's all right. I'm perfectly capable of doing it myself."

"Nonsense." He held out his hand. "At least allow me to help."

She recoiled. "I can't. I couldn't." After a moment's hesitation, she added, "I don't want to compromise your rehabilitation."

Emily could see his cold smile. "Funny you should use that word." He reached out and literally tugged a carpetbag out of the woman's hand. "My doctor told me today I needed to start lifting weights." He demonstrated the bag's evident weight by shaking it. "I think this meets with his new prescription."

The woman shrugged. "If you insist."

The next moment was a blur. The woman stretched out a booted foot and knocked away Mr. East's cane. When he failed to topple over as she expected, the woman dropped her two other bags to grasp the one he held. A tug of war ensued, and Mr. East seemed to have the better of her until the woman released the bag. As he stumbled backward with his newfound treasure, she took the opportunity to snatch up the cane and give him a good rap on the head. He dropped the bag and clutched at the offending cane instead, trying to wrench it from her grasp.

Somehow, the woman managed to seize the bag, shoulder him out of the way, and run toward the door. Emily shouted for help, which startled the night manager. He fell out of his chair, disappearing behind the counter.

Emily watched in amazement as Mr. East leaped at the woman, tackling her and causing them both to sprawl to the floor. Her bag flew across the room . . . and skidded to a stop at the Major's feet.

He stood there, his arms crossed.

"Is there a problem?"

The woman spoke first. "He's gone crazy, Major Payne. I found the poor fool out here wandering around and muttering to himself. Then he attacked me."

She scrambled to her feet far faster than Mr. East, who appeared slightly groggy and none too steady. The woman sidled up to the Major, grasping his arm. "Save me!"

The hackles rose on Emily's neck. Surely the Major wouldn't fall for her trick. What if he believed the woman?

Emily ran down the stairs. "No, wait. She's lying. I saw the whole thing."

The Major quirked an eyebrow. "You did? Just what did you see?"

Emily cleared her throat. She had to be careful. "I watched her come down the stairs and then Mr."—she came a hairbreadth close to calling him Mr. East—"Galludat asked her what was wrong. She said she was leaving, and he offered to help carry her bags. Then she got agitated and began to fight with him over the bags." Emily stared at the woman. "She knocked away his cane, took it, and hit him with it."

To Emily's surprise, the Major nodded. "That's exactly what I saw." He turned to the woman, placing an iron clasp on her arm. "As it happened, I decided to take a late-night stroll, and I witnessed the entire thing." He lifted her bag. "This is rather heavy, don't you think? Would you mind if I took a look?"

Miss Brady bristled. "Indeed, I do mind. These are my . . . personal and private effects." She colored prettily. "My unmentionables."

Emily helped Mr. East to his feet, not sure whether his heavy weight against her was a part of his crippled count act or whether he had suffered some sort of injury. At least his voice rang out strong and clear.

"Then why not let the maid go through the bag? She's seen unmentionables before."

Miss Brady stiffened, snatching the bag from the Major's grasp and clutching it to her chest. "If you do not desist, I'm going to . . ." She searched for the proper threat.

"Scream?" Mr. East supplied. "Call the police? I don't think so. The cops are the last folks you need to see." He reached over to the bag, which the woman held to her bosom with two protective arms. Rather than try to wrench it away, he grasped a small string that protruded from the bottom of the bag.

One tug of the string, and the bottom seam of the bag split open, releasing a shower of knives, forks, and spoons to clatter against the floor.

Emily reached down and retrieved one knife, holding it up so that the hotel crest reflected in the light.

The Major smiled. "Thank you, Mr. Galludat. Your powers of observation are commendable. Miss"—he stuttered only briefly over her name—"D-Drewitt. Your services are over for the night. You will be excused from tomorrow's morning muster and your morning duties will be assigned to another for one day." He glanced at his captive. "You and I will wait in my office until the marshal arrives." He turned to Mr. East. "Sir, you look a bit unsteady. I'd be glad to call for an attendant to help you back to your room."

Mr. East momentarily tightened his grasp on Emily, filling her with a sudden flood of warmth. "Perhaps Miss Drewitt would be willing to help me."

"C-certainly, sir," she stammered. To her surprise, the Major nodded his consent.

"Very well, then. Good night—and, again, my thanks."

Miss Brady uttered a very scandalous epithet as the Major unceremoniously hauled her toward his office. The night manager peeked over the counter and wiped his brow, evidently having escaped the Major's notice. Sleeping on the job was a court-martial offense in the Major's hotel military.

But to the man's chagrin, the Major stopped just short of the doorway leading to his office and pointed at the manager. "I'll deal with you after I'm through with her."

The man paled visibly and sank back out of sight beneath the counter.

Delgatto tried not to laugh at the man, but Emily's suppressed giggle got the best of him. As they stumbled down the hallway, they covered their joint laughter in an effort not to wake up the other guests.

As they reached his door, his dizziness abated and he began to realize how delicious it felt to hold and be held by Emily. A clean scent rose from her hair as she used her passkey to open his door. As they entered, he used his foot to shut the door.

She stopped and glanced at him. She wore a look that was a mixture of curiosity, desire, fear, and excitement.

He knew that look.

He shared that look.

Suddenly he forgot all his reasons why it made no sense to fall in love with a woman in the past. He forgot why he was back in time. He forgot what the Heart of Saharanpur looked like.

All he could do was think about her, anticipate what she'd look like in the throes of passion. What sweet music her voice would be, saying his name over and over again.

He kissed her and felt her breath catch in her throat. He could feel her pulse thrumming through her body, her heart racing. And it wasn't in fear.

She ran her hand around the back of his neck and pulled him closer, her kisses frenzied, demanding. He returned her passion tenfold, which in turn inflamed her.

A few precious moments later, they were almost tearing the clothes off each other. Beneath her stark uniform, she wore lace-edged undergarments, old-fashioned by his standard, but twice as enticing as modern lingerie. He slowly untied the ribbons that kept her chemise shut, revealing the pale skin of her breasts and then slowly exposing each dusky nipple.

He drew one into his mouth, marveling over the sweet taste of her skin and the even sweeter sounds of her moans of pleasure. He felt himself harden in desire.

She tangled her hands in his hair and began a rocking rhythm that echoed both her gasps for breath and the intensive tempo of her heart as well as his.

He found the bow tie that held her bloomers closed and pulled it, loosening the string. Sliding his hand down her waist and toward the V between her legs, he was rewarded with her strong reactions to his touch, her lovely shudder as he reached her, and her gasp of pleasure as he began to stroke her.

She pulled at his hair, forcing him to abandon her breast and slide up to take her mouth instead. She was wanton in her desire, exacting, demanding, and he was pleased to do her bidding.

She found his free hand and splayed it on her breast. He complied, grasping the rosy nub between his fingers and supplying the right amount of pressure to make her arch her back in response. He returned the favor by guiding her hand to his crotch, where she began a tortuous rhythm that would soon drive him totally mad.

They fell to the bed where, after only a few moments of delicious torment, he broke away long enough to kick himself free of his pants. Then they returned to their efforts with even stronger passion and a more frenzied rhythm.

Somewhere in his brain, he realized this act was like nothing he'd ever experienced. There was something magical and different about being with Emily, about sharing with Emily more than just his body, but something deep inside of him, too. Just the thought of her set him on fire. The act of touching her, being touched by her, was almost more than he could take.

Just as he feared he was going to explode right then and there, she guided him into entering her. Their motion became as one as their hearts and bodies united. She came first, her breath in strangled gasps and her body jerking in reflex to each soul-shattering wave of sensation that crashed over her. It was even more intoxicating to watch her writhe and moan in pleasure. The sight of her extreme satisfaction brought him to his own pinnacle of sensation and he came, knowing she was watching him surrender to his own pleasure.

Spent and exhausted, they lay in each other's arms, unwilling to break the divine silence that hung about them like an afterglow. Breathing was difficult enough. But after a while, he found the strength to say the words he really longed to hear aloud.

"Emily, I love you." She caught him in a soulful gaze and he felt compelled to elaborate. "I can't imagine when I didn't love you."

She shifted his arms so that she lay on top of him. Instead of replying, she ran the gentle tip of her forefinger down the side of his bristled jaw.

"Why?"

He managed to shrug. "If I could explain it, then I'd be the king of the world. All I know is that I want you forever. . . ."

His conscience cut it short about a dozen words too late. *But you don't have forever. You barely have today. She's yesterday and you're tomorrow.*

She must have read his face and seen the sudden wave of doubt wash over him.

"But . . ." She swallowed hard. "But you have your duties. Your responsibilities." And to his surprise, she added a quiet, "I understand."

He wanted to scream, *No you don't!* But this was a discussion they could never have. Time travel was a concept he barely understood himself and could never explain to her. But didn't she deserved an explanation that had some resemblance to the truth?

He cleared his throat. "Let me tell you a story. Once upon a time there lived a pretty happy family.

They had a nice house, liked their community, and were content with the world at large. Then one day, someone came into their life and stole one of their most precious belongings. Suddenly, their world wasn't so great. They lost their house, got kicked out of their town. In fact, the town sorta dried up and blew away, all because someone stole this . . . special belonging of theirs.

"So they plotted to get it back. The only trouble was, they didn't know where it was. All they could do was prepare and plan. They taught their children all about this missing article and schooled them on every way possible of finding it and getting it back. And their children taught their children. And so it went. So many years have passed by that you may wonder if the missing article will bring them any happiness. They can't get their house back. They can't rebuild their community. What if the only thing they'll end up having to show for their eventual success will be the return of the item itself? Is that enough to inflame each successive generation, who don't remember the house or even when their family was just a family?"

At her confused look, he shook his head. "Ignore me." He pulled her into his arms. "I think the point I'm trying to make is that my duties have always superseded all aspects of my life." He kissed the top of her head. "And you're the first person I've ever met who has made me wonder if I should forget my family and just go on with my own life."

To his surprise, she nodded. "I think I understand. It wasn't my idea to come here to work. My family asked me to, for reasons of their own. The day we met, I was to return home, unfortunately not having completed the task I was sent to do. But then an illness hit our town and they've been quarantined. I was forced to stay here."

"Are your family sick?"

She graced him with a smile for asking. "No, they're fine. But the town's been quarantined. They can't leave and I can't come home. I should be homesick, but I'm not. I'm secretly glad I'm not going home to face their disappointment for failing in my duties."

Although neither had spilled too many details, Delgatto saw the common thread in her story that matched his.

"So what do we do?" he asked.

She shrugged. "We complete our tasks and then we get on with our lives."

It was the unspoken word that gave him hope.

Together.

Fifteen

They slept in each other's arms for several hours, until the weak winter sun broke into a pale daybreak. Emily woke first, discovering that she wore no clothes and that she fit well against him, curve for curve. Curiosity led her to peek beneath the sheets. She'd never actually seen a man unclothed before. The night before, she'd been too caught up in the moment to take a proper assessment.

But she saw . . . it, nestled in a patch of black curls. For such masterful actions performed the night before, it seemed almost anticlimactic now, peacefully slumbering like its master.

She dragged her attention up his body, admiring the tight waist and the muscles that rippled above, leading to a properly furred chest and, above that, broad shoulders. Her gaze threatened to dip down again to his nether regions, so she forced her attention on a scar below his belly button. The scar was a rather neat-looking slash with only slightly puckered sides. It had healed incredibly well. She lifted the sheet to get a better look at it, even reaching out with her hand to touch it, when a deep voice stopped her.

"Excuse me?"

She could hear the smile in his words. "Exactly what are you doing under there?"

"Admiring you."

He coughed. "I never had it put that way before."

"I want to touch . . ."

He laughed. "Be my guest."

She ran her finger across the ridge of the scar tissue. "How'd you get this?"

"Uh . . ." He coughed again. "Oh, that. Nothing exotic. My appendix burst when I was twelve."

"And you survived?" Harsh memories pressed against her temples.

"Sure." He even shrugged as if talking about having the sneezes. "It really wasn't that bad. I got to stay home from school for two weeks."

The image of a sweet face flashed in her head. "I lost a friend to that a few years ago. Evidently her doctor wasn't as good as yours."

There was a moment of silence, and then he spoke in a low voice. "I guess not." He paused, then added, "I'm sorry for your loss, Emily."

For some strange and perhaps reassuring reason, his words actually helped to alleviate some of the pain. "Thanks. Me too. I still miss her."

There was another moment of silence. Then she could hear welcome laughter in his words. "You going to come up for air, or am I going to have to come in after you?"

Emily remained still.

"Well?" he chided.

She traced a circle over his washboard muscles. "Don't rush me. I'm thinking."

Suddenly the covers shifted, exposing her face as

well as his chest. "Don't tempt me, woman," he said with a mock scowl.

She looked up with her best look of innocence. "Tempt you how?"

He growled and grabbed her, making her both squeal and laugh at the same time. Suddenly he put his hand over her mouth. She licked his palm, but he shook his head, shushing her.

She heard a knock, then a voice.

"Mr. Galludat, it's Major Payne. May I speak with you for a moment?"

Emily shot her Mr. East—and she had already come to think of him as solely hers—a look of panic.

His eyes opened wide. "Uh, just a moment, Major. Uh . . . I'm not decent." He pointed to himself. "I am naked, you know," he whispered. Then he scanned the room. "You've got to hide."

"Where?"

He slid off the bed, grabbed her hand, and pulled her with him. "In the bathroom," he commanded.

Emily complied, only to find herself pushed into the bathroom and the door shut behind her. She shivered, opened the door, and stuck her head out.

Mr. East saw her and while trying to pull on his pants, frantically waved for her to return to her hiding place. She pointed to her clothes, which were unceremoniously draped all over the room.

He nodded and began to hop around, collecting her clothing while still trying to pull on his pants. She tried not to laugh at his antics, but her control was weak.

"Just another moment, Major," he called out while tossing her uniform and other items toward her. One shoe went wild, slipped through her grasp and hit the bathtub with a large metallic thud.

"Are you all right, sir?"

"Just peachy," Mr. East growled as he discovered his shirt was inside out. He paused by the door to give Emily one last stern *Don't you make a sound and shut the door while you're at it* look.

Emily silently pulled on her clothes, straining to hear the conversation through the solid wooden door.

". . . is trying to suggest that you broke into her room and placed the items in her luggage."

"Then how did she explain trying to leave in the middle of the night without paying her bill?"

"She says she received a telegram saying her father was ill, but the telegraph office has no record of it."

"Because it doesn't exist. If I were you, I'd investigate and see if she really is who she says she is. It's a classic scam to assume the identity of another person, preferably a rich one who might be able to run up a large bill without question or opposition."

"You speak as if you have experience in this field."

"I do. I've seen it happen before."

"Then I'll send a few wires and see if this Miss Brady is authentic or not."

"Good idea. Is there anything else, Major?"

"No, no, just wanted to keep you informed and to express my appreciation for identifying her to us. I'll wish you a good morning, sir." There was a pause, and then he added, "That's odd. This appears to be a maid's apron."

Emily looked down at her half buttoned dress, looking around and discovering to her horror that she had lost her apron.

"I suspect it belongs to the young lady who helped me back to my room, this morning. She was afraid I'd cut my head in the melee and had removed her apron to staunch the flow of blood."

There was a moment of uneasy silence. "But I see no blood on the material."

Mr. East sounded perfectly natural and at ease. "She was just so earnest and so anxious to make sure I was all right. I didn't have the heart to tell her I wasn't bleeding, but that I'd received a different sort of injury."

"Come now?"

Mr. East lowered his voice and whispered something that made the Major bray in laughter.

"Indeed, indeed. It would have upset her sense of propriety to have been privy to that bit of information. I see why you carried on the charade. I'll wish you a good morning, then, sir."

The door closed sharply and Emily almost burst out of her hiding place.

"What would have upset my sense of propriety?" she demanded once she decided the Major was out of hearing range.

Mr. East stood in front of the mirror, combing his hair. He wore a look of secret amusement. "Oh, nothing."

Nothing, her foot! She stomped over to him and, rather than pout, decided to wheedle the information out of him.

"What?" she asked again, wrapping her hands around his waist.

"Just a little . . . man talk. That's all."

She started working one hand down. *"Little . . .* man? That's not what I recall from last night." She watched his reaction in the mirror, noting the fine blush that started at the tips of his ears.

"C'mon, Emily." He reached for her hand to guide it away, but she was persistent. She found a sensitive spot and he flinched. Then she went after it again. They began to wrestle, she trying to tickle him and he trying to stop her. They ended up on the bed, Emily on top and Mr. East, her willing victim, on the bottom.

"Now," she said in false triumph. "What were you two talking about?"

His blush deepened. "I had to come up with a good excuse. We're just lucky it was your apron he saw and not your bloomers. That would have been difficult to explain."

She leaned down and nipped him on the ear. "So," she whispered, "what did you tell him?"

"That you thought I'd been hit in the head and was worried about me bleeding all over the carpet, but in reality, I'd been . . . injured somewhere else and didn't want to tell you about it."

"Where?" she insisted.

He turned his head so that his hot breath scorched her cheek. "I told him I'd been kicked where it counts—in the privates—and that you were far too delicate and innocent to be informed of that tragedy, so I allowed you to believe I'd been popped in the head."

She lifted up as if to stare at the injured member. "That's funny. I didn't notice any problems with it last night." The fabric at his crotch twitched.

"And it still seems to be working quite well."

With a sudden movement, he reversed their positions, putting her on the bottom and him on top.

His wicked grin promised many things, pleasure being the utmost pledge. He bent down, only to be interrupted by a knock at the door.

"Maid service."

Emily took advantage of his distraction to begin unbuttoning his shirt, kissing each bit of exposed chest.

He shot Emily a pained grin, then turned his head toward the door. "No service today, thank you," he said between gritted teeth.

He turned back to Emily, only to be interrupted once more.

"Shall I leave fresh towels, sir?" asked the plaintive voice.

Emily pushed his shirt aside, exposing his taut, flat nipple, which she nipped with her teeth. He flinched in pleasure rather than pain.

"No," he said in a strangled voice. "No towels, no soap, no toilet paper. Just leave me the hell alone. OK?"

Emily pretended to be shocked, pointing to herself and offering a silent, "Me?"

He made a face, shook his head, and swooped down to catch her in a kiss that made her toes tingle in anticipation.

"Yes, sir. Sorry, sir." The voice sounded teary.

They both heard slow footsteps and her voice, somewhat more chirpily, addressing the next room. "Maid service."

Emily pretended to pout. "That was mean. All she was doing was her job."

His wicked grin filled her heart and fired her imagination with renewed desire. "I have all the maid service I can handle right now. Don't you agree?"

She pulled him down toward her. "Indeed I do."

They made love twice more and Delgatto finally fell asleep, exhausted by her unending source of energy and rather strong imagination. When he woke up, he realized she was gone, then remembered her benevolent boss had given her only half a day off.

He contemplated their adventures together in bed. He'd fallen asleep out of sheer exhaustion, spent but happy. And he couldn't really blame himself. After all, she was younger than he and had a natural stamina he had long since lost. Mind you, he wasn't out of condition and still kept a fairly rigorous training schedule, but training was no substitute for exuberant youth.

Of course, she'd admitted to him between lovemaking sessions that she was considered an old maid, but he figured that was merely the prejudices of the late nineteenth century. She couldn't be more than twenty-five, but in a world where women married and had several children by the time they were twenty, she was considered beyond her prime.

He laughed in spite of himself.

Any more prime and he wouldn't be able to walk straight. As it was, she had exhausted him with her unflagging energy, her natural curiosity, and an imagination that had no boundaries. The only downfall was the fact that once, while in the throes of passion, she'd called out, "James." For one confusing moment, he thought she was calling out a previous lover's name. Then he realized that to her he was James. *But . . . what's in a name?* he told himself. After the initial shock, he allowed himself to savor the passion in which she almost screamed the name. Her sentiment was honest, even if the name wasn't.

However, despite her enthusiastic desire, he had a feeling she was inexperienced in making love and might have even been a virgin. Be that as it may, she'd definitely enjoyed the experience, giving as good as she got.

A warm glow settled over him.

OK, maybe giving better than she got. The woman had been insatiable, and he'd been enticed into doing things he hadn't done in a while.

Who was he kidding? In years.

Eons, even.

He'd been damned-near celibate the past few years, not because he'd wanted to, but because the chase for the Heart of Saharanpur had been all encompassing, demanding his total time, attention, and dedication. Sometimes, he wondered if the chase was worth it, whether he'd be better off living with his family's disgrace than spending every waking hour trying to redeem it.

After a while, it all seemed somewhat fruitless. Even impossible.

But he would have thought it impossible to travel back in time, and yet here he was, lying in bed having just experienced the most intoxicating and captivating sessions of lovemaking he'd ever hoped to survive. And with a woman from the repressed nineteenth century.

He should be so lucky in his own century.

Delgatto pushed away his thoughts and pulled back the curtain, surprised to see that dusk had already settled over the landscape. He must have slept for hours, not even hearing Emily as she dressed and slipped out.

I hope she's not mad.

As he got dressed, he contemplated his next move—not with Emily, but in his search for the Heart. Then a sobering thought hit him. What happened when he found the cursed thing? Miss Sparrow had said he could return with it to his rightful time on the next solstice, and that was in June.

But that would mean leaving Emily behind.

His stomach flip-flopped.

Will I do that? He stared blankly across the room. *Can I do that?*

The bit of his conscience permanently imprinted with the needs of his family whispered, *How can you not go back?*

He wadded up his pillow and hurled it across the room.

Damn!

Delgatto's next suspect was a widow whom he'd not seen before. Evidently, she kept to herself in her Tower suite. She took her meals in her room and seldom came out.

He wanted to find Emily and let her use her staff contacts to ferret out information about the woman, but for some reason, Delgatto wasn't quite ready to face her again. He needed to sort out some very serious feelings first.

At the risk of alerting the terminally curious Rupert, Delgatto decided the young man would provide the most information.

Rupert scratched his head. "Miss Donovan? I really don't know anything about her. I've heard she's a real looker. I know she hasn't been a widow for long." He lowered his voice. "They say she inherited almost a million dollars from her husband and that he was a great deal older than she."

"How much older?"

Rupert raised a knowing eyebrow. "Old enough to be her grandfather." He motioned Delgatto closer. "I'm not one to gossip, but there were some rumors about foul play."

"You think she killed him?"

Rupert stepped back, waving his hands as if to erase the words from the air. "I didn't say that. As far as I know, there's no proof of anything like that." He shrugged. "I'm just telling you what I've heard others say."

Delgatto thanked the young man and then wandered to the stairs. By the time he'd climbed to the top and stepped into the hallway leading to Miss Donovan's suite, he had a plan formulated.

When he reached her door, he leaned hard against it, making sure his cane struck it with sufficient force to make a clattering sound.

Sure enough, she opened the door to discover poor Count Galludat leaning against it for support, deathly pale and wheezing for air.

"Sir, are you all right?"

He managed to nod and squeeze out his apology between gasps. "Sorry . . . overexerted . . . myself . . . need to . . . sit . . . and rest."

She helped him into her room and eased him into a chair, pulling up a hassock for his feet. A moment later, she pressed a brandy into his hand. He took an appreciative sip.

"Thank you."

Under the guise of recovering, he took a close look at his hostess. She had a Grace Kelly thing going for her—blond hair, blue eyes, flawless skin, a smile that radiated all-American goodness and a body made for all-American wickedness in bed.

"Allow me to introduce myself. My name is Count Robert Georges Galludat and, as you might guess, I am from France."

"Charmed, I'm sure. I'm Madelaine Donovan."

He kissed her hand in his best continental manner. "If I may be so bold as to ask, is there a Mr. Donovan?"

She lowered her head. "I was recently widowed. My Roger passed on last month."

Delgatto wore the appropriate look of sorrow. "My condolences. Was it sudden?"

She nodded. "We met a little over a year ago here—he was taking the cure. We fell madly in love and thought he was recuperating. But"—she sighed artfully—"I'm afraid the cure didn't take." She looked around the room. "I decided to come back on what would have been our first anniversary to remind myself of our happier times here at The Chesterfield."

Delgatto made eye contact with her. "I am genuinely sorrowed by your loss."

The eyes that met his were not those of a bereaved widow. They were those of a hungry woman looking for her next inheritance.

He decided to counter her sad story with one of

his own. After all, they always said misery loved company.

"I understand what it feels like to lose someone. When my accident occurred and it appeared as if I was no longer"—he coughed—"a complete man, my fiancée left me."

"How horrid," Madelaine cooed in sympathy.

"However, the hot springs have rejuvenated me, bringing back life to that which was lifeless." He indicated his cane. "I could not walk and now I can." He met her hungry stare with one of patented innocence. She was possibly savvy enough to see through anything but a well-planned, mostly plausible con. "My abilities are improving each day, and so I ignore the pain and exercise, climbing the stairs in hopes of building my strength and returning myself to my former condition."

She was almost salivating. "Do you hope to win your fiancée's heart back again?"

He shook his head. "She abandoned me when I needed her most. There is no place in my life, old or new, for her."

Her mouth said all the right things in sympathy but her eyes were calculating his wealth and measuring his health. Somehow he felt that under her tender nursing care, he'd be dead inside of six months.

He reached out and took her hand. "You are a marvelous listener. I've not talked about myself to anyone since I've been here."

She ducked her head coyly. "I find you fascinating. I could listen to you talk forever."

It was the perfect opening. He lifted her hand to

his lips. "May I be so bold as to ask you to have dinner with me tonight?"

She lifted her face, a single tear sitting strategically at the corner of her eye. "Tonight is the anniversary of my marriage with my late Roger. I promised myself I would not leave the suite."

Playing hard to get, eh? She was smart. If she'd jumped at the offer, the count might have belatedly found her actions suspicious. The ball was in his court now. "Perhaps I could have a meal brought up here that we could enjoy together. Nothing extraordinary—just one of Chef Sasha's specialties."

She contemplated the idea for the perfect amount of time, letting hesitation and desire wage a war across her features. Finally, she nodded. "I'd be delighted."

He stood. "Eight, then?" She nodded, then helped him toward the door. He performed one more perfunctory hand kiss then allowed himself to be ushered into the hallway.

After the door closed, he closed his eyes.

So how do I tell Emily I have a date tonight with another woman?

Sixteen

Although Emily had been excused from morning muster as well her morning duties, she had plenty of work left for the afternoon. The newly christened Fannie had been given Emily's morning responsibilities, and Emily had to go back and repair some of the many mistakes the girl had created in her haste and inexperience. After getting yelled at by two different guests who blamed her for Fannie's mistakes because they paid no attention to the face above the apron, Emily returned to her room, drained of all energy.

But as she sat on her bed, memories of her adventures the previous night and that morning surfaced. She'd never known making love could be so . . . so satisfying, so delightful, so addictive. As exhausted as she was, she'd like nothing better than to crawl into bed with Mr. East.

She stopped.

Mr. East.

Here she'd made love to the man, and she was still referring to him in such a proper manner. He had a first name. Why didn't she use it?

"James," she said aloud. She wrinkled her nose. For some reason, he didn't seem like a James to her.

"Jim?" she tested. "Jimmy?"

None of them sounded . . . right.

She leaned back and closed her eyes. Who cared what she called him, as long as she could be with him.

She bolted up in bed. How long *could* she be with him? He'd told her about his mission. Presumably, when his duties were complete, he'd go away to his next task.

He'll leave.

She turned around and buried her face in her pillow, letting it muffle her rage and her sorrow and her fears.

There was a knock at her door and a hurried whisper. "Emily, it's me. Let me in."

Mr. East.

Half of her wanted to throw open the door and the other half wanted to stay where she was, allowing the pillow to absorb her emotions. Instead, she lifted her head and called out, "Go away."

"C'mon, Emily, someone's going to see me. Open the door."

"No," she said, sniffling.

There was an odd noise, a click, and then her door opened by itself as if it had never been locked. He stepped in, pocketed something, and closed the door behind him. "What's wrong?"

"You," she said, fighting the urge to break out into a fresh wave of tears. "You're going to leave."

He looked confused. "No, I'm not."

Her lip trembled despite her best efforts to stop it. "Eventually."

He seemed to contemplate the revelation, then nod. "Eventually, but no time soon."

"But what about us?" She tried desperately not to cry. There was nothing she could abide less than a hysterical woman. She was bound and determined not to become one herself. "Is there an 'us'?"

He moved quickly across the room and knelt beside her bed. "At some point, I *will* have to leave. But it won't be because I want to go—or want to leave you."

An idea began to creep into her head. "Can I go with you?"

He sat back on his heels and concentration formed furrows in his forehead. "I honestly don't know. Maybe. I could ask Miss Sparrow."

Even in the depth of her emotions, she realized his statement was deucedly odd. "Miss Sparrow? What does she have to do with it?"

He made a face. "It's hard to explain. But if you went with me, it would mean leaving everybody you knew, this place, your family, everybody and every *thing* familiar to you. And then I'm not even sure it's possible."

He seemed so intent, so concerned, and yet his words didn't make sense to Emily. She was about to say something when yet another knock interrupted them.

They both heard Fannie wailing in the hallway.

"Not now!" Emily felt a rush of tears prickle her eyes. She had enough troubles in her life, let alone to have to stop and address Fannie's manufactured problems.

"Fannie," she called out. "It's not a good time."

Instead of answering, Fannie broke out in a new set of loud sobs.

Mr. East sighed. "She's not going away, is she?"

Emily shook her head. "No." Her heart skipped a beat. "And she can't see you here, either." She glanced around the room. "You have to leave."

He stood, brushing off the knees of his trousers. "How? I can't go out the door, because she's there." He shifted to the window and glanced down at the bushes below. "Those are hollies. I'll rip myself to shreds if I try to go out this way."

Emily scanned the room for a solution, her attention settling on the armoire. "In there," she commanded, grabbing him by the arm. She opened the cabinet door, slid back the hanging clothes as best as possible, and pushed him inside, giving him no time to register any complaints.

"Now be quiet. I'll try to get her out as soon as possible."

He stopped the door from closing. "Emily, I love you."

She swallowed hard. "And I love you, too." She closed the door.

Delgatto tried to find a comfortable position, but he was about four inches too tall for that. He ended up resting his back against one side of the cabinet and bracing himself with his knees against the opposite side.

Outside, he could hear Emily talking with the woman, but he couldn't distinguish their words. Whatever the problem, this Fannie was terribly upset. Every other moment, she broke out in loud gulping sobs.

He waited patiently, if uncomfortably. Something kept jamming him in the ribs. Finally, he worked his arm around and tried to push it out of his way. It was some sort of cloth-covered wire shape—maybe not cloth, but some sort of fine net. He began to examine it in the dark, tracing its outline—the series of curves it formed. It was somewhat familiar in shape, but recognition sat just on the edges of his memory.

He began to rebuild the item in his mind, the wire shape, the netting. They felt like . . .

Wings!

His heart skipped a beat. They *were* wings. Costume wings, and he'd seen them before.

On his fairy princess.

Delgatto suddenly had a hard time drawing a breath. Emily was his fairy princess?

Impossible.

She was a maid, and maids didn't crash parties at The Chesterfield. He knew she valued her job too much to take that sort of chance. And as far as that went, where could she have gotten such an obviously expensive costume?

The answer came to him in a flash, releasing the band that had tightened across his chest.

Someone gave the costume to her.

After the ball.

He began to see the possibilities. Emily would tell him who gave her the costume, thereby identifying the mysterious fairy princess. Suddenly he became impatient, having to restrain himself from throwing open the armoire door and revealing his presence to the terminally upset Fannie.

The air in the enclosure grew stale and hot.

He heard Emily's voice as she stepped closer to the armoire. "Let me get . . . a clean apron out of here and then we'll go see the Major together."

The door opened partially and Emily blocked any

view into the armoire by positioning herself in the door. When she reached in, he grabbed her hand and spoke in the lowest whisper he could manage. "Where did you get this?" He pointed to the costume.

She flushed. "Now, where is that clean apron?"

"Where?" he prompted, mouthing the word.

She swallowed hard and spoke between clenched teeth. "Lady Arkling." Closing the door, she said in a loud voice, "Oh well, I can't seem to find a clean apron. Let's you and I leave and go talk to Major Payne in his office, all right?"

Her companion didn't seem to notice anything strange about Emily's loud and pointed delivery because she emitted an equally loud, "Oh, thank you, Emily! I really appreciate this."

Moments later, he heard the door slam shut loudly.

Delgatto literally fell out of the armoire, still clutching the fairy outfit. After his eyes grew accustomed to the sudden change in light, he examined the wings, almost mesmerized by the way the bits of glitter caught the light. They were definitely the same set of wings.

Lady Arkling, eh? So who was she? Even more important, *where* was she?

If Emily was temporarily indisposed, then he'd have to rely on someone else for the information.

Several minutes later, he approached the Major's office. Unfortunately, the man wasn't in, but the clerk on duty assured Delgatto the Major would arrive "any minute now."

Delgatto hung around the front desk, trying to affect an idle air, when all he really wanted to do was find this Lady Arkling and get his necklace back from her.

His necklace.

Not technically his, but at least he was one of the rightful owners, albeit over a hundred years in the future.

Delgatto betrayed his nerves by drumming his fingers on the counter. Evidently annoyed by the sound, the clerk found an excuse to retire to the room behind the counter. Delgatto began to fiddle with the papers on the counter, straightening them. On top was a folded piece of paper, addressed to the Major. Lifting a corner of the paper, he discovered it was a telegram for the Major. But even more alarming, he saw the words "James East."

With his smoothest motion, he slipped the telegram into his pocket and headed toward the gentlemen's bar. He headed through the cloud of smoke that met him at the entrance of the room and chose a booth in the very back of the room, waving away the bartender's silent request for a drink order.

Once satisfied he was alone in the rear of the room and likely to stay that way, he unfolded the telegram and read the hand-printed block letters.

NO RECORD OF AGENT NAMED EAST IN SS NO PLANS FOR PRESIDENTIAL VISIT TO YOUR AREA STOP SUGGEST YOU DETAIN MAN AND TURN OVER TO AUTHORITIES STOP GOOD INSTINCTS AS ALWAYS STOP REDJACK

Damn it . . . he'd been made! And by some short squatty martinet who still thought he was running the army.

What now?

The solution was obvious. A new telegram. He pocketed the paper and waved the bartender over.

"I need to send a telegram. How would I do that?"

The man smiled. "We have blank forms at the front counter. Just fill it out and we'll have one of the porters run it down to the telegraph office. They'll post the charges to your room, afterward." He paused. Then his face brightened. "I think I have some blanks here." The man reached behind the bar and pulled out a piece of paper. "Here you go, sir."

Delgatto reached into his pocket and tipped the man well with Count Galludat's money. "Thank you very much."

He began to compose the new reply in his head.

EAST ONE OF BEST AGENTS IN SS STOP KEEP DETAIL OF VISIT SECRET STOP SUGGEST YOU OFFER EAST WHATEVER ASSISTANCE REQUIRED STOP GOOD INSTINCTS AS ALWAYS STOP REDJACK

That would do nicely. All he had to do now was find a pen and duplicate the telegraph worker's scratchy handwriting and *voilà.*

Instant authority.

He ambled back to the front counter where the Major stood, thumbing through a sheaf of papers. "Are you sure nothing has come for me?" he was asking the clerk on duty.

"No, sir."

The Major looked up and almost managed to hide his look of mild distrust. "Mr. Galludat, good to see you."

Delgatto pointed to the man's office. "May we talk for a moment? In private?"

"Certainly."

A moment later, they were seated around the Major's desk. The Major looked as if he wanted to speak first, but Delgatto beat him to the punch.

"My sources tell me you've asked for confirmation of my identity, and I must say I'm pleased you've taken this step. It goes even further to show how dedicated you are to the security of The Chesterfield and its patrons."

The Major was unable to hide his shock at being discovered, nor his secret pleasure at being praised for his thoroughness.

"I suspect your friend Redjack should be responding quite soon to alleviate your fears. Meanwhile, I have another individual I'd like to investigate, and I need some background information."

The Major leaned forward, now fully enthralled with the hunt. "Who?"

"Someone named Lady Arkling."

The Major rolled his eyes and leaned back in his chair. "Oh. Her."

"You're familiar with the name?"

The Major reached into his drawer and pulled out a large file, dumping it unceremoniously on the desk. "Here's everything we have on the woman—every bogus charge, every underhanded action, every false claim, and most important"—he moved a sheaf of papers fastened together with a straight pin—"every bill she left unpaid."

Delgatto's stomach tightened. "Left . . . unpaid? Left, as in no longer here?"

The Major nodded. "She left in the dead of night

in a manner quite similar to our Miss Brady—who by the way, is actually one Zelma McGruder of Yonkers. Evidently she has a long history of impersonating heiresses."

"Forget her," Delgatto demanded. "What about Arkling?"

The Major consulted the file. "She showed up here six months ago, a week before our Summer Jubilee. She charmed every man in the place, present company excepted. I knew there was something . . . not right about Lady Arkling. I have a good ear for accents, you know, and found some discrepancies in hers."

And not mine?

"And?"

"She inveigled herself into the good graces of everyone—hotel staff, guests, and shopkeepers alike. On the evening of the summer ball, instead of attending, she stole anything and everything that wasn't nailed down, and escaped into the night carrying away a veritable fortune and leaving behind nothing but bills and broken hearts."

"She . . . she hasn't been seen since? Not ever? Not, let's say, last week or so?"

"If I saw that . . . that *female* again, I'd run her out on a rail."

Delgatto stared at the mountain of paper. So if Lady Arkling was a con woman extraordinaire, why had she given Emily an expensive costume? Had Emily been an unwitting confederate? Or—he swallowed hard—a witting one?

Doubts began to creep up in his mind, whispering terrible things. Emily had been awfully willing to help him when it came to breaking into people's rooms. Was it merely a matter of falling into old habits?

Had Lady Arkling returned to the scene of the crime to attend the Christmas ball?

His stomach fired in pain.

Had Emily helped the woman sneak into the hotel and been paid in trinkets? Even worse, had she helped the woman escape detection?

"What's wrong, Mr. East? You look decidedly pale."

Delgatto fought against his growing revulsion and tapped the file. "Is there any way she could have returned without your knowing it?"

The man shook his head. "Absolutely not. Everyone on staff here, plus all the merchants in town, know what she looks like. If she as much as set one foot within the city limits, they'd send up a hue and cry louder than fireworks on the Fourth of July."

Delgatto nodded, his mind captivated by a thousand different thoughts, some of them whispered accusations, others loud voices of denial. He stood and started walking toward the door. He needed to get away and think. Long and hard.

"Mr. East?"

He heard the name, but it didn't register.

"Mr. East, don't forget your walking stick."

Delgatto spun around, retrieved his cane, and exited, remembering only a few steps beyond the door to affect the count's awkward gait.

He went back to his room, pulled out a piece of paper, and began to write out what he knew. The fairy princess had been wearing the Heart of Saharanpur. It didn't take a jeweler's loupe to establish that it was authentic. Emily now had that costume and said she'd gotten it from Lady Arkling. However, Lady Arkling had left six months ago. As far as anyone knew, she hadn't returned.

So who had been wearing the costume and the necklace at the Christmas ball?

Emily? If she possessed such a priceless necklace as the Heart, she wouldn't be working as a maid in a hotel.

Delgatto suddenly saw a bit of light at the end of the tunnel. Maybe she'd lent the costume out to a guest. Or, even better, rented it out. That made sense: She got the costume from Lady Arkling, realized that it was of no use to her personally, but made a bit of money on the side by renting it out to a female guest.

His panic began to subside and turn into elation. *Then that means Emily knows the fairy princess!*

It was all really quite simple. Even worse, the answer had been under his nose the entire time. He had to speak with her. Now.

He remembered his cane this time as he headed for the servants' hallway. Unfortunately, there was too much activity, too many people in the area for him to go straight to Emily's room. Left with no other recourse, he stepped outside, pulling his jacket closed around the light snow that was falling. He counted off the rooms until he felt certain he was at her window. The holly bush helped mark the spot as well as prevent him from getting close enough to knock.

Luckily, the curtains were pulled back and he could see her sitting on her bed, talking in earnest with another maid. The other woman looked somewhat familiar, as if he had seen her around but not really noticed her face. The anonymous servant syndrome, he supposed.

He took a closer look. She was tall, gangly, and made rather broad gestures with her large-boned hands. It was evident she was upset and Emily was trying to calm her down. After a few minutes, the two of them stood up and hugged. Then the other maid left.

Alone at last.

He was too far from the window to knock on it and get her attention. He was left with only one recourse. He knelt down, patting the ground in search of pebbles small enough to throw at the window and not break it. He stuck himself on too many pointy leaves as he felt along the dirt, only to discover a few twigs and several rocks large enough to shatter the glass. He widened his search area and finally found three or four suitable missiles.

He straightened up, selected a pebble and cocked his hand to toss it toward the window.

He froze. The pebble tumbled out of his hand.

Emily stood framed in the window, tears on her face. She cradled something in her hand and then held the object toward the light.

A large emerald suspended from a gold rope chain.

The Heart of Saharanpur.

Seventeen

Emily held the necklace to the lamp, letting the stone spin lazily, suspended by its gold rope chain. The green shards of light spilling from it still possessed the ability to captivate, to mesmerize her just as they had when she was a child.

Every time she saw the emerald, she was instantly transported back in time to when she was a little girl, playing elaborate dress-up games and holding tea parties with her stalwart companion, her grandfather. As they sipped their imaginary tea and dined on invisible sandwiches, he would tell her the most marvelous stories about a pretend prince and princess in a land far away whose families were on opposite sides of a great war, but who had fallen in love with each other the first time they met. They enlisted the help of a stable boy, who dutifully carried their love notes to each other. And when the princess discovered she was to be married to an ugly ogre of a duke, the stable boy risked his life to steal a carriage and alert the prince. Together they returned to her castle, where the prince whisked the princess away to freedom and safety.

Both the prince and princess knew the young stable boy could never go back to the castle, so they gave him money for safe passage to the new lands and a very special gift: the Heart of Saharanpur. The prince explained that one of his ancestors had brought it back from the Holy Lands. Reportedly, the stone was blessed and would help whoever owned it find true love. The prince, having already found his true love, gave it to the stable boy with his thanks and best wishes for the future.

Emily loved that story, because although her grandfather never suggested it, she had the assurance of a child that he must have been that stable boy. Not only did he have the Heart of Saharanpur, which he'd let her wear with her dress-up clothes, but he'd had a long and wonderful marriage with her grandmother whom he'd always referred to as True Love. Even Emily had grown up calling her Truly, rather than Grandmother or Oma.

One day, when Emily had grown older, she had asked him, point-blank, if the story of the prince and princess was true, but he never quite gave her a clear answer.

Not until the day he lay on his deathbed.

As Emily knelt beside him, trying to contain her tears, he patted her hand, then directed her to retrieve the velvet-lined wooden box that housed the necklace.

"I'm giving this to you," he'd said. "Your father has already found his true love in your mother, so he doesn't need it. You take it. You've always cherished it more for its beauty and history than for its wealth. Let it help you find your true love."

Later, after her grandfather passed on, she learned her father had been angry with the old man's decision. He felt slighted, having been denied an asset that he could sell to help his ailing business. After a short while, he approached Emily, not demanding, but asking her to sell the Heart, but she couldn't do it. She felt compelled to keep it, to honor her grandfather and his last wishes.

Nothing was the same between Emily and her father after that. Even when she offered to work at The Chesterfield and send all her money home, it didn't seem good enough to please her father, especially when he learned she'd fooled him by leaving the wooden case behind and taken the Heart of Saharanpur with her for safekeeping. Not enough money, he'd complained. But she took the job just the same, trying to prove to him she was still a good daughter and cared about her family. For two long years, she'd performed as a maid, doing tasks that she'd never had to perform at home. She did them well and without hesitation. But at the end of her two-year contract, she was secretly ready to go home. Facing her father's disapproval would be far less taxing than another year at the Major's beck and call.

But when the quarantine hit the town, his financial difficulties tripled. Her mother had sent a letter that revealed what the first telegram didn't: not only was the family business in jeopardy, but now the bankers were considering taking away their home and their land.

Emily knew the time had come to sell the Heart of Saharanpur and that her father would be much too happy to help find a buyer. But she didn't offer to sell it to please him. She was willing to do whatever she could to keep a roof over her brothers and sisters and keep them fed. It was her duty to them, one her grandfather would understand and accept.

And, she thought, watching the stone spin to a stop, then reverse directions, *perhaps the Heart's legacy has already come true.*

Her vision blurred for a moment as she thought of Mr. East and their enthralling moments together. Was he her true love? She honestly didn't know. She hoped so. Perhaps they needed a stable boy to help them escape.

Nonsense.

Emily gave the stone one more spin, the refractions making green light dance around the room.

"I don't want to sell you, but I must," she said aloud, addressing the stone as if she expected it to hear her. "Tomorrow will be our last day together. I'm sorry to give you up, but you will make the difference between my family surviving or being carted off to the poorhouse." Then she looked heavenward. "I hope you understand, Grandfather. . . ."

Emily placed the necklace back into its case and noticed the curtains were open. She reached over and tugged them shut, then returned the case to its hiding place in the secret compartment at the bottom of her sewing basket.

She stashed the basket in the bottom drawer of her armoire, then opened the door above to remove her nightgown. Seeing her wrinkled clothes, she remembered Mr. East's look of dismay at the hiding place she'd chosen for him. Then he'd certainly made a quick about-face.

Why had he been so all-fired interested in her dresses? Had he heard the evil stories about Lady Arkling?

She stiffened. Was that why he was at The Chesterfield? Searching for clues as to the whereabouts of that very deceitful lady?

But now that she thought about it, Emily wondered if he hadn't been pointing to the fairy costume, instead.

She pressed her palm against her mouth, trying to contain her laughter. So Mr. East had learned he wasn't the only one with secrets. When he'd put on a mask to enter the Molderhoffen's suite, she recognized at that very moment that he'd also been the dashing masked highwayman at the ball. Although they'd never made their planned assignation at the gazebo, circumstances had thrown them together again, as if it were fate's wish that they meet and fall in love.

Although she knew of his identity as the highwayman, he'd had no idea that she was his fairy princess.

What a laugh he must be having now!

Delgatto stared at the curtains, cursing them for interrupting his view of one of the most marvelous sights he'd ever hoped to see.

She has it. She's had it all the while.

He stood there, frozen in the spot for an indeterminable amount of time. The light snow changed into a heavy one, and finally the cold penetrated his attention by making him start to shiver uncontrollably.

He stumbled toward the front of the building, numbed by shock and the growing cold. The ever present Rupert must have seen him trip up the porch stairs and rushed out to offer aid. Delgatto allowed the young man to continue believing his dazed condition was due to weather, rather than shock. He wasn't going to explain why he'd been standing out in the snow, playing Peeping Tom with one of their staff members.

The young man led him directly into the bar, where the bartender thrust a drink in his hand and cleared a seat closest to the roaring fire.

"What were you doing out there, sir?" young Rupert chided, using his scarf to rub life back into Delgatto's gloveless fingers. "You could have caught your death of cold, Mr. Galludat."

Delgatto felt an unpleasant tingling in his limbs as well as his heart. "Emily," he said in a leaden voice. "She was the fairy princess."

To Delgatto's surprise, the young man reacted with a flush of guilt, looking away. "At the Christmas ball? No, sir. You must be mistaken." He began to rub even harder.

Delgatto pushed away Rupert's efforts. "I'm not mistaken." He read the look in the young man's eyes. "And you knew about it, didn't you?"

Rupert glanced around, as if worried they were being overheard. He lowered his voice to a whisper. "Not so loud, sir. If anyone else finds out, she'll lose her job. Me, too. The Major has very strict rules about guests and staff mixing in social situations."

"But why? Why did she do it?"

Rupert shrugged, gave the area another critical once-over and kept his voice low. "She'd completed her contract with the hotel, but she couldn't go home because of some quarantine. She had to stay here, but where? She couldn't afford to be a guest, and someone had already been hired to take her place." A small smile replaced some of the young man's earlier concern. "Miss Sparrow was the one who came up with the answer."

"Miss Sparrow?"

The young man nodded enthusiastically. "She arranged for Emily to stay in an empty Tower suite as a sort of a Christmas bonus from the owner of the hotel. A real Cinderella situation. So we, her friends, decided she ought to take advantage of the situation. One of the town seamstresses had all these dresses that Lady Arkling had ordered but never paid for, including that fairy costume. One thing led to another . . ." His voice trailed off.

Delgatto's head began to clear. "And Emily became the belle of the ball as the fairy princess."

"Exactly." Rupert shot him a shrewd look. "So why was it such a shock to you, sir?" What he wasn't saying was, *What's Emily to you and why do you suddenly care?*

With his brain cells sufficiently warmed, Delgatto knew a good explanation was in order, and he was going to have to pour it on with thick sentimentality for it to stick. "As you know, I attended the ball for a short while. But while I was there, I saw the fairy princess. There was something about her—something almost magical. One look and I was smitten." Delgatto felt the old talents begin to unthaw, the ones that allowed him to spin believable lies to protect himself.

"And even more importantly, feelings began to return, feelings I feared were lost forever. I took my first steps that next morning, and I must credit her beauty for inspiring me, for filling me with energy and renewing my desire to walk again." He stared into the fireplace, adding a note of awe in his voice.

"And to think it was a simple maid who stirred me so."

Thoroughly entranced by the story, Rupert could do nothing but nod.

"So you can see why I'm so shocked by the revelation."

"Sure."

"So please don't say anything to anybody about this. Especially Miss Drewitt. I need to"—he paused and sighed—"sort out my feelings for her before I take any actions."

"Actions . . ." Rupert repeated, now lost in his own thoughts. He looked up, seemed to snap back to reality, and added a hearty, "Yes, sir. Not a word to anyone. Now you just sit back and sip that brandy. We've got the outside warm enough. You work on the inside."

The young man disappeared from the bar, presumably to return to his duties in the lobby. Just as long as he didn't fire up the hotel grapevine with the headlines: *French Count Has Hots for Maid, Film at Eleven.*

Delgatto took a tentative sip of the brandy.

Why did you have to make this so . . . complicated, Emily?

Delgatto suffered through his dinner with Madelaine Donovan, trying to play the attentively suave count, but with his mind constantly wandering to the all-encompassing subject of Emily.

His dinner companion seemed quite miffed with his constant distractions, and he had to create a whopper of a lie to turn her pout into a sympathetic purr. Madelaine had a late husband to talk about, so Delgatto created news of his former fiancée's impending delivery.

As he told of his disintegration of his relationship with his fiancée, he let it slip that one of the chief reasons they'd broken up was his inability to perform, his incapacity to give her the gift of life she so desired.

He watched Madelaine's interest go from hot and bothered to merely bothered. Within twenty minutes, she made an excuse and ended their dinner early, leaving him and his alleged erectile dysfunction problems behind, probably—hopefully—forever.

That night Delgatto couldn't stay away from Emily, but he couldn't confront her yet.

A little breaking and entering was called for.

He waited until the employees' hallway was empty, then made quick work of picking her lock. He slipped in and shut the door soundlessly behind him. Once his eyes grew accustomed to the dark, he could see her on the bed, sound asleep, only a few highly tempting feet away. But this wasn't the time for a midnight game of tickle me, Elmo. He had work to do.

He searched her room in total silence.

It wasn't that he intended to steal the necklace right then and there, but he had to see it for himself. Hold it. Admire it. If he could make himself let go of it, he would. Then again . . .

He continued searching, not finding it in the usual places. Wherever it was, she'd hidden it well.

Noiselessly, he slid open her desk drawer, only to find little beyond a few sheets of paper and a couple of stubby pencils. Spotting the corner of paper peeping from beneath the blotter, he allowed curiosity to get the best of him. He pulled the paper free and unfolded it, revealing a telegram addressed to Emily Drewitt and sent from a Marcus Drewitt.

As Delgatto read it, every muscle in his body grew taut. Although it didn't mention the Heart, per se, the jewel was most likely the only thing of any worth Emily possessed and could sell.

And if he hadn't lost track of the days, tomorrow was New Year's Eve.

Damn! It gave him precious little time to figure everything out. All his life, he'd waited for this moment—to regain what rightfully belonged to his family. Up until mere hours ago, he'd been assured he was merely stealing it from a stranger, a faceless, nameless criminal who had no right to own it.

But this was no faceless, nameless person.

It was Emily.

And she wasn't a criminal.

Somehow, he'd bet her family's reasons for owning the stone were almost as compelling as his family's.

He read the telegram again and a plan began to blossom in his head. He couldn't, he wouldn't steal the necklace from Emily. She deserved better than that.

But there was nothing to keep him from stealing the necklace from its *new* owner after the transaction was completed.

It was so simple it was almost ludicrous.

Emily would get paid. He'd get the stone. All would be well in the world—past, present and future.

Delgatto slapped his hands together in glee, belatedly thankful for his gloves, which muted the sound into something harmless. Emily reacted to the slight sound by shifting in bed. To his pleasure and his dismay, her blanket slipped back, revealing the rather sheer front of her nightgown.

Look but don't touch, he reminded himself. And look he did. After all, they'd been together in the most provocative of positions, doing the most inventive things with each other for the sake of pleasure.

What was the harm in noticing? And admiring . . .

. . . and wanting her so bad he thought his legs would give out?

The Heart of Saharanpur, he reminded himself. *Wouldn't you rather see* it *instead?* He dragged his attention away from her very enticing curves and returned to his search. Three minutes later, he found the false bottom in her sewing basket and pulled out the jewelry case.

The box was different, lacking the royal crest, but he knew what was inside. He hefted the case, feeling the proper weight, the proper sense of movement within. Placing it on the desk, he stripped off his gloves. They'd been an old and important habit for a thief such as himself. But fingerprints weren't accepted evidence in the courts of this day, why deny himself the thrill of real contact?

His palms literally itched in anticipation. Rubbing his hands together briskly, he knelt down, getting at eye level with the desk and its precious cargo. Using his left hand to steady the case, and poising his right to lift the lid, he drew a deep breath.

. . . and couldn't move.

He couldn't do it.

If he took one look at the Heart of Saharanpur, the lesser man inside might not be able to give it up.

That would foil all his grand plans about waiting and stealing it from the next owner, rather than from Emily.

He sat back, sighed, and plowed his fingers through his hair.

Why was it so difficult?

Why couldn't he just open the case and take a quick peek? Why didn't he have the strength of character to view it and then leave it?

Why? He knew why.

He'd been waiting all his life to see it. To touch it. To admire the smooth coolness of the stone's surface. To admire its green clarity.

He stopped himself. *Get a grip, man. It's just a thing. Not a person.*

Not a person like Emily. He glanced at her. A warm, loving person who made him laugh, who wrapped him in warmth and acceptance. Who could make him ache for her like he'd never ached for a woman before.

He closed his eyes, afraid to even see the case, much less the treasure inside. With renewed control, betrayed only by his slightly shaking hands, he returned the case to its hiding place in the sewing basket and replaced the basket in the drawer of the armoire.

"You may never know how much I love you, Emily," he whispered, fighting the urge to caress her face. Instead, he pulled on his gloves, turned his back on the two treasures in the room, and slipped out the door.

Eighteen

The morning muster was longer than usual, full of special tasks in anticipation of the New Year's celebration. After the Major finished his tirade, Emily tried to talk to him. Unfortunately, he was in no mood to listen to anyone, much less her, and brushed her off instead with a "Later."

After performing most of her morning chores, she took her concerns to Miss Sparrow instead. She knocked on the frame of the small room that served as Miss Sparrow's office. It was little more than a closet crammed with a desk and two chairs.

"Ma'am, do you have a moment?"

The woman looked up and smiled. "Always for you, Emily. How may I help you?"

"I have a . . . situation that has occurred and I need advice. Actually, I was hoping to speak to the Major and ask him for some guidance in the matter."

One eyebrow shot up. "Guidance? From the Major? My goodness, but this is an unusual request. So you would like me to intercede on your behalf?"

"Yes, ma'am. I would."

"May I ask what it's about?" Her look of amazement faded into something more wary in appearance. "You aren't suddenly overwhelmed by the need to confess your sins to the man, are you?"

At the word *sins,* Emily immediately thought about Mr. East and all the delightfully forbidden things they had done together.

Luckily, Miss Sparrow continued. "Please say you're not going to tell him about attending the ball in costume."

Emily's mouth gaped open. "You knew about that?"

The woman offered her a tight little smile. "Of course. I know almost everything that goes on around here. And if I had thought there was any harm to you in attending it, I would have stopped you. But you weren't technically an employee, so I felt it was high time you had a chance to kick up your heels." She leaned forward in conspiracy. "You had a good time, didn't you?"

Emily nodded shyly. "I certainly did."

The woman's smile was warm. "I'm so very glad you did." Her posture and her expression went from friendly to professional in a blink of an eye. "So, what sort of help do you need from the Major?"

Emily spoke very slowly, hoping her explanation made sense. "Someone is supposed to come to The Chesterfield today and ask for me. My parents have arranged for this person to buy a family heirloom that I have in my possession. I only found out about it yesterday."

"And you want the Major not to let them know you're a maid here and have them believe you're a guest, instead?"

Emily shook her head. "Oh, no, ma'am. That's not it. I just wanted the Major to oversee the transaction and make sure that the buyer is honest and that his payment is, as well. I don't know much about these things. Someone could very easily cheat me and I wouldn't know it."

"I doubt anyone could cheat you, Emily. You're a very bright girl. It *is* a very wise idea to bring in someone on your behalf who is more worldly and more familiar with high finance. But I'm afraid the Major is going to be tied up for the rest of the day in anticipation of the New Year's celebration tonight." At the sight of Emily's disappointment, Miss Sparrow smiled. "Not to worry, Emily. I will personally make sure to provide you an experienced champion to protect your interests."

"You will?" Emily wanted to hug the woman, but knew it wasn't exactly proper behavior. "Oh, thank you, Miss Sparrow. If there's ever anything I can do for you . . ."

The woman's smile grew larger. "I'll make sure to mention it to you. Now, if someone asks for you at the front desk, I'll let you know and I'll arrange for you to meet in one of the private parlors." She glanced at Emily's uniform. "And you might think about changing clothes and putting on one of those lovely dresses Maria lent you. Your price negotiations might shift more to your favor if your buyer takes for granted that you are what you appear to be: a well-dressed, well-heeled hotel guest. We won't lie to him about your profession, but we certainly won't correct any assumptions he might make based on your guest-like appearance."

Emily forgot about the differences in their stations in life and threw her arms around the woman and embraced her. "Thank you, Miss Sparrow. Thank you so much . . ."

"You're welcome," the woman whispered back. She broke their hug and nudged Emily toward the door. "Now run along. I have to arrange for your champion."

"You want me to what?" Delgatto crossed his arms, trying to contain the rage that wanted to break free.

"You heard me well enough the first time." The woman wore an insufferably calm smile. "Emily is going to be selling her jewelry today, and she's afraid she's too inexperienced at such high finance and that the buyer might take advantage of her." She leaned forward. "You wouldn't want that to happen, now would you?"

He began to pace the impossibly small room. "I'm here to steal the bloody thing. You know that and I know that. If you involve me in the sales negotiations, then you're severely hampering my ability to steal it."

"How so?"

"The buyer will have seen my face, that's why."

She wore a look of complete innocence. "But why would he believe Miss Drewitt's representative would be a thief?"

OK, she had him there. But he'd be damned if he'd give her the satisfaction of knowing she was right.

She continued. "The scenario is relatively simple. You act as her negotiator, getting a fair, if not generous, amount for her. Once we are sure the money has been properly deposited in her account, the buyer gets the necklace. You insist on buying him a drink, preferably in town and not at the hotel. After you two are sufficiently in your cups, you offer to walk with him to the bank or the train or wherever he is going. You are attacked by masked hoodlums who rob both of you, stealing the necklace. Perhaps you are even injured in the melee, bringing more credence to your role as hapless victim."

She was good. Damned good. The scenario might work, too, if not for one small problem.

"After all," she continued, "for all anyone knows, you are a French count visiting here for recuperation's sake. And perhaps you have a passing interest in precious gems and are willing to apply what knowledge you possess to help an unfortunate young lady."

He swallowed hard. And therein lay the problem. "Well . . . not everybody believes I'm a count. Or crippled. Or French."

"What do you mean?" Her gaze narrowed, and alarm began to creep into her face. "You didn't tell someone who you really are, did you?"

Delgatto stopped pacing and turned his attention to a picture hanging at a slightly off angle. "Of course not. Who'd believe I was from the future? I barely believe it myself." He straightened the picture twice, stalling for everything he was worth.

"Mr. Delgatto . . ."

He didn't even correct her. "And speaking of people not believing things, it was the Major who caught on to my little impersonation."

"He what?"

Boy, now he really had Miss Sparrow's attention, minus her calm, cool, and collected smile. She looked almost distraught.

He turned his attention back to the picture. "The Maj is pretty sharp, sharper than I gave him credit for. But as a wise man once said, 'Never underestimate great talent, especially mine.' I managed to salvage the moment. He now believes I am a Secret Service agent, here as an advance scout for a possible presidential visit."

He knew she was staring at him; he could feel two holes being drilled into the back of his head. He turned around and shrugged. "What was I supposed to do? He saw through the crippled count gimmick. I turned things around so that penetrating my disguise proved how really good he is at his job. The man loves to be praised. And he loves intrigue, too. I threw in some mumbo-jumbo about quiet negotiations with foreign powers and had him eating out of my hand."

She shook her head. "Don't you understand that for all his blustery ways, Major Payne still has some very strong contacts with his former superiors in Washington? He could easily penetrate this new disguise as well."

What was she? A mind reader?

He stuffed his hands in his pockets. "He almost did already. The Major sent one of his buddies a wire, asking for confirmation of my identity. How was I to know he was that well connected? Luckily, I was able to intercept the telegram which suggested they lock me up and throw away the key, and substitute my own answer, which gave me a rather glowing recommendation."

She started to speak, but he held out his hand to stop her.

"I know, I know. It could still blow up in my face.

But all I have to do is wait until Emily's transaction is finalized, witnessed, whatever. Just as long as she is paid for the thing. Then I can steal it from the new owner, and literally make off like a bandit. I'll disappear and then come back here—with a new identity—in June for my return engagement."

"You seemed to have found a suitable solution to spare Miss Drewitt any financial distress."

Delgatto felt telltale color flood his cheeks. Since when had he started wearing his feelings on his sleeve? His Tuesday night poker buddies were going to have a field day with his new sensitivities once he got back.

"I can't hurt Emily. I won't hurt her. I think she's had a hard enough life without my stealing the only really valuable thing she has."

Miss Sparrow caught him in an uncomfortable glaze. "Haven't you done that already?"

An eerie silence fell across the room. His voice sounded broken and unsure even to his own ears.

"What do you mean?"

"You're making such pains not to steal her Heart of Saharanpur. But what about her own heart?"

He made three false starts, trying to dismiss their moments together as nothing more than a mutually satisfying roll in the hay, but even *he* couldn't bring himself to say it, much less believe it. He dropped into the chair by her desk.

The King of Thieves was a royal has-been.

"What do I do?" he whispered. "I think I love her. Hell, I know I love her. I've already told her so. And it's scaring me to death. I mean, I know what I'm supposed to do. It's been drilled into me from the womb, and I'm the family's last hope. There is no *next* generation to take up the shield and go on with the crusade. I've been too busy chasing the damned thing to have a life, a family. If I fail, then the family fails. There's no one after me to continue the quest, noble or otherwise." He paused. "What do I do, Miss Sparrow?"

"It's a question only you can answer."

She heaved a sigh that made him think of his great aunt Beatrice, the only member of the family not caught up in a single-minded quest for the necklace. She used to sigh like Miss Sparrow, and he knew it meant, *I don't want to be disappointed in you, boy. Do the right thing.*

But he'd be damned if he knew what the right thing was at that moment.

She stood. "I'm afraid I must go. Duties call. But before I do, let me ask you one question." She placed her hand on his forearm. "Is the honor of a family more important than the honor of an individual?" She squeezed his arm, nodded her farewell, then left him sitting at the end of her desk.

The honor of an individual. Meaning him, of course. But hadn't he already found the honorable solution—to steal from the next owner and not from Emily? Hadn't he found the ideal answer that served both Emily's family and his own?

Then the significance of Miss Sparrow's words hit him between the eyes. Both he and Emily were acting on behalf of their families, but not taking into account what they wanted themselves. Sure, the idea of selfless devotion to the family was noble, but should it take over—commandeer both of their lives?

Forever?

He saw how she'd looked at the Heart of Saharanpur. What he saw in her eyes wasn't greed or false pride of ownership, but a sense of sentimentality. She didn't want to sell it. It meant something very special to her.

And he didn't want to steal it from her.

The honor of the family . . .

He'd never been given a choice of occupations. It was expected of him to carry on as the family's thief. Sure, he was good at it, but he might have been good at a dozen other vocations.

But he'd never know.

Just as he'd never know if he and Emily could have made a go of it. He couldn't stay to find out because of his duty to bring the Heart of Saharanpur back to his family.

He buried his face in his hands. *Why isn't there a way out of this?*

Emily had a hard time concentrating on her duties at hand, fretting about her meeting with the unknown buyer. Miss Sparrow had promised to find someone to negotiate in her stead, but who? Quite frankly, Emily didn't trust the town's only jeweler. She had waited patiently to speak to him soon after she'd arrived in town, but he had been too busy with several rich customers to serve a lowly hotel employee. Literally forgotten by the jeweler, Emily had watched one large woman "ooh" and "aah" over various pieces of jewelry. A second woman made a timely appearance, expressing equally enthusiastic interest over several of the same pieces of merchandise. Incensed at the idea of competition, the first woman doubled her offer, the second woman countered, and finally the first woman left, having paid almost triple the original price.

A short time later, Emily saw the jeweler handing money to the second woman, praising her for having helped him "gouge the old battle-ax."

If he was to be her champion, Emily would insist on handling the transaction by herself. Who knows who he might decide to cheat: the buyer, her, perhaps even both of them.

Emily pushed away her thoughts as she faced the last room she had to clean: Mr. East's. She'd put it off until last for some reason she couldn't readily explain. She hadn't forgotten his parting words last night, nor had she forgotten her own response.

I love you.

And she did love him. Why? She had no earthly idea why. She'd asked her grandfather once about finding true love and distinguishing it from ordinary love. His answer? It was easy to describe ordinary love: you loved how someone looked, you loved how they touched you, you loved how you felt when you were with them. True love was much harder to define and therefore just as hard to explain.

But you'll know it when it happens, he'd said. *It'll be like nothing else you've ever experienced.*

She held her breath as she knocked on his door. There was no answer. She entered his room, finding it less neat than usual. Was there any wonder? He'd been distracted. By her.

Dutifully, she picked up his clothes. She lifted his shirt to her nose and inhaled, recognizing the slightly spicy scent of cologne she had come to think of as uniquely his.

Folding his garments neatly and placing them on

the chair, she turned to his bed. The sheets and covers were haphazardly thrown to the side, but she could still see the imprint of his body in the mattress, as if he had just risen. She touched the spot gingerly, almost expecting to still feel the residual warmth from his body.

The sheets were cool.

But if only she were.

As Emily stripped the sheets, her mind wandered to forbidden places. She daydreamed about him, remembering how his touch made her shiver, how his kisses made her burn. She closed her eyes, clutched his pillow to her chest and savored the commanding memories that filled her mind, swaying to a love song of the soul only she could hear.

"Emily?"

Her eyes sprang open, but the allure of her memories made it hard to focus on the figure standing in the doorway.

It was Miss Sparrow. "Are you all right? You were just . . . standing there."

"Uh, s-sure . . . I'm fine," Emily sputtered. "Just resting my eyes for a moment."

Miss Sparrow nodded. "It's been an unusual week." She paused to give Emily a knowing look. "And it's about to get even more unusual. He's here. The buyer, I mean. I was at the front desk when he came, so I have him safely tucked away in the Red Parlor and told him you'd be there in fifteen minutes. I've alerted your champion, and he'll be there as well."

Emily drew in a sharp breath. Fifteen minutes. Possibly enough time to finish here, run to her room, change clothes, and then dash to the parlor. She took two big handfuls of sheets and tugged.

"Merciful heavens, girl. You don't have to do that. I'll get someone else to finish the room. You run along."

Emily could have kissed the woman. She stepped over the pile of sheets and made a beeline for the door. "I'll never forget this, Miss Sparrow. I appreciate this so much."

"It's the right thing to do," the woman declared. "I'm certain of it."

As Emily shot out the door, Miss Sparrow held out her hand. "One question before you go. Have you seen Fannie this morning?"

"No, ma'am. But she was mighty upset yesterday."

"I think the fool girl has run off. She's not cleaned any of her rooms this morning, and no one has seen hide nor hair of her since muster."

Too excited to stand still, Emily started down the hallway, walking backward so she could still address Miss Sparrow. "She said nothing to me about leaving, but I wouldn't be surprised if she's sitting on the platform waiting for the next train. I don't think she was suited for this job."

By now she was halfway down the hall and almost shouting.

Miss Sparrow waved goodbye, then held up crossed fingers, a gesture which Emily imitated with a smile. Emily knew she couldn't run to her room. The Major frowned upon such actions because they drew "unnecessary attention" to the staff. So she employed a hurried gait that fell just below his definition of running. Anyone looking at her would simply believe she was moving with efficient speed to her next task.

She ran into Cornelia in the intersection of their hallways.

"Have you seen that . . . Fannie around anywhere? At all?"

Emily shook her head. "Nope. Miss Sparrow is looking for her."

"I am, too. The silly chit was supposed to trade rooms with me. Instead of doing mine, she's disappeared. I'm furious. The Major thought she had completed her duties and I was the slackard, when it was actually the other way around." Cornelia balanced her fists on her hips. "She used me. That's what she did. No one thought to look for her until now because all her rooms were cleaned." She stabbed a finger at her own chest. "Why? Because I cleaned the things. Myself. Now I have to clean another set as well." Her face folded into a very unpleasant scowl. "I ought to hex her."

Emily inched away. "Perhaps so. I'd love to help, but I have . . . a meeting to attend."

Cornelia ignored her. "A hex. That's a good idea. Warts and such wouldn't work; she's already a horse-faced, big-boned clod of a girl. I know." Cornelia spun in a circle two times, and crossed her arms, and twined her fingers together. It looked terribly uncomfortable.

"Fannie," she intoned in an artificially deep voice, "or Tiffany or whatever your name was, may your return home be fraught with disappointments. And along the way, I hope someone tricks you as successfully as you tricked me." Cornelia opened one eye and added a quick, "And may you break out in boils and hives."

She unclenched her arms and shrugged at Emily's look of disapproval. "I had to throw that in," she whined. "The other parts were so vague. I need to know she's going to suffer some sort of physical torment."

Emily sighed, waved goodbye to her friend, and entered her room where her best dress waited, laid out on the bed. She changed clothes quickly, then turned to Cornelia's bag of cosmetics to attempt to repeat some of the magic her friend had created for the ball.

Having little experience with the pots of paints and fearing that her attempts would make her look more like a dancing girl, Emily limited herself to a small amount of rouge and a touch of lipstick. Luckily for her, her hair cooperated by falling in suitable curls when she removed her combs.

She admired herself the best she could in the tiny, warped mirror above the dresser. Retrieving her sewing basket, she removed the case that held the Heart of Saharanpur, allowing herself one last moment to admire it.

Somewhere in the back of her mind, she heard her grandfather's voice offering his usual defense when her father would get angry at the idea of a child playing dress-up with such a valuable possession.

"Come now, Marcus," her grandfather would chide. "A beautiful object like this wasn't meant to be hidden away in a safe. It looks its finest when placed around the neck of a beautiful woman. And look at our Emily . . ." Coaxed from her usual hiding spot behind his leg, Emily would shyly approach her father, finding support and solace in her grandfather's smile.

"Have you ever seen the Heart look so beautiful? Or, as a matter of fact, your own child? They compliment each other." Then her grandfather would reach down and kiss her. "Run along, child. Say hello to the queen for me and tell her I'll return to the royal tea in just one moment."

I miss you so much, Grandfather. . . .

Dragged back to the present, Emily stared at the necklace safely nestled in its velvet-lined case. She let her gaze sink into the seemingly infinite center of the stone.

Her grandfather was right.

A necklace such as this was meant to be worn and appreciated. Perhaps the buyer would find it even more desirable and therefore more valuable if she wore it herself. Plucking the necklace from its case, she put it on, carefully fastening the difficult clasp with experienced fingers. She hadn't noticed until that moment that she'd instinctively chosen the one dress she owned—the dark green velveteen—that showed the necklace off to its best advantage.

If nothing else, it would allow her one last time to wear the necklace, to pretend she was someone worthy enough to gossip with the queen over tea. . . .

She held her head up high as she walked down the hall. When she emerged from the employees' area and into the Grand Foyer, none of the guests noticed an impostor was in their midst. However, several of the hotel's lobby employees noticed.

Carl, behind the front desk, gave her look of open shock. But O'Riley, a bit unsteady on his feet, blew her a kiss. Rupert saw her, then clicked his heels in attention, dipping his head as a gesture of respect. Then he broke his heretofore solemnity by giving her a thumbs-up. Emily walked . . . no, glided across the room toward the Red Parlor, overwhelmed by a very odd and very calm sense of belonging, as if the necklace gave her the confidence to be there.

She paused at the door, took a deep breath, then stepped in.

A medium-sized man stood by the fireplace, sipping from a steaming cup of something. He was casually leaning against the mantel, then straightened when he saw her.

"Miss Drewitt, I presume?"

She nodded. "You have me at a disadvantage. My father's wire didn't mention your name."

He placed his cup on the mantel, brushed his palm against his leg, and strode toward her, hand outstretched. "William Kidder. Pleased to make your acquaintance." He shook her hand, but failed to let go. As he continued to hold her hand, he cocked his head slightly. "I have the strangest feeling we've met before."

She extracted her hand, but allowed her gaze to linger on his face. He was young, perhaps not much older than herself, and had a smooth peaches and cream complexion. He stared at her with big blue eyes that gave him an air of youthful innocence. He did seem somewhat familiar, but she couldn't readily remember meeting him.

"I don't believe so. Are you from Chicago, too?"

"No, no, I was just passing through when I just happened to run into your father and learned your necklace was for sale. From his descriptions, he made it seem as if it were quite unique." His attention slid instantly from her face to her neck. "And he wasn't kidding a Kidder . . ." His laughter was just a bit too loud and a bit too braying.

She took an instant dislike to him.

But, she reminded herself, *you don't have to like him. All you have to do is take his money. Hopefully, lots of it.*

"So this is the infamous Heart of Saharanpur." He stepped close enough to lift the stone and examine it. "I must say I thought I'd never see it." He lifted hauntingly familiar eyes to meet hers. "I suppose you know the story behind it?"

A chill crept up her spine. "I know what my grandfather told me."

"Ah, yes, your grandfather—a stable boy in his youth, if I'm not mistaken. A very bad stable boy, from what I've heard. Not bad as in uncomfortable around horses, but bad as in"—he wagged a finger in her face—"naughty, naughty."

She stepped back from him, reaching for the chain to make sure the necklace pulled away from his grasping fingers. "That's not what I was told."

He nodded. "Of course not. You probably heard some sanitized version of it, some fairy tale about star-crossed royal lovers. A Romeo and Juliet epic with a much happier ending."

"S-something like that."

The amusement went out of his eyes, leaving them flat and lifeless. "Well, you were lied to. The princess didn't run away with the prince. She was kidnapped by him, and the stable boy was his accomplice. The prince stole the Heart of Saharanpur at the same time. Maybe he wasn't sure which the king valued more. In any case, he kept the princess and ended up giving the Heart to the boy as payment for services rendered, not to mention as a bribe to keep his mouth shut." He smiled, but the expression never entered his eyes. "It really was the perfect scam. The kid couldn't palm it, he couldn't sell it, and it was far too valuable for him to simply throw away. So he kept it, which meant if he didn't keep silent, the prince could rat him out. Any bat-time. Any bat-place."

Emily took another step away from the man. He was simply mad. "I think you'd better go."

A new voice filled the room. "You heard the lady. Leave." Mr. East stepped into view, his hands in fists and a fierce scowl etched across his face.

Then a look of shock replaced his anger.

He stared at the young man.

"Oh, shit. You?"

Nineteen

The Kid.

Delgatto instinctively shifted his weight to the balls of his feet.

"How in the hell did you get here?"

The young man shrugged. "Same way as you, I suppose. Big swirling vortex, bright colors. A little *Star Wars,* a lot of *Star Trek.* Very impressive. But that's right." He paused to tap his temple with his finger as if being seized by a memory. "You probably don't remember the trip. You were already safe in the arms of Morpheus."

"More like morphine. You booby-trapped the chain."

The young man smiled. "I did, didn't I? It was a brilliant idea, if I say so myself. What's the old saying? 'It takes a thief to catch a thief'?" He clapped his hands together, the sudden sound making Emily jump. "Track you, drug you, and get your ass hauled to jail." He made a face, then doffed an imaginary hat at Emily. "Pardon my language, Miss Drewitt."

"Don't worry about me," she said with surprising strength. "I've heard the word 'ass' before." She leveled him with a steely stare. "I've even met my share of them."

He nodded in acceptance. "Touché. But do we want to sit here and play with words—and I do realize the popular culture references are completely over your head—or shall we get down to business? Name your price, Emily. I want the necklace."

Delgatto took a step closer. "Why? You stole it already." He stopped himself before adding the damning phrase, "In the future."

The Kid lost some of his bluster. "You know, there's a rather funny story about that. After all the work it took to get into the place, you know what I found in the safe? Same as you. Almost nothing. Just that damned empty case. Turns out the collector never had the Heart, just the box it came in. But we were able to salvage the moment. We decided to pin the theft on you and split the insurance money."

His face darkened. "Only you missed your cue by about a hundred and ten or so years. I saw you enter the tunnel with a woman, and I decided to follow. Simple as that."

Emily crossed her arms. "Would one of you start making sense, please?"

"It's a long story," Delgatto offered, "but trust me, he's not who you think he is."

Her face remained expressionless. "He introduced himself as William Kidder. For some reason, I have no problem believing the *kidder* part."

You don't know how right you are.

She turned to The Kid. "You want to buy the Heart of Saharanpur?"

He nodded. "Name your price, sweetie."

She crossed her arms and met The Kid's gaze with her own. "Twenty thousand dollars."

The Kid blinked, then smiled. "Five thousand."

"Twenty thousand," she repeated.

"Six thousand."

She wore an impossibly calm expression, saying the words with unerring clarity: "Twenty thousand."

The Kid made a face. "Evidently you're unclear on the concept, Emily. You're supposed to come down while I go up."

She barely twitched. "Twenty-five thousand dollars."

The Kid released a ragged sigh and turned to Delgatto. "Would you talk to her? Explain how these things are done?"

Delgatto smiled and turned to Emily. "Thirty thousand dollars."

"Hey, wait." The Kid's eyes grew large. "You can't bid against me."

Delgatto smiled. "Yes, I can. My money is just as good as yours."

The Kid stared at him, his wide blue eyes betraying all the little gears turning in his head. Both of them had unlimited funds. However, all of their invisible bills had pictures of invisible presidents on them. "T-thirty-five thousand dollars," he finally stuttered.

Delgatto crossed his arms, parroting Emily. "Forty grand."

"Fifty."

"Seventy-five."

The Kids almost shouted, "One hundred thousand dollars."

Delgatto kept his cool and displayed his most genuine smile, knowing exactly how it would infuriate the man. "We can go on forever. I'm willing to top any figure you mention."

The Kid contemplated his options, then held out

both palms in mock surrender. "He's left me no choice, Emily. One million dollars."

Although the figure was absurdly high, especially in nineteenth-century dollars, Emily looked as if she were unwilling to summarily turn down the offer if there was any remote possibility it might be honest. Her look of determination started to waver.

The Kid began to smirk.

Delgatto knew he had only one chance to stop this charade, but then again, what he was about to do was no bluff. He moved between Emily and the young man and dropped down to one knee. The look of anticipation on her face almost made him stand back up again and grab her.

And kiss her.

"Emily, we haven't known each other long, but I know your heart and you know mine. I can see you don't want to sell the necklace, that it means more to you in terms of fond memories and sentimentality. So . . . don't sell it. Let me give you my heart instead, and we'll find a way to help your family without selling the necklace." He looked up and saw tears in her eyes. "Will you marry me?"

She held him spellbound for several seconds until she nodded. "Yes, Mr. East. I'll marry you."

The Kid began to laugh. "Mr. East?" he mocked.

She stiffened. "He's James East of the U.S. Secret Service."

The young man almost doubled over in laughter. "James East? Have you no shame, old man? No imagination? You couldn't come up with anything better than that? I hope Robert Conrad sues you for everything you're worth." He began laughing so hard tears trickled down his face.

Growing recognition dawned on Emily's face, along with a bit of revulsion. "Wait," she said, pointing at The Kid. "Now I know who you remind me of." Her gaze narrowed. "No, not remind. I know who you *are.*" She stepped closer to him as if to get a better look at him, and caught him by surprise by hauling back and slapping him as hard as she could. "How dare you? How dare you pretend to be my friend?"

The Kid rubbed his cheek. "In a word. Ow." He turned to Delgatto. "What does the bad guy usually say about now?" He spoke in a theatrical voice with a villainous lisp. " 'Quite a little spitfire, isn't she?' "

Emily almost shook with rage. She turned toward Delgatto. "He . . . he's . . ." She sighed and closed her eyes. "He was . . . Fannie." A tremor of disgust coursed through her.

"One and the same!" The Kid took a bow with several flourishing hand gestures. "I've been doing successful female impersonations for years now."

Delgatto stepped closer, wanting to get between the young man and Emily, who was too wrapped up in her own revulsion to realize the danger she was in. "That's because you're not much of a man."

"Ooh . . . he shoots, he misses. Can't you do better than geriatric retorts, old man? Of course, what else could I expect from a geezer like you? You know the difference between us, old man? Besides twenty years or so?"

Delgatto motioned for the young man to come closer. "Let's take this outside. I owe you one for the stunt in the closet."

At The Kid's look, Delgatto nodded. "Yeah, I realize now that Fannie wasn't your first role. You also went to the Christmas ball. As the court jester, right?" Delgatto crooked a finger at him. "You and me. *Mano a mano.* Winner takes all."

The Kid paused as if to contemplate the idea. "Winner takes all, eh? Hmm. Why go through the hassle of a fight? We both know who's going to win. Winner takes . . . her!" With lightning-fast reflexes, he grabbed Emily, slamming one arm around her waist, pinning her arms to her side, and placing his other hand around her throat. He could just as easily snatch the necklace as break her neck, and Delgatto wasn't sure which he might do first.

"Let's not waste my time. I've come for the necklace and I intend to take it back with me."

Delgatto took a step closer, but the young man tightened his grip on Emily's throat.

"You *would* like for her to breathe, wouldn't you?"

"Don't hurt her." Delgatto held up his hands in pseudo-surrender and took a step in retreat.

"Good." The Kid nodded, then relaxed his grip. "Very good."

Emily gasped for air, but rather than seeing debilitating fear in her eyes, Delgatto noticed some very healthy anger. Hopefully he could channel that to their advantage.

The Kid released her neck and used his free hand to fumble with the chain's clasp. He made a face, evidently unable to manage it one-handed.

"It's hard to do, even with two hands," Emily offered quietly.

"So I see. I suppose I could let you do it." His free hand snaked into his jacket pocket and reappeared, clutching a very modern automatic. "Lucky for me, I'd just put a new clip in before I set off on my . . . trip to Oz. It's hard to find the right type ammunition around here, but I've been quite thrifty with what I brought, so rest assured I have plenty for this little problem."

Although Delgatto knew Emily had never seen a gun quite like that one before, she seemed to recognize its inherently lethal qualities. With rather steady hands, she undid the clasp, allowing The Kid to snatch the necklace away. His hand betrayed only the slightest tremor of excitement.

"Well con-gra-tu-la-tions," Delgatto drawled. "You got yourself a priceless necklace. But let me ask you one little question: how do you get it . . . home?"

The Kid waved the gun in Delgatto's direction. "I was hoping you could help me with that."

Delgatto held up his hands. "Don't look at me. Courtesy of you, I was asleep when it happened, remember? I have no idea how I got here or how to get back."

"I did it."

Miss Sparrow stepped into the room, her thin face calm and serene. "I brought him here. And if you promise not to harm them, I'll send you back. With the Heart of Saharanpur."

Delgatto couldn't help but gape at the woman. "But I thought you said—"

Miss Sparrow silenced him with a schoolmarm-like stare. "No time for arguments, sir. The young man has a gun. I suggest we give him exactly what he wants."

"Sounds like a brilliant idea to me. Now where's the case that goes with this thing?"

"I have it." Emily dipped her hand slowly into the pocket of her dress and pulled out the wooden case.

Behind her back and out of The Kid's view but fully in Delgatto's, she made an odd gesture, her fingers closing quickly.

What are you trying to say, Emily?

"Now, put it inside," The Kid ordered.

She dutifully opened the case, dropped the necklace inside, then held the open case out to The Kid. When he reached for it, she snapped the spring-hinged lid shut on his outstretched fingers.

Delgatto realized what she was going to do about a split-second before she did it. While The Kid yelped and reacted to the pain, Delgatto leaped at the man, trying to get himself between Emily and the gun. Miss Sparrow fell behind the sofa. Delgatto didn't know if she'd fainted or was simply diving for cover.

The Kid made the fatal mistake of trying to retain possession of both objects, necklace and gun, evidently unable to decide which was the lesser evil to lose. As they fought, he lost control of both; the gun flew off in one direction, the ammunition clip skidded in another and the emerald in a third direction, leaving the two of them in a tangle on the floor.

Delgatto landed a good foot in the young man's face and reached out, hoping to find the gun. First he found the clip, which he batted away, and then his hand landed on the open box, his fingers grazing the smooth emerald.

Electricity shot through his arm. Green sparks flew from the stone. Then a pinpoint of light formed in the middle of the room. It began to rotate as it grew larger and brighter. A great roaring sound emanated from its center, as if wind was rushing into a vacuum.

Loose papers began to flutter around the room, being pulled into the vortex that had begun to form.

The spinning tunnel grew larger and larger, demanding their attention. Delgatto scrambled away from the swirling light, backing into his opponent, who had unfortunately recovered his gun.

The young man grabbed him and jammed the gun barrel against his temple.

"The necklace," he demanded. "Now."

Emily stooped down and retrieved the case.

"C'mon, faster—or lover boy here gets it."

She took a step toward them.

In the span of a single second, Delgatto knew what he had to do, exactly how far he had to go in the name of true love.

"Stop, Emily."

She halted.

He tried to draw a deep breath, but his lungs refused to cooperate. "My name's not James East. And I'm not an agent with the Secret Service."

"Oh great," The Kid muttered. "*Now* you decide to play true confessions. I don't have time for this." He ground the gun even harder into Delgatto's skin. "Shut the hell up, please?"

The look Emily gave him almost broke his heart, but he continued. "I'm no better than this idiot," he shouted in order to be heard over the roar coming from the vortex. Luckily, it seemed to have reached its full size and had stopped expanding.

"He"—Delgatto gave his captor a sidelong glance, afraid that a nod might set off the young man's trigger finger—"pretended to be Fannie, to be your friend in hopes of finding the necklace. I . . ." He faltered. The words were harder to say than he ever could have imagined possible. "I-I was just as bad. Worse, even. I didn't merely become your friend. I pretended to fall in love with you, but for the very same reasons. I came here to find the Heart of Saharanpur, just like he did. I lied, I schemed, I broke into those rooms, all because I was searching for the necklace."

She continued to stare at him.

Oh God, please let her believe me.

There was no way he was going to let her give The Kid the necklace. She was going to keep it, even if it meant he would have to die to protect her.

The Kid twisted the barrel, just for spite. "Aw, c'mon. Tell her everything. Get to the good part. I want to watch her try to twist her brain around the time travel part."

"Time t-travel?" she repeated.

"Yeah, me and lover boy aren't from your century. Heck, we're not even from the one after that. We're what you call twenty-first century guys. Cool, eh? And we'll be going"—his voice adopted a sudden television announcer-style polish—"back to the future." He shrugged. "At least I will, with the Heart of Saharanpur. You guys can stay here and rot as far as I care."

While The Kid prattled on, Delgatto glanced down, spotting the ammo clip that had been knocked under a chair.

Hope flared in his heart.

The Kid had at most only one round, possibly already jacked into the chamber. Only one bullet which could be used against two . . . no, three possible opponents. Miss Sparrow had just made an appearance, holding on to the sofa as she pulled herself upright.

All Delgatto had to do was make sure that bullet

came nowhere near either woman, especially Emily. Miss Sparrow slipped behind Emily, offering Delgatto an oddly serene smile as she placed her hand on Emily's shoulder. The two women shared a fleeting look. Then Emily faced him again.

Her look of utter devastation was gone. In its place, she wore a smile that spoke of love and acceptance and, best of all, forgiveness.

"I know what you're doing. And as much as I appreciate your efforts, it's really quite unnecessary." She shifted her attention to The Kid, holding the wooden jewelry case out toward him with two hands.

"If you want this badly enough to kill for it, then take it."

The gun muzzle eased back. "Now you're talking my language, lady."

As the young man reached out for his prize, Delgatto pushed backward with all his might, throwing The Kid off balance. As they fell, The Kid managed to snag the sleeve of Emily's dress, pulling her into the fray. Delgatto jabbed an elbow in The Kid's gut, but the young man recovered too quickly, coming up and catching Delgatto beneath the chin with his head. Stars exploded in his head. Or was it the gun?

Emily!

Delgatto's vision cleared in time to see The Kid cock a fist back and let fly a punch that knocked Emily to his feet. Yet somehow she had managed to hang onto the jewelry case. Delgatto's vision not only sharpened to twenty-twenty, it went blood red.

No one touches her . . .

"Give it to me, you bitch," The Kid screamed in a shrill voice.

Delgatto lunged at The Kid, and their momentum

carried them over Emily without landing on her. They rolled on the floor, Delgatto giving as good as he got. They traded punch for punch, dirty trick for dirtier trick. In a perfect world, experience would have triumphed over youth.

But this world had its flaws.

Finally, The Kid stood over Delgatto, delivering a kick to the stomach just for spite. He turned to Emily and reached out for the box. But instead of taking it from her, he backhanded her.

"That's for not giving me what I asked for the first time."

Dazed, bruised, and bleeding, Delgatto tried to stand, but could barely make it to his hands and knees. Emily sat on the floor, holding her hand to her bleeding mouth. The wooden box was sitting in the folds of her dress.

"Now give it to me," The Kid commanded, standing over her, hand outstretched.

She picked up the box, and gave Delgatto a glance he couldn't quite interpret. Then she turned her attention to The Kid.

"Here," she said, holding out the box. "Fetch."

And she flung the box into the whirling vortex.

The Kid didn't hesitate for a moment to dive into the gaping maw of the tunnel.

They could see him tumble and fall, but he reached the box, pulling it tight against his chest and smiling. His laughter of triumph echoed within the vortex, multiplying until it sounded like that of a hundred men, all laughing hysterically.

"Good-bye, Delgatto," a chorus of identical voices sang. "So long, sucker . . ."

The laughter and the words combined in hideous echoes that turned into a terrible roar.

Delgatto crawled over to Emily and pulled her into his arms. As the noises grew louder, Delgatto pulled her closer, cradling her head against his chest, trying to cover her ears and shield her eyes from the awful light that poured from the vortex.

Then, with no warning, the vortex suddenly closed, silencing the noise. The light collapsed on itself until it was nothing more than a brilliant pin-prick.

And then it disappeared.

"Emily?" He pulled her away slightly to inspect her injuries. "Are you all right?"

She offered him a brief smile that faded into a wince. "It hurts to smile."

He reached up and wiped away a drop of blood forming at the corner of her mouth. Then he pulled her closer, never wanting to let go of her again. "Just as long as you're safe."

Emily sighed and settled into his shoulder, then pulled away with a jerk. "Where's Miss Sparrow? She didn't . . . he didn't . . ."

"I am unharmed." Miss Sparrow reappeared from behind the sofa. Her usually neat bun had been knocked lopsided and several hairs dared to dangle in her face. Her perfectly pressed apron now had some distinct wrinkles, as well as several soil marks. She calmly nudged the offending bits of hair from her eyes. "Are you two all right?"

"He hit Emily." Delgatto felt the anger build up in him at the mere thought.

"But I'm not hurt," Emily added. She stared into his eyes. "What about you . . . Mr. Delgatto, is it?"

"I've had worse." He tried to shake his head, but the room threatened to spin. "And it's not *Mister* Delgatto. Just Delgatto."

"That's your real name?"

He shrugged. "It's what I go by."

Miss Sparrow dragged herself to her feet, and came over to them, trying to affect repairs in her appearance. "Then it appears we have all survived this rather unsavory encounter." She glanced toward the spot where the vortex had been. "With one unfortunate exception."

"Unfortunate? I wouldn't say that. He got the proverbial last laugh. He got the Heart of Saharanpur and a one-way ticket back home."

Emily squinted at the spot where the vortex had existed, then turned her furrowed attention to him. "Exactly where is 'home?' "

He swallowed hard. "Not where as much as . . . when."

"When?" she repeated faintly.

"That . . . thing connects with the future. Only the future it connects with is actually my now."

"You're from the future." She stared at him with total disbelief.

He nodded.

"How far in the future?"

He closed his eyes. "2001." He cracked open one lid, curious to see her expression. She sat there as if pondering a great mystery.

"So you came back in time to steal the Heart because you couldn't find it in your time. Somehow you knew I'd worn it to the Christmas ball."

"There was an article in the paper about it, describing the stone."

"So in your future, you have the ability to go places . . . in time?" Before he could answer, she turned around and faced Miss Sparrow. "Wait. You told Mr. Kidder that you did it, that you brought them here."

Miss Sparrow stiffened slightly. "I only intended to bring Mr. Delgatto, not the other gentleman."

"It's Delgatto," he repeated out of habit. He turned to Miss Sparrow. "So you lied when you said the vortex-time tunnel thing worked only on the winter and summer solstice?"

"I never lie," the woman said with a sniff. "On those two days, the vortex connects The Chesterfield with its counterpart in the future. I didn't know until today that I could open it at any other time. Until today, I never had the need . . ." Her expression darkened. "But I'm fairly sure that tunnel wasn't like the others. It did not connect with the future from which you came."

"Then, where did he go?"

She heaved a troubled sigh. "For the life of me, I have no idea. It could have been anywhere. Any time. Past, present, or future. Essentially, he's lost in time."

Delgatto shook his head. "Poor bastard." Then he looked at Emily's bruised face. "Maybe he deserved it. I don't know. I'll let someone higher up be in charge of his fate. Who knows? Maybe he's happy wherever he is. He got the Heart of Saharanpur. That's what he wanted more than anything"—he massaged a sudden pain that flared in his temple—"other than using my head as a football, that is." The pain subsided with a new, more uplifting thought.

"Hey, I just realized something. It's gone. Forever.

The Heart of Saharanpur, and I couldn't be happier." Delgatto felt as if a weight had been lifted from his shoulders. "He can have it. I give up."

His sense of relief turned into giddiness. "This feels wonderful!" He reached over and kissed Emily. "It really does. I don't care if I never see the thing again, and I don't want to go back to my future. I want to stay here. With you."

A strange look dropped over Emily's face and he grew alarmed.

"What's wrong?" He suddenly remembered the words he'd been forced to say in order to protect her. "If it's about those . . . those terrible things I said, I'm sorry. They were all lies." His conscience pricked him. "Well, most of them were lies. I did come here to steal the necklace, and I was planning to charm it out of the hands of the woman who owned it. But what I felt, what I feel for you is real. It has nothing to do with the Heart of Saharanpur, but with this heart." He tapped his chest.

He took her hands in his. "Emily, I fell head over heels for you long before I discovered you were the fairy princess and you were the one who owned the necklace." He was starting to babble now, unable to anticipate her response. "Honest." He drew a solemn cross on his chest. "On my honor, Emily."

She caught him with a straightforward gaze from which he couldn't turn away. "Your honor . . . as a thief?"

He winced. "As a reformed one."

She graced him with a wincing smile. "I realized why you were saying what you did. I didn't believe you for one moment." She stopped suddenly, concern blossoming in her face. "Wait . . . you're talking about the 'I don't love you' part, not the 'I want to marry you' part, right?"

He grinned enough for both of them. "Exactly. I do love you, and I do want to marry you. But there is one small problem."

"What?"

"I'm not sure what reformed thieves do for a new career. I've never made a living any other way but"—he gulped—"stealing things."

"Like hearts?" Emily supplied.

He shrugged. "Only ones made out of stone. I've never had time until now to deal with the other types."

"My heart's still made out of stone."

His own heart crammed itself into his throat. Maybe her forgiveness was harder to receive than he'd expected. "Emily . . . you have to believe me. I—"

She placed her finger on his lips and shushed him. "I'm talking about *this* heart." She reached into her dress pocket and pulled out . . . the Heart of Saharanpur. "I slipped it out of the box before I threw it into that . . . hole."

To Delgatto's surprise and delight, his own heart didn't skip a beat. He didn't yearn to hold it, to have it, to do anything with it, other than move it out of his way. The only desire he felt was for Emily.

He pointed to her pocket. "Put it back, please. I don't want to ever see that thing again." He pulled her into his arms and started kissing her, but Emily broke away.

"Will you at least help me sell it?" she asked.

"Gladly." He leaned forward and began nibbling her ear. "I do know a bit about precious jewels."

"See?" she said in triumph. "A potential career."

"Sure . . ." He was more interested in kissing her than discussing his professional future.

She wrapped her arms around him, nestling her chin in his bruised shoulder. He didn't even mind the twinge of pain if it meant holding her.

"I'll send this thing back home to Chicago and let my father sell it." She slipped the stone into her pocket. "According to his last letter, he already has elaborate plans on how to use the money to save the family business."

"How?"

"He's going to join a group of men who are financing one of the buildings that's being built at the Columbian Exposition."

The hairs rose on the back of Delgatto's neck. "You mean the exposition in Chicago?"

"Yes." She arched her head back, exposing her very luscious throat. It took all his willpower to control himself.

"What building?" he prompted.

She pulled back, a bemused look. "I'm not sure. Something about mining, I think." She wrapped her arms around his neck. "What difference does it make?"

Delgatto stiffened as his mind jumped back . . . er . . . ahead to history as he had memorized it. One of the many unsubstantiated stories about the Heart of Saharanpur was its supposed demise in the great fire that gutted a large portion of the exposition in 1894.

He reached up and pulled her arms from around his neck. She still had the Heart of Saharanpur in her hand. "A big difference." He turned and saw

Miss Sparrow watching them. From her expression, he couldn't tell if she was playing voyeur or was merely lost in her own pleasant thoughts. When she realized his attention was on her, her usual aloof but serene expression dropped into place.

"I . . . know something. About the exposition," he explained. "Are there some sort of . . . cosmic rules against this sort of thing? You know, telling people about the future and screwing around with the space-time continuum or whatever?"

She contemplated his question for a moment, then asked, "Would it result in your personal gain?"

He shook his head. "Not really."

"Then I see no reason why you should remain silent."

"Good." He turned to Emily. "You can't let your father invest in any building at the Columbian Exposition. Sometime in 1894, I don't remember the date, maybe summer, there's going to be a huge fire. It's going to destroy several of the buildings. I can't exactly remember which ones."

"How do you know this?" she asked in a hushed voice.

"I've memorized every fact, every figure, even every rumor—anything that has to do with the necklace. The stuff was drilled into my head from the day I was born. One of the stories—actually a rumor—was about how the stone was destroyed in the fire that decimated the exposition. I don't know if that was true or not, the bit about the stone, but the fire—that's a sure thing. It's going to happen."

Emily mulled over his explanation for quite some time before she looked up and gave him a resolute nod. "Then we don't give father the money if we sell it. We invest it for him." She rose to her feet, then held out her hand to help Delgatto up. Her smile bordered on the slightly wicked. "Perhaps you can remember something from your history lessons that might make a good investment for him."

He accepted her hand and stood as well, albeit with a little more difficulty. He stretched, trying not to groan. "I might be able to remember a thing or two that could be . . . profitable for him."

"Good." They started out of the parlor, but Emily stopped before reaching the door. "Is your name truly Delgatto? Just the one name?"

His collar started to tighten around his neck.

She stared at him. "You're blushing. Why?"

Miss Sparrow provided the answer. "Because he's the Prince Charming to your Cinderella."

Emily's brow knitted in confusion. "Come again?"

"May I introduce you to His Royal Highness, Crown Prince Charlemagne Alphonso Thierry of Bendavia."

Delgatto closed his eyes, willing the thin woman with the big mouth to go away.

Emily stuttered over the name. "C-Charlemagne Alphonse . . ."

"Alphonso," he corrected automatically. He opened his eyes. "Now you see why I refused to use it."

"But you're a p-prince . . ."

"Not really. It's just a title. There's no country, no kingdom, no land, no royal treasury. Just a pretentious title that I've had to lug around all my life. And Bendavia? It's nothing but a forgotten small blue spot on maps that even you'd consider to be old. The only royal title I've ever been entitled to was

King of Thieves. And my cat burgling days are behind me forever."

She cocked her head. "Charlemagne Alophonso Thierry. C. A. T. Cat. Delgatto means 'Cat,' right?"

He nodded. "Great Uncle Antonio was the very kind individual who took pity on the kid with the unpronounceable name and nicknamed me 'Delgatto.' It's stuck ever since."

"Prince Delgatto," she said as if testing the sound.

"It's just plain—"

"Delgatto," she supplied. "I know, I know . . ."

They continued on until Emily stopped again.

"Where's Bendavia?"

Epilogue

Esmerelda Sparrow knelt beside her hope chest and placed the gold chain beside the pistol, the badge, and the polished brass nameplate. Delgatto had seemed to understand why it was important for her to have the chain, and he had no difficulty getting Emily to agree to give it up.

However, it had taken him a while to accept the fact that Emily did not want to sell the stone. He understood her sense of attachment to it, even if her father didn't. But Esmerelda knew how hard it was for him to look at it and be reminded of the life of crime it had fueled.

She wasn't sure what brought about his change in thought until Emily confided that they'd been discussing the future of children in their lives. When the two of them began to discuss the idea of having children, he realized he had a chance to bring his family's honor to fruition. His child, be it a daughter or a son, would eventually inherit the token of honor that his family had held so dear.

The circle was complete for the House of Bendavia, even if there was a slight hundred year or so setback in one of the branches of the family tree.

It would be a boy. Esmerelda knew that already.

even if the child hadn't been conceived yet. He would be. And he too would help complete another very important circle.

And she hoped the Heart of Saharanpur would help him find his true love, just as it had helped his parents.

And would someday help Esmerelda herself.

She closed the lid of her hope chest.

One more to go.

Dear Reader,

STOLEN HEARTS, as well as the other books in the Hope Chest series (ENCHANTMENT by Pam McCutcheon, FIRE WITH FIRE by Paula Gill, GRAND DESIGN by Karen Fox and coming next month, AT MIDNIGHT by Maura McKenzie) were all born around a restaurant table covered with butcher paper. Armed with purple and orange crayons, we plotted like mad and came up with The Chesterfield, Major Payne, Rupert and most of the secondary characters. Then, each of us began to shape our own stories within this framework. Of the five books, STOLEN HEARTS underwent the greatest transformation from initial idea to finished book. But one element never changed during the metamorphosis—the character of Delgatto.

Astute watchers of television, more specifically of XENA and HERCULES might notice some similarities between the character of Delgatto and that other "King of Thieves," Autolycus. Rest assured, this was no accident. As a lifelong lover of television, I can't resist the urge to cast my books—albeit mentally—with actors. In this case, from the very first moments the story started to coalesce in my mind, I knew that my King of Thieves would share the same "heart of gold" as that other royal rogue, Autolycus as portrayed by Bruce Campbell. To that end, I have not-so-cleverly included some Autolycus/Ash/Brisco lines in this book.

Did you find them?

E-mail me at *delgatto@suspense.net* and let me know.

And don't forget to get Maura's book and find out what Miss Sparrow has been up to. . . .

Laura Hayden